D1385547

I 1986870

OGILVIE
AND THE TRAITOR

OGILVIE
AND THE TRAITOR

Philip McCutchan

Severn House Large Print
London & New York

This first large print edition published in Great Britain 2003 by
SEVERN HOUSE LARGE PRINT BOOKS LTD of
9-15, High Street, Sutton, Surrey, SM1 1DF.
This edition first published 2001 by
Severn House Publishers, London and New York.
This first large print edition published in the USA 2003 by
SEVERN HOUSE PUBLISHERS INC., of
595 Madison Avenue, New York, NY 10022

British Library Cataloguing in Publication Data

McCutchan, Philip, 1920 -
    Ogilvie and the traitor. - Large print ed. - (A James
    Ogilvie novel)
    1. Great Britain. Army - Fiction
    2. Ogilvie, James (Fictitious character) - Fiction
    3. India - History - 19th Century - Fiction
    4. Historical fiction
    5. Large type books
    I. Title   II. MacNeil, Duncan, 1920 - . Wolf in the fold
    823.9'14 [F]

    ISBN 0-7278-7208-7

Printed and bound in Great Britain by
MPG Books Ltd, Bodmin, Cornwall.

One

Snow lay thickly over London, a white Christmas to gladden the hearts of children if no one else: in Piccadilly the street urchins ran, shouting with laughter, casting snowballs until chased by angry constables who cuffed ears red and swollen with chilblains. In Kensington Gardens, in Green Park, the children of the aristocracy walked demurely alongside their nannies, eyes bright with eagerness, with the strong desire to escape the apron-strings and cast a snowball with the *hoi polloi*. From Buckingham Palace the old guard, found from the Grenadier Guards, now relieved by the Coldstream, slow-marched with snow-muffled footsteps out of the great gateway, their bearskins and grey greatcoats flecked with the snow that still fell lightly from a leaden sky, the fifes and drums, backed by the brass, beating out 'The British Grenadiers' as the sharp command came to break into quick time. They moved away towards Wellington Barracks, fading into the snow, looking like Napoleon's retreat from Moscow. The palace flagstaff stood bare of the Royal Standard: Her Majesty's court was currently at Balmoral on Royal Deeside, with Her Majesty dreaming sadly of Prince Albert and her ghillie John Brown. Along the Mall, coming down Constitution Hill from the cavalry barracks at Knightsbridge, a troop of the Life Guards moved circumspectly through the snow, their scarlet and blue cloaks making bright splashes of brilliance against the white of the trees in the Green Park as they cascaded over the rumps of the horses. The horses' nostrils steamed like the railway engines that pulled up the steep gradients of the West Highland line...

Captain James Ogilvie, on leave from the 114th Highlanders on the North-West Frontier of India, glanced down at the woman by his side: he felt a shiver run through her body. 'You're cold, Mary. I've kept you out too long – we'll walk back now.'

She smiled and he felt the pressure of her fingers on his arm. 'Blood still thin from India, I think, James.'

'It should have thickened again by now. It's years since—'

'Yes, I know. Don't talk to me of passing years, please, James. *Too* depressing ... and I

6

don't know how *you* take the weather!'

He shrugged. 'I'm a Scot.'

'Even the Scots have blood, I imagine.'

'And the Khyber has winters. Don't tell me you've forgotten winter in Peshawar, Mary. Come on, we'll go back to Brown's.' He held her tight as they stepped into the road, crossing the Mall to walk up Marlborough Road towards St James's Street into Piccadilly.

Already here the snow was turning to a grey-brown slush, churned up by carriage wheels and hooves. They came past the old brick palace of St James, glanced at the sentry marching his snow-cleared post with bayoneted rifle at the slope, watched him halt with a crash of boot-leather, turn to face his front with another crash, order arms and stand at ease, eyes staring dead ahead, seeing nothing, guarding history. Originally St James's had been a hospital for leprous maidens, metamorphosing into Holbein's royal palace in 1532, becoming, after the burning of Whitehall, the principal residence of the court from the reign of William and Mary to that of George IV. In its chapel royal Her current Majesty, Queen Victoria, had been married; from its dim chambers Charles I had walked to his beheading; and there Charles II, and the Old Pretender, and George IV had been born.

'You're quiet, James.'

He laughed. 'Ghosts!'

'India?'

'Not this time: my sense of history. All that's happened between those walls.' He waved a hand, backward towards the palace.

'Think of the dust,' Mary Archdale said lightly, and he felt some irritation; she'd always tended towards flippancy and had no sense of history or tradition. In that respect – this he knew – she thought him stuffy, too bedded down into the regiment. Often it had come between them in the past, the past of some three years ago since when, seeing nothing of Mary in the interval, she had receded from his mind. He had not altogether welcomed the sheer fluke of chance or fate that had thrown them together again: only yesterday, coming down from Corriecraig Castle on Speyside to spend his last two weeks in England at Brown's Hotel, he had seen Mary Archdale upon the platform at King's Cross, looking somewhat bewildered, surrounded by trunks and hat boxes, hurrying porters and barrows, train noises and escaping steam. Recognition had been mutual and instant: news had been exchanged and all the polite enquiries made. Was James's father, Sir Iain Ogilvie, still commanding in Murree, was his mother well, and how was Lord

Dornoch and the regiment? They had stood there in the bustle and uproar, oblivious of all but themselves and an Indian past, of more than a degree of passion aroused in the hot Peshawar nights or in Simla behind the verandah of Mary Archdale's bungalow. Ogilvie had thought again of poor Tom Archdale, Brigade Major, many years older than Mary, a pompous bungler whose first care upon the march had been his thunder-box or field lavatory, but who had died a soldier's death in action. Mary had not married again; Ogilvie had a suspicion that he himself was the reason for that. And currently she had come down from Hunting-don, where she had been staying with old friends. Coincidentally, she too was going to Brown's Hotel, news that had made Ogilvie frown. He had no wish for scandal, and to arrive in one cab would be scandalous. But luckily Mary had seen the point, and had herself, though with a sardonic twinkle in her eye, suggested separate arrivals at the august Brown's Hotel. Worse was to come: at their subsequent meeting as if by chance, when, in the residents' drawing-room, the past was briefly and circumspectly re-examined for the benefit of listening ears, Mary dropped her bombshell: she was returning to India by the next P & O for Bombay on an extended visit to a cousin married to a major on the staff of the Twenty-Second Division, attached to the Northern Army Command at Murree.

'In which case,' Ogilvie had said rather coldly, 'you must have known my father was still the GOC.'

'Yes, I did. I'm sorry.' There was the sardonic twinkle again. 'I didn't feel King's Cross Station was the place for too many explanations. You look cross, James.'

He shook his head. 'Not cross.'

'Worried, then. The Colonel – or your mother?'

'Neither,' he said sharply. 'Well – anyway, not my mother. But you know what India is, Mary.'

'And you have your career to think of. Do I have to remind you I'm a widow, James?'

'Of course not, but—' He broke off in some confusion: he was not at his best with female company, and lacked tact. However, the smile at the back of Mary's eyes, a sad though understanding one, told him she knew what was in his mind: in Peshawar, in Simla, she had had a reputation. It had been, except in regard to James Ogilvie himself and only he, an unjust one and attributable wholly to the drawing-room poisonings of Mrs Colonel This and Mrs Major That, but in Indian garrison life gossip stuck cruelly. It had to be accepted as an immutable fact of life, bred by jealousy and enlarged upon by spite. It had to be accepted not only by the woman talked about, but also by regimental officers who cared about the army; and in James Ogilvie's case it could not be denied that he had also to consider his father's position as General Officer Commanding the Northern Army in India.

Knowing all this, Mary Archdale rested a gloved hand lightly on James's arm. 'Don't worry, love. Murree's not so close to Peshawar.'

'No...'

'All the same, you might sound a little less unhappy.'

'Oh, damn it! I'm not unhappy.'

She nodded. 'Just prudent. I do understand. And anyway...' She lowered her voice, but not her eyes. 'For now, we're not in India. We're in London, James – foot loose and fancy free!'

Walking into Piccadilly towards Brown's Hotel, Ogilvie knew he had sounded like a damn prig and that he'd acted like one too – up to a point. But Brown's was Brown's and the cloth of the Church of England was well represented amongst its guests; no one would be asked to leave more quickly than anyone interrupted in a nocturnal bedroom flit, and if that should happen, and never mind discretion on the part of the management, the fat of scandal would flame in the fire of gossip. So other means had had to be found; the willing assistance of Jackie Harrington had been sought and given. Harrington, now a captain in the Grenadier Guards, still maintained his rooms in Half Moon Street and was delighted to be contacted again by an old friend of Sandhurst days. Last night, as it happened, he had been Officer of the Guard in St James's Palace, and as such confined to the palace limits and the expensive dinner party customarily laid on by the officer having the guard duty. Half Moon Street was available and no questions asked. Mary, knowing she was being hidden away from respectability, hadn't minded in the least, and had given herself passionately and with a total abandon. They had been slow to wake, and had lain a long time in each other's arms when they had done so, not speaking, not needing to speak, satisfied and content. In their minds was Jackie Harrington's promise: he was going on leave at the end of the week, and was happy to loan Ogilvie his rooms, regretting only that he was unable also to allocate his soldier servant to look after his guest – in the singular: Harrington, as befitted an officer whose duties included

12

those of the London season, was a tactful man. Mary had no objection to tidying up before they left in the morning.

They entered Brown's Hotel together – they were known to be friends now. An elderly man in a porter's green baize apron, bent and wizened, approached.

'Is it Captain Ogilvie, sir?'

Ogilvie nodded. 'Yes.'

'Captain James Ogilvie, of the Queen's Own Royal Strathspeys, sir, the 114th—'

'Yes, yes, that's me. What is it?'

'There's a message, sir. A gentleman called, sir, an officer. Captain Jourdain, sir, from the War Office.' The old man consulted a piece of paper in his hand. 'On the staff of Major-General Featherstonehaugh.'

'Well?'

The porter scratched his head. 'Do you know how to use that there telephony instrument, sir?'

'Yes, I do. Am I to telephone – is that it?'

'Yes, sir. Major-General Featherstone-haugh's secretariat, sir. If you'll kindly follow me, sir.'

Ogilvie turned to Mary. 'Sorry. I'll try not to be long. I'll find you in the drawing-room directly.' He went with the old retainer, who shuffled creakily towards a cubby-hole where the new-fangled instrument of communication, jointly served by the National

Telephone Company and Her Majesty's Post Office, lay in its mystery. Ogilvie slid a florin into the old man's ready palm and lifted the receiver from the instrument's hook, thus calling the exchange. After much delay and a curious sizzling in his left ear, the number of the War Office was obtained and Ogilvie was connected to Major-General Featherstone-haugh's extension. By error rather than design, he was connected direct to the Major-General and not to Captain Jourdain. This he deduced initially from the strange noises at the other end. A good deal of background interference and more sizzling became overlaid by a series of damns and bloodies.

'Hullo, hullo, hullo, hullo. God damn! How d'you work this bloody thing – hey? Who's that, who's that at the other end, what? Hullo, hullo.' The sizzling increased. 'Oh, bugger.'

'My name is Ogilvie, sir.' It came out as a shout.

'What? No need to blow my bloody head off, is there? I'm not deaf. Who is it?'

'Captain Ogilvie, sir, 114th Highlanders. Captain Jourdain—'

'Jourdain, Jourdain. Oh – *that* Ogilvie. Yes, yes. By God, I'd like to wring the neck of that bugger Bell. HRH would *never* have stood for this! Damned if I see why I should!

14

What's wrong with a bloody runner – hey? Ogilvie, are you there?'

'Yes, sir—'

'Well, get a move on, then! Come here! At once!' There was a crash in Ogilvie's ear and he hung the receiver back on its hook, grinning. He went to find Mary, told her where he was going, and sent the porter for a cab. Another florin changed hands and Ogilvie was ushered into a hansom cab, a snow-covered vehicle, presided over by a gaunt man in a many-caped greatcoat flicking a whip over the ears of a horse that blew twin jets of steam into the London air. The hansom drove into Piccadilly where the wooden blocks forming the roadway were wet and slippery with the slushy snow. Ogilvie shivered; it was a dreary scene now, all freshness gone, and the passers-by looking miserable, frozen to the marrow, many of them with thin clothing that could surely keep out no cold, and with pinched faces, red and blue as the snow made its way down their necks. Within fifteen minutes Ogilvie was waiting upon Major-General Featherstonehaugh, left to sit, until the General was ready for him, in an ante-room furnished with a roaring fire that flamed and spat into its highly-polished brass fender. An officer who introduced himself as Jourdain came in after five minutes.

15

'Captain Ogilvie? Good. The Major-General's ready to see you.' Jourdain gave a wink. 'I warn you, he's still in a foul mood. Loathes the telephone, but insists on answering it himself when the bell rings – don't ask me why. I can only suggest he's practising.'

'What does he want to see me about?'

Jourdain, who wore the green tunic and badges of the Rifle Brigade, said, 'Something nasty. But he'd prefer to tell you himself.' He turned away towards double doors at the end of the ante-room, pushed them open before him, stood aside and announced Captain Ogilvie. From before another immense fire a loud and hectoring voice smote unjustly at Ogilvie's ears.

'So it's you. Take your damn time, what? India makes a man lazy if you ask me!' There was a harsh laugh. 'Either that, or produces too much bloody misplaced energy!' The Major-General, a very short, very round old gentleman with a whisky-coloured face and snow-white side-whiskers, began flapping up the tails of his morning coat and moved a little way from the fire: his backside was getting too hot. 'Don't damn well know what I'm talking about, do you, Ogilvie?'

'No, sir.'

'Rape,' the Major-General shouted suddenly, his face going darker. 'Bloody rape, young man, that's what! Feller wants you. Damn sepoy, or is it sowar? Never served in India myself – thank God! Off you go,' he added, flapping Ogilvie out of the room with waves of his arms.

Ogilvie gaped. 'Go, sir? Where, if I may ask?'

'Police cells. Happened out of barracks – rape usually does, no doubt – damn civil power's got him. Tell him, Jourdain, tell him. I've got my hands full.' As Ogilvie turned away, he saw the Major-General leave the fire and advance upon the telephone, his blue eyes glittering. Perhaps, Ogilvie thought, it was a fatal fascination that could not be denied.

Two

Captain Jourdain, who had led the way to his own office, gave a sigh, caught Ogilvie's glance, and smiled. 'Never seek to become an ADC,' he said. 'At any rate, not to a Whitehall warrior. I'm prepared to grant it's different in the field! That's just between you and me, of course.'

'Of course.'

'And now you want to know what's going on.' Jourdain waved towards a chair. 'Bring your arse to an anchor, Ogilvie.'

Ogilvie raised an eyebrow. 'A nautical turn of speech?'

'My father's. He was in the navy.' Jourdain sat behind a desk littered with papers which he looked at with irritation, running a hand through thick dark hair and blowing out his cheeks: he seemed ill-at-ease in an office, as though he couldn't wait to get back to the barrack square and the shouts of the drill sergeants and corporals. 'Now look, Ogilvie, you wouldn't think it, but even His Nibs knows he can't order you to take this on –

you're on leave, and you've nothing to do with Whitehall.' He grinned in a friendly way. 'We're taking liberties with you. If you want, you can tell us to go to the devil – though I don't advise it, mind.'

'Volunteers – you, you and you!'

'A fair description, Ogilvie. But I dare say you'll want to help.'

'If you'll tell me the facts—'

'Just about to. I expect you know we have a detachment of squadron strength of the Kohat Light Horse temporarily attached to London District?'

Ogilvie nodded. 'I've read about it, and in fact I've seen them in the Mall—'

'Quite. It was a whim of Her Majesty's, to show some appreciation of her Indian Empire. They've been carrying out guard duty at the Horse Guards.' Jourdain paused. 'I understand the KLH are recruited in your divisional area?'

'That's right. They're part of the First Division's cavalry at Nowshera. Am I to understand that one of them has committed rape?'

'I'm afraid so,' Jourdain said. 'A lance-*duffardar*, by name Akhbar Mohammad Khan—'

'A Moslem. He'll have his god to answer to!'

'No doubt he will, Ogilvie, but looming

rather closer is the Bow Street magistrate, and after that, I suppose, the Old Bailey.'

'You're assuming he's guilty?'

'He's been identified.'

'By the woman?'

'Yes.'

'I see. When did this happen?'

'Last night,' Jourdain said. 'He jumped a girl in an alley off the Charing Cross Road.'

'Girl?'

Jourdain waved a hand. 'A euphemism. She was a trifle worn. All he had to do was pay, but he wouldn't have known that.'

'And the police intend to prosecute?'

'I don't think they have any option. The woman laid a complaint.'

'And the man himself?'

'He denies it flatly. Wasn't there, he says. But he can't establish an alibi.'

'And where do I come in, Jourdain?'

Jourdain didn't answer directly. He asked, 'Do you know the man?'

'I don't recall the name, that's certain. It's unlikely I'd know him in any case. We meet the officers of the Indian regiments, of course, but not—'

'Not the rank and file, naturally. But he says he knows you – and he knows you're over here because he saw you once when he was riding down the Mall with his troop. I gather you've been in London earlier? War

20

Office has your address as Brown's only from yesterday, but six weeks ago—'

'Yes, I spent ten days here looking up old friends.'

'That's when he saw you, Ogilvie. Now he's asking for you. Asking for your help, if only as an interpreter. He hasn't much English, and he has no friends.'

'His troop, surely?'

'He seems a bit of a loner ... but what I really meant was friends at court.'

Ogilvie frowned. 'What about his squadron commander? What's his name, by the way?'

'Soames. But he's been recalled to India – he left his wife behind there, and she's sick. Soames sailed on the last P & O from Tilbury. The acting squadron commander's a VCO – a *risaldar* named Jalala Khan.'

'How much longer have they over here?'

'Three months, about,' Jourdain said, checking a list. 'They go back in the *Malabar*, the next troopship after the *Jumna* sailing from Portsmouth at the end of next week—'

'That's the ship I'm sailing in – the *Jumna*.'

'Yes, I know. I'm dashed sorry to ask you to mess up the last week of your leave, old man. Once you get involved with the law, it's not easy to disentangle. Well?'

21

Ogilvie slumped in his chair, blowing out his cheeks. This could be a case of a single visit or it could take up much time, and it would be many years before he saw England again, unless the regiment itself should be ordered home before its time was up, which wasn't likely. But he saw no alternative: a man was asking for his help, a man who, far from home and family in a strange and largely hostile land, would be in black despair in a police cell. Abruptly he said, 'All right. Will you take me to him?'

There was no doubt of the way in which the Metropolitan Police mind was working: the female plaintiff might be, and was, a slut, with convictions for prostitution behind her; but her attacker, shrilly identified by her at a parade consisting of other NCOs from the lance-*duffardar*'s squadron, was a bloody Indian. Not only that, but a soldier. An Indian soldier would clearly find it almost impossible to seduce a willing woman: the man would have been missing his home comforts, and it was a case of QED. As such it was spelled out for Ogilvie by the Station Inspector.

'We have no doubts at all, sir. The identification was positive.'

'There's a case for saying that all Indians look alike to people who've never been out

22

of England.'

'Be that as it may, sir.' Inspector Fitch was unmoved behind a large walrus moustache that gave his bloated face an air of immense sadness as it hung like a crescent moon over a tight blue tunic.

'I'm told he denies the charge?'

'They all do that, sir, begging your pardon. A military gentleman, used to dealing with defaulters, ought to know that. He has no alibi, sir. His statement says he wasn't in the vicinity, that he was walking along a road the name of which he couldn't say but which we think we've identified as being Victoria Street.' Fitch pulled at his moustache. 'There's no witnesses, sir, to what he states. None.'

'Somebody would have seen him. An Indian cavalryman in uniform is no everyday sight in London, Inspector Fitch.'

'No doubt, sir. If he was there. But as you said, sir, all Indians look alike. To my way o' thinking, that acts *both* ways.'

'But justice, surely—'

'Now look, sir.' Fitch's moustache blew upwards at its ends, rising on an angrily puffed breath: Ogilvie recognised a strong similarity between this policeman and his own Divisional Commander in Peshawar, Bloody Francis Fettleworth; each worked on prejudice, each mind was as unresilient as a lump of rock. 'What you're suggesting – there's only one way to find out, and that's to question the whole population of London—'

'Nonsense,' Ogilvie said irritably. 'The police surely have their methods of enquiry – even an appeal in the newspapers? Someone would come forward, wouldn't they?'

Fitch glared and sucked at a tooth. 'Begging your pardon, Captain Ogilvie, it's none of your affair, not that side of it. The native was arrested and charged, and the charge was properly accepted by the Reserve Inspector. The native will be up before the beak – magistrate – this afternoon.' Once again the moustache was blown upward. 'Do you now wish to see him, sir?'

'Yes, please.' Ogilvie hung on to his rising temper. He followed Fitch to the cells, descending stone steps into a dank, dismal basement. They were met at the bottom of the steps by the gaoler, a constable who swung open the door of a cell after first peering through a small aperture. 'May I go in?' Ogilvie asked.

'That's as you wish, Captain Ogilvie. At all events, the man is not violent.'

Ogilvie went into the cell: Fitch and the gaoler, with Captain Jourdain, remained outside, looking in. The native cavalryman, who had been sitting on a low shelf-like bunk bed, with his head sunk miserably in his hands, got to his feet in soldierly fashion as Fitch announced his visitor's name. He bowed his head, then stood at attention, a tall man, straight-backed as befitted his calling, a man with a proud and almost imperious face, clean-shaven and hook-nosed, his uniform showing the two chevrons of a lance-*duffardar*, equivalent of a full corporal of the British Army.

Ogilvie said, 'Stand easy, *duffardar*.'

With a crash of knee-booted feet, the native moved to the at-ease position. There was a chink of medals: Ogilvie noted a general service medal with three clasps, a long service medal, the 1880 Kabul to Khandahar Star, and an award for bravery. The man's head was high now, and the eyes seemed to flash fire at Inspector Fitch and the gaoler. Ogilvie said, 'You are Lance-*Duffardar* Akhbar Mohammad Khan, of the Kohat Light Horse?'

'Yes, sahib.'

'You asked to see me. I have come. How can I help you?' Then he added, 'But first a question. Did you commit the crime with which you have been charged?' He had been speaking in Pushtu: he heard the hoarse suspicious whispers from Fitch, the quiet assurance from Jourdain; Fitch forbore to interfere.

The lance-*duffardar* answered his question. 'Ogilvie sahib, I have committed no crime. I was walking peacefully, returning to the cavalry barracks where your Horse Guards live.' The gaze was level, but full of hurt and reproach. 'Such a crime I would never stoop to commit. In time we go home to my own country. There I have a wife and three sons, three sons, sahib, who wish to follow me into the armed service of the Raj. I would not do this thing.'

Ogilvie made no comment on that: men did things from time to time that were wholly out of character. Yet this time he was convinced of a forthcoming miscarriage of justice. The man's voice held conviction. He appeared to be in his early thirties, a responsible NCO of excellent service. His papers would give evidence to that effect. Ogilvie asked, 'Have you any complaints as to your treatment, since your arrest?'

'Sahib, I have been correctly treated physically, but the policeman with the face like a sheep's bladder painted red, and who was not born of woman but of a cow, speaks to me as though I were not human. I do not understand what he says, but I know it is not pleasant, and it is my hope that his soul and those of his ancestors—'

'That is enough.' Ogilvie held up his hand, relieved that Inspector Fitch would be no

26

more understanding of this tirade than the native had been of his own ill-tempered harangues. Currently Fitch's face held nothing more than a baffled scowl. 'I must tell you this, Akhbar Mohammad Khan, that I cannot interfere with the processes of the law. You have been charged and you must answer. It may be possible for me to arrange for your proper defence and also to advance your record of service to the Raj in support of your good character. In order to see that this is done, I shall have words with your *risaldar* as soon as possible.'

'That is good, Ogilvie sahib, and I am grateful.'

'But it is possible, in our system of law, that the magistrate will feel it necessary to refer you to a higher court. If this happens, do not despair. You will not have been found guilty, and I shall be doing all I can so that a full defence is ready. Do you understand?'

The native nodded. 'I understand, Ogilvie sahib. I believe also that the *risaldar* sahib will help. He is a good officer, Ogilvie sahib.'

'I'm sure he is. I shall leave now, and go to see him.'

'Ogilvie sahib, do not go yet. This I beseech you.'

Ogilvie, who had started to turn away, paused and looked back. 'There is something else?'

'A matter of much importance, Ogilvie sahib, and of much urgency.'

Ogilvie glanced at Fitch and Jourdain: Fitch clearly would understand nothing, and it was doubtful if Jourdain would; and he had the feeling that that was the way the lance-*duffardar* wanted it. He said, 'Then you should speak at once, Akhbar Mohammad Khan.'

'I shall do so, Ogilvie sahib. In your hands this will be safe – I know this, for I have known your reputation in India, where I serve in your division. Also in the command of your illustrious father, the Lieutenant-General sahib commanding the army in Murree, with whom I wish you to communicate. This is why I asked to speak with you, Ogilvie sahib.'

'Go on.'

'I wish to speak of the Captain sahib.'

'Your captain ... Soames sahib?'

'That is so, Ogilvie sahib. He has already returned to India—'

'On account of a sick mem-sahib. I know.'

'Not on account of a sick mem-sahib. That she is sick may be true, but that is not the reason, Ogilvie sahib, for his return.'

Ogilvie's eyes narrowed, and again he glanced towards Fitch, noting growing impatience in the sheep's-bladder face. 'What, then, is the reason?'

28

'Do you know of the man they call in India the Wolf of the Salt Range, a man whose real identity has never become known, Ogilvie sahib?'

'I have heard of him.' All at once, the atmosphere in the police cell seemed to have changed. Ogilvie felt a prickling in his scalp, a shiver down his spine. The confines of the cell below the London streets opened up into the barren landscape of the Salt Range, the great gaunt hills south-east of Peshawar, dotted here and there with the outpost forts that held the line for the Salt Department of the Indian Government against the smuggling operations of the bandits out of Waziristan and elsewhere. He had indeed heard of the Wolf of the Salt Range, of his raids and his killings and of his habit of taking no prisoners. It appeared from the tales of men along the North-West Frontier, and in the messes of the garrisons at Peshawar and Nowshera, that no living man except his own brigand band had ever seen the Wolf: if you saw, you died, and that was that. Simple and effective! Ogilvie asked, 'Have you, then, word of the Wolf? And if so, how did any knowledge come *your* way, Akhbar Mohammad Khan?'

The native looked at the three men in the doorway, then back at Ogilvie. 'What I am about to tell you, Ogilvie sahib, will sound

29

like lies, but it is the truth. This I swear upon my father's soul, and my grandfather's soul, and my great-grandfather's soul, and upon the Koran, and upon the Prophet himself. If it be lies, then I shall be condemned by the Prophet.'

Ogilvie licked his lips: now, even Jourdain and the two policemen seemed to be sensing the strange atmosphere, the aura of ancient gods that reached out from Akhbar Mohammad Khan, the emanation of age-old treacheries and murders and rituals. From the corner where he stood by the bed, the lance-*duffardar* seemed to loom, powerful, omniscient, growing in physical stature as he began once again to speak.

The cell door shut; there was a hollow boom that sounded like a knell. For a moment there was silence; then Inspector Fitch rubbed his hands briskly together. 'Well, Captain Ogilvie, did you get anything from all that?'

'It's hard to say, Inspector,' Ogilvie answered with his tongue in his cheek.

'Bloody Bombay Welsh, begging your pardons, gentlemen! Rattle, rattle, like a Maxim gun, fifteen to the dozen! Well now, you've seen him, you'll realise he's been properly treated in all respects, and no doubt you'll also appreciate how that great brown body'd 'ave put the fear of Gawd into that pr – poor young woman last night...'

Ogilvie and Jourdain emerged into the street. Jourdain raised his cane for a hansom cab. Ogilvie asked, 'If he goes for trial, what does he stand to get?'

Jourdain shrugged. 'Don't know. I suppose it could be anything up to ten years' hard labour. Rape's rape, isn't it?'

'He mustn't be found guilty,' Ogilvie said.

'What's that?' Jourdain was watching the cab draw up. 'What did you say?'

'I think you heard, and I meant what I said. To hell with the law! Strings have just got to be pulled, that's all. I—'

'But look here, Ogilvie—'

'That man,' Ogilvie said quietly but firmly, 'has to sail for India with me at the end of next week. That's vital to the Raj. In any case, I'm convinced he's innocent. I'm asking you to see to it that he doesn't go for trial.'

'On your say-so? Listen, Ogilvie, what the devil did he tell you?'

'I'm sorry. That'll have to keep till we get back to your Major-General.'

They got into the cab. Jourdain pulled out a watch. 'The General will be at luncheon – Guards' Club. I'm hungry too.' He called up to the cabby. 'Not the War House, cabby.

31

Café Royal. All right, Ogilvie?'

'There may not be time. When will the General be back?'

'Give him till three thirty. He's a glutton and likes his brandy too.'

'I can't give him till then, Jourdain. I must talk to him at once – before our lance-*duffardar* goes before the justices.' He turned on Jourdain impatiently. 'More hangs on this than a General's lunch, more than a damn dimwit London bobby's susceptibilities, too! And the General seems addicted to the telephone, whatever he says. Get hold of him, for God's sake!'

Major-General Featherstonehaugh was at first angry, making loud reference down the telephone line to Indian mumbo-jumbo and the damn nuisance that brown skins were in London; but Captain Jourdain knew how to handle his master and spoke in gravely urgent tones about the security of the Raj. Ogilvie was put on the line to state his case personally. He was, he said, about to leave London for Her Majesty's prison at Princetown on Dartmoor and it was vital that the lance-*duffardar* be released in the meantime. Upon his return to London he would, of course, report fully to the War Office; for now it would be inadvisable to say much more on the open telephone.

The little he had been able to reveal was convincing. 'Hand the telephone back to Captain Jourdain,' Featherstonehaugh shouted. When the ADC came on the line again the General passed precise instructions: Jourdain was to go back to the police. The General didn't give a damn how he did it, but the charge was to be dropped. If there was no other way, the lance-*duffardar* must face the magistrate and be found not guilty and discharged. 'They'll do it if I say so. God Almighty, they're only *policemen* – they're there to do what they're damn well told, are they not? If you have difficulty, tell the Inspector I'll have the Commander-in-Chief on his back who'll give him orders from the throne. Goodbye.'

Major-General Featherstonehaugh hung the receiver on its hook and made his way back to the dining-room, his face truculent. Never mind that the man in the police cell was no more than a common soldier and an Indian at that: Her Majesty's armed forces stood supreme and this was an excellent opportunity, a well-authenticated opportunity, of putting the civil power firmly in its place. The police had tended to become uppitty of late ... on his march to the dining-room the General saw a fellow member ahead and bawled at him.

'Hardy, I say. I say – Hardy! Come here.'

The man paused, turned, walked back. Featherstonehaugh put a thick arm across his shoulder. 'Your cousin's the Bow Street feller, isn't he, the stipendiary? Thought so. I want you to have a message sent to him at once by runner...'

Three

Once clear of Paddington and the western outskirts of London, all the countryside seemed to lie under a blanket of snow. In his first-class compartment James Ogilvie listened to the train's rhythm as he swayed towards Reading, Devizes, Taunton and Exeter, a rhythm that settled into the back of his mind as he reflected upon the strange story told to him by Lance-*Duffardar* Akhbar Mohammad Khan; Ogilvie had passed on only parts of this story to the General, enough, he hoped, to satisfy that choleric old gentleman until he, Ogilvie, returned from Dartmoor Prison.

The native cavalryman, if his story was to be believed and Ogilvie was, perhaps illogically, convinced that it was, had been framed: if anybody had attacked the prostitute, it had been another man from the Kohat Light Horse. It was more probable that money had changed hands and the woman had made up her story from start to finish. And the lance-*duffardar* had insisted that the man behind his troubles was none other than his departed British officer, Captain Horatio Bendersley Soames. Knowing India, knowing the loyalty of the native NCOs to their officers and to the Raj – knowing also the power of white officers to make or break, a knowledge shared to the full by Akhbar Mohammad Khan – Ogilvie found himself unable to believe that any native would invent such a yarn. Even if mistaken, Akhbar Mohammad Khan must *believe* his accusation to be the truth; and mistake could scarcely have come into the rest of the story.

'Why,' Ogilvie had asked, 'should your Captain sahib wish to bring this trouble upon you?'

The NCO, it seemed, had discovered secrets about his Captain. One night, not long before Captain Soames had returned to India, the lance-*duffardar* had been unable to sleep, thinking thoughts of homesickness for a land he had never before left, and a family managing without his presence: he had got up from his bed in Knightsbridge Barracks and left the barrack-room, going down to the stables below, quietly so as not to disturb his comrades. He had become aware of low voices from the stables, and he had moved even more quietly to listen, considering it to be his duty as an NCO and fearing, perhaps, horse thieves or such. He had recognised the voice of Captain Soames, Captain Soames sounding surreptitious, hurried, and nervous. Very clearly, the Wolf of the Salt Range had been mentioned. The conversation had been in Pushtu, but from the context of what was said, the lance-*duffardar* did not believe the other man to be a soldier of the regiment. Captain Soames had said that the Wolf was not to worry: all would be well, but he himself would arrange a speedy return to India in advance of the regiment. A cable was to be despatched to this effect; the lance-*duffardar* did not know to whom this cable was to be addressed but made the assumption that the Wolf was unlikely to be reached by such means himself and that there must be an intermediary. Another name had been mentioned: Sergeant Zachary. An uncommon name, and one that Ogilvie knew. A year ago a Sergeant Zachary of a line regiment in cantonments at Peshawar had been Court Martialled on a charge of taking bribes from Pathan bandits along the Frontier; he had been reduced to the ranks, dismissed from Her Majesty's service, and sentenced to a long term of civil imprisonment, for which he had been sent home to England. The lance-*duffardar* had not caught what, if anything, was Zachary's involvement with current matters. When indications had come that the unknown visitor was leaving – and he appeared to have come into barracks by scaling a wall and to the displeasure of Captain Soames – Akhbar Mohammad Khan had retreated upstairs, but had made some sound that had brought Captain Soames out of the stable.

'The Captain sahib,' the native NCO had told Ogilvie, 'was angry and frightened. He made me come down, and he seemed about to strike me with his cane, and threatened me with punishment for eavesdropping. I said I had heard nothing. I think he did not know whether to believe or not to believe, Ogilvie sahib. But he controlled himself, and said I must be very careful if I wished to see India again, and that he would be watching me. He said no more, but I understood. Then he went away, and later he went back to India.'

'But left his orders behind, to be executed when he was safely out of the country?'

'As I truly believe, Ogilvie sahib.' The eyes had remained level throughout the whole recital. 'In England, no man would have believed what I have said, and I would have been out of the way of the Captain sahib.'

Long before Exeter, dark had come. The lights from the train windows flickered on lying snow, but the fall had stopped long since. At Exeter Station transport was waiting: a brake from Princetown, a prison vehicle pulled by two heavy horses. The brake was an open one and the air, as they climbed towards the moor, was cold in the extreme. Ogilvie found himself shivering despite his thick greatcoat: Mary had wanted to come, but it was as well he had forbidden it. She would have had no liking for such a journey; now, he envied her the friendly warmth of Brown's Hotel in Dover Street. The wind increased as the brake climbed past Moretonhampstead, the horses' hooves sliding on the narrow roadway between the drifts of snow.

'Are we going to make it?' Ogilvie asked the warder who was driving.

'We'll get there, sir, never fear. I've been out in worse weather than this, sir.' The man drove on, saying nothing more: he was a taciturn fellow, Ogilvie thought. The wind blew its freezing breath into a face toughened to near leather by many winters on the moor; he seemed not to notice. Ogilvie, as the moon came up and lit distant snow-capped piles of high granite, the tors left high and stark by the early centuries of soil erosion, fell to thinking about the terrible life in Princetown gaol, and of ex-Sergeant Zachary serving out his time, perhaps bitterly reflecting upon the different days of the Sergeants' Mess on Indian service, of sweepers and bearers to call him 'sahib' and do his instant bidding: how had the mighty fallen! But there was little point in wasting sympathy on Zachary: the man had let his regiment and his country down, had acted selfishly against the British Raj. There was just the one point of interest left: would Zachary talk now?

Through Postbridge over the East Dart river, spanned by the road bridge and the ancient flat-stone bridge built by primeval man and standing yet. On to Princetown, almost totally in darkness at this late hour: it was past midnight. A few lights burned in the warders' homes, a few dotted the tall buildings of the prison. With a rumble of its wheels the brake turned into the main gate to be stopped by a guard. A lantern was held high, its beams bringing up the faces of Ogilvie and the driver. The body of the brake was briefly scanned.

The driver said, 'Captain Ogilvie from London, to see the Governor.'

They were waved through into the prison yard, where they headed for the block that housed the Governor's office. Ogilvie climbed down stiffly, feeling chilled to the bone. He stamped his feet, flung his arms about his body, breath steaming into cold air to

40

rival that of the horses. What a bloody place to spend five, ten, fifteen years of a man's life! Sergeant Zachary had gone down for five, had four more yet to do.

The Governor was Colonel Francis, late The Border Regiment, 34th and 55th Foot. On the wall was a portrait of himself in full regimentals, all blue and scarlet beneath a gilded helmet. On another wall was a carved replica of the Border Regiment's helmet badge with the Chinese dragon bestowed in honour of the regiment's service in China during the opium war of 1839. Francis was a tall man, splendidly built, with an imperious face that should quell any prison riot, and he was a man of few words.

'Whisky?'

'Thank you, sir.'

Francis waved an arm. 'Decanter's there. Help yourself. Don't stint. Look damn cold. I'll not join you if you don't mind.' His face was flushed: he'd had one or two already, Ogilvie thought without any trace of blame: whisky would be the only way to keep Dartmoor out.

'Now – Zachary.'

'He's agreed to see me, sir?'

'Agreed, did you say?' Francis gave a short laugh and tweaked at one end of his moustache. 'Agreed my arse. Been damn well *told*. I've had a telegram from Feather-stonehaugh. I doubt if I need say more.'

Ogilvie smiled briefly. 'No, sir.'

'Zachary's ready when you are, Ogilvie. Don't hurry. Get warm. Zachary has plenty of time. Want to see him in here?'

'May I leave that to you, sir?'

Francis nodded. 'In here, then. Want me here?'

'I think it would be better, sir, if I saw him alone.'

'Secrets?'

'Not that, sir. It's just that ... well, I may need to be harsh.'

'And you respect my position. I understand, of course. I'll rely on you not to overstep the mark too far. I doubt if you'll have any trouble with the man – no violence, nothing like that, or I'd not leave you alone.'

'A good prisoner, sir?'

'Yes. Wants as much remission as he can get. Married with a boy of six.'

'Thank you, sir. I'll bear it in mind.' Ogilvie, warmed through by an immense fire burning in the grate, finished the whisky.

'Ready?'

'Yes, sir.'

Francis pressed a bell-push on his desk. 'He'll be wheeled in right away.' They waited; within a quarter of a minute a familiar

42

commotion started outside – they might just as well have been in a regimental orderly room when the bugles had blown Defaulters.

'Lef', right, lef', right ... '*alt!*' There was a crash of boots and the door was opened by a stout man who bore all the markings of an ex-Regimental Sergeant-Major. This man stood back against the opened door and shouted. 'Prisoner and escort, quick – *march!* Lef', right, lef' ... '*alt! Stand still!*' A salute was snapped at the Governor. 'Sir! The prisoner Zachary, Jonathan 'Enry, present as ordered. Sir!'

'Thank you, Mr Boniface, kindly dismiss the escort and leave yourself. I shall join you. Captain Ogilvie will see the prisoner alone.'

'Sir!' More salutes and shouts, and everyone withdrew but Ogilvie and Zachary. Ogilvie moved to the Governor's desk and sat down, looking at the prisoner standing at attention before him, a man still smart and military-looking. Was there a trace of shame? Staring into the face, Ogilvie wondered.

'Stand at ease, Zachary,' he said.

'Sir!' The left foot was carried smartly sideways, the hands went behind the broad back. The eyes remained staring a little over Ogilvie's head in accordance with the drill book.

'Look at me, Zachary. Forget the army.'

'Yes, sir. Though it don't seem to 'ave forgotten me.'

'Did I ask you to comment?'

The throat moved in a swallowing motion. 'No, sir.'

'Then hold your tongue until I ask you a question.'

The mouth shut, forming a hard line. There was a sulky look in the face now, and the eyes failed to meet Ogilvie's for long, flickering off sideways and then taking refuge in the over-the-officer's-head angle as per regulations; Ogilvie let it go. He said, 'For your information, I have served in Peshawar. I was there at the time of your Court Martial, Zachary, and I'm going back next week.'

'Yes, sir.'

'Tell me what you know of the man they call the Wolf of the Salt Range.'

There was a slight flicker of movement in the face, some sort of automatic response, but not necessarily one of alarm, Ogilvie fancied. 'The Wolf of the Salt Range, sir. I've heard of him, who hasn't? A nasty bastard, they say, sir.'

'A killer, Zachary. A killer of very many men, both British and native.'

'Yes, sir.'

'As were the people you took bribes from a year ago.'

'If you say so, sir.'

'Do you deny it?'

'Not the bribes, sir. That's down in black an' white.'

'The fact the men were killers?'

'I couldn't say about that, sir.'

'Killers of your own comrades, men in your own barrack-room?'

'I was a sergeant, sir.'

'You know very well what I mean, Zachary. In fact, as a sergeant, your crime was the worse. Do you know Captain Soames?' The question came very suddenly.

'Captain Soames, sir?' This time, Ogilvie felt sure of a reaction. 'I don't think I do, sir. What regiment would he be, sir?'

'The Kohat Light Horse. Currently in London at Her Majesty's command.'

'A native lot.'

'Is that relevant, Zachary?'

'Sir?'

'Why do you make a point of it?'

'I'm sorry, sir. I didn't mean to.'

'I see. You were covering certain thoughts. Zachary, I ask you again, do you know Captain Soames?'

'No, sir, I can't say as I do, sir.'

'And I think you're telling lies,' Ogilvie said flatly. 'I have reason to believe you know Captain Soames very well, and have done so for some time, starting well before your arrest in India. I have come from the War Office, Zachary, with a Major-General's authority behind me, and behind him the Commander-in-Chief, Field-Marshal Lord Wolseley. There are big guns in the field, Zachary, and aimed at you.' He picked up a pen from the Governor's desk and pointed it in Zachary's face, now dead white. 'Remission is a desirable thing – I needn't remind you. It can be lost – and it can be gained also. I suggest you think about that. There is another point. You have a wife. You've gone a long way already towards bringing her world around her ears. Don't make it worse.'

Zachary's mouth opened and shut again, fish-like. His pallor increased. He almost gasped, 'Is that meant to be a threat, then?'

Stiffly Ogilvie said, 'I believe the security of the Raj to be threatened by acts of disloyalty. Nothing will be allowed to stand in the way of the full defence of the position of the Queen-Empress in India.'

'Big words,' Zachary said softly, sneering. 'I say you're a bastard – an' that's *all* I'm going to say!'

Ogilvie rang the bell on the desk: they came back in, Governor, Mr Boniface and escort.

'Done with him?' Francis asked.

'Yes, sir.'

'Take him.' Francis gestured at Boniface. Zachary was marched away, back to his lonely cell. Francis cocked an eye at Ogilvie. 'You're sweating like a pig. Get what you want?'

Ogilvie said, 'He broke.'

'Took his time over it.' Francis looked up at the clock on the wall. He had been out of the room for nearly two hours. 'Not easy?'

'I feel as rag limp as I suspect he does,' Ogilvie said. 'I wouldn't have your job, sir.'

'We don't normally do what you've been doing,' Francis said drily. 'Don't brood. You'll recover. Thing is – was it worth it?'

Was it worth it? A hard question, that. But Ogilvie believed the answer to be yes. Zachary, he believed, had at least told all he knew; there would be plenty to report to Featherstonehaugh in London. But it had been an unpleasant task, a hateful one: threat, even the suggestion of threat, was alien to Ogilvie. In regimental life, an officer dealt out punishment when necessary and that was that. The act was done, or it was not: there were no innuendoes, no trailing ends. He was well aware that tonight threat had won out, that Zachary had been well and truly browbeaten – and, at the same

47

time, bluffed: Ogilvie would not have put the threats into execution, though Featherstonehaugh might well, he supposed, have done so over his head.

Spending what was left of that wintry night in the Governor's house, as a guest, with a fire burning in his bedroom and casting flickering shadows over walls and ceiling, Ogilvie found sleep hard to come by. He woke, when called at a dismally early hour by a servant with morning tea, to headache and cramp in his limbs. It was still pitch dark but when he pulled the curtain aside he saw lying snow in plenty. Breakfast came almost at once: before going to bed, he had stressed a need for a quick return to Whitehall. As soon as the meal was finished, the prison brake was waiting and Ogilvie went out into freezing cold and the beginnings of a dawn that was going to reveal a steel-blue sky. The brake took him south across the moor to Plymouth – the Governor had advised this as a faster route into London: the excellent express service of the Great Western Railway covered the 225 miles into Paddington in not much more than four hours. Nevertheless it was late afternoon before Ogilvie's hansom cab dropped him at the War Office, where he reported to Jourdain.

'The old man's impatient, Ogilvie.'

'I'm sorry about that,' Ogilvie said a trifle bleakly, and asked, 'The lance-*duffardar*?'

'The magic worked, old boy. He's free as a lark. Fitch is said to be rumbling like a volcano, but Featherstonehaugh is sublimely unperturbed.'

'Where is he – the lance-*duffardar*, I mean?'

'Wellington Barracks. It was thought best he didn't rejoin his squadron, at any rate till they're back in India. He's been attached as a supernumerary to the mess servants.'

'And in the *Jumna*? He's still coming with me, I hope?'

Jourdain nodded. 'The Major-General's idea is to attach him to you personally while at sea.' He paused. 'What about Zachary?'

'An interesting talk,' Ogilvie answered. They were now in the corridor leading to Featherstonehaugh's room. 'You'll hear all about it presently.' They approached the door, and Jourdain announced Ogilvie. Featherstonehaugh stared from behind a cloud of cigar smoke: this afternoon he was in the uniform of the General Staff, a mass of scarlet and gold, with gilded tassels hanging from his right shoulder in indication of his august status as ADC General to Her Majesty.

'Ah, Ogilvie. Just in time. I'm due for the night express for the north – bidden to

Balmoral. Like to get this wretched business out of the way before I go to my club.' More smoke was blown. 'Zachary?'

'In deep, sir. And he's positively involved Captain Soames.'

'Good God.' The eyes bulged: this was terrible. 'What, precisely, is the involvement?'

'The Salt Department, sir. Smuggling through the customs line, the hedge.'

'Hedge?'

'The customs barrier, sir. An earth embankment, a wide one, covered with a thick cactus hedge – it runs right through from Attock on the Indus, more than a thousand miles of it, to Saugor in Central India. The line's crossed at distant intervals by tracks cut through the hedge, and at each cutting there's a customs post.'

'Manned by whom?'

'The Inland Customs Department, sir, who have their own attached sepoys.'

'H'm. I don't know much about India, Ogilvie ... but Soames is attached to your Division, as I understand. Attock, Saugor ... they're nowhere in your area, are they?'

'Attock's not far, sir, but in any case that's only one of the smuggling areas. We have salt deposits to the south of us, bordering the Punjab—'

'And Soames?'

'According to Zachary, sir, Captain Soames is concerned chiefly with the Punjab.' Like Zachary the night before, Ogilvie stared over the General's head, speaking formally and without particular inflexion in his tone. 'Captain Soames – according to Zachary – is deeply involved in the smuggling operations, and is in the pay of the Wolf of the Salt Range. There's something else, sir.'

'Well?'

'Chakwal, sir. Two years ago a battalion of native infantry was massacred there. It was believed, though never proved, that advance information had reached the Wolf concerning our troop movements—'

'Was Soames involved?'

'As I said, sir, there was never any proof. But Captain Soames ... yes, sir, there was some suspicion.'

'I see. And Zachary? Did he have anything to say on that score?'

Ogilvie shook his head. 'Nothing, sir.' He added, 'As to what Zachary did tell me, I think I should say that I gave him my word that I would protect his statement to me and that Captain Soames would not know. I gave him an assurance it would be a privileged statement vis-à-vis the law, too. He's serving his time, sir, he's paying for what he did. There can be no further charge

51

against him.'

Featherstonehaugh said irritably, 'You sound unctuous, Ogilvie ... however, I take your point.' He drummed his fingers on his desk, his face worried. 'I don't care for seeing a man kicked when he's down,' he went on somewhat surprisingly. 'I'll do what I can. Is there anything else?'

'I'm afraid there is, sir. It appears Princetown gaol has an effective grapevine. Word has reached Zachary that the Wolf of the Salt Range intends mounting a concerted attack by the tribes on the forts and outposts guarding the salt line south and east of Peshawar. It's possible Captain Soames may be assisting him with information.'

'A large-scale attack, eh? What do you suppose that would involve – from your experience of India?'

Ogilvie shrugged. 'A lot of bloodshed, sir. Possibly a general rising along the Frontier. These things are catching, and we could be made to fight on two fronts at once. If I may suggest it, sir, I think the Commander-in-Chief in India should be advised immediately by cable.'

Four

Featherstonehaugh clearly was not going to get the 'wretched business' out of the way before leaving for the Queen's court at Balmoral: nevertheless he took himself off to the Guards Club, leaving the draft of a communication for Lord Wolseley who, he said, would inform Sir George White in India if he thought it necessary. He would, he said again before leaving, keep ex-Sergeant Zachary's interests in mind though he was damned if he saw why he should bother his head about a traitor.

'Wife and family,' he said. 'That's the nub! They shouldn't suffer.' He looked shrewdly at Ogilvie. 'D'you suppose Soames is involved there? Paying out funds as the price of silence?'

'I don't know, sir. It's possible.'

'Well, we can check his bank, though I doubt he'd have taken the risk – there'd have been other ways, most likely.'

'Yes, sir. There's another point I've considered. Zachary could have covered for

Captain Soames—'

'Taken the blame – the Court Martial?'

'Yes, sir. In addition to his own part in it, that is – he's certainly no innocent lamb for the slaughter.'

'Did you press him on that?'

Ogilvie nodded. 'He gave nothing away, sir.'

Featherstonehaugh pursed his lips. From a pocket came a turnip-shaped gold watch to be studied. 'I'm rushed for time. Off you go, Ogilvie. Thank you for your help. Enjoy the rest of your leave. Jourdain will contact you at Brown's when necessary.'

In truth, the remaining time in London didn't seem like leave at all: mentally, Ogilvie was re-orientated Indiawards already, and all the while he was half expecting communication from the War Office. The nights in the Half Moon Street rooms were oases that he and Mary Archdale enjoyed with abandon: he knew he was going to miss her even while he reflected, with a degree of anxiety, on the likelihood of their being thrown together in the normal course of garrison life in India. Mary Archdale was looked upon with reserve to say the least by his Colonel, and the regiment was ever his first consideration. Then there were his parents: his father, a man of roving eye who liked to display an ageing gallantry, had a soft spot for Mary; his mother, on the other hand, would not receive her. Lady Ogilvie, James knew well, feared Mary's emergence as a daughter-in-law. Besides the fact that Mary was some seven years his senior in age, Lady Ogilvie quite failed to see her, in due time, as mistress of Corriecraig.

During those last days of leave there was no contact with Lance-*Duffardar* Akhbar Mohammad Khan and only one message reached Ogilvie from the War Office, a summons to report to Captain Jourdain. Ogilvie was told that a cable had gone to Sir George White and that after his arrival in Peshawar he would be informed when it would be convenient for the Commander-in-Chief to hear his report in person. In the meantime his passage orders stood: he was to sail for Bombay in the *Jumna* to rejoin his regiment in cantonments, and the lance-*duffardar* would report to him at Waterloo Station and attend upon him during the voyage. Four days after this Ogilvie scrawled a note of thanks to Jackie Harrington for the use of his rooms, said goodbye to Mary Archdale, took a cab to Waterloo where he received a smart salute from the tall native in the uniform of the Kohat Light Horse, a colourful figure for the London crowds to stare at as the two made their way to the

55

Portsmouth train accompanied by a porter pushing a barrow crammed to capacity with baggage.

At their meeting, tears shone in the lance-*duffardar*'s eyes. 'I am grateful, Ogilvie sahib. May you and all your ancestors and descendants be truly blessed. My life is now yours, to be defended to the death.'

'It was a matter of simple justice,' Ogilvie said. 'We shall speak no more of it.' As the Portsmouth express moved out, Ogilvie stared from the windows. Coming into open country, now largely clear of snow, he looked his last on England for many years to come, and found a sudden sadness in his thoughts. There were compensations in India, but a lot was left behind whenever a troopship sailed. The abundant green of English summer fields was a very dear memory when the sun blazed down from burnished skies along the Afghan border, when the cry went up along the marching files for the regimental *bhistis* to fill the water-bottles to slake the raging thirsts of men whose throats were as dry and harsh as sandpaper. Even the rains of England, gentler and fresher than those of the Indian season of wet, became part of the nostalgic picture that every man carried before him until the singing bullets of the snipers brought him back to the realities of Frontier

56

service. Driving later to the naval dockyard from the railway station in Portsmouth, Ogilvie saw the *Jumna* lying at the South Railway Jetty with smoking funnels and a scene of great activity along her decks as she embarked her foreign service battalion and a host of other, miscellaneous reliefs. The 1st Battalion The Wiltshire Regiment, The Duke of Edinburgh's, were being trooped to India from Le Marchant Barracks at Devizes, and were now marching aboard in their scarlet tunics with salmon buff facings to the fifes and drums beating out 'The Vly be on the Turmat' from the jetty. Ogilvie knew that this would not be the regiment's first spell on the sub-continent: the 62nd Foot had greatly distinguished themselves at Ferozeshah in the First Sikh War, advancing unsupported against the Sikh artillery firing point-blank into the ranks. That day the 62nd had seen half their number fall, including all their officers. The sergeants had brought the Colours out of action, and in commemoration of this the Colours ever since had been handed to the safe custody of the Sergeants' Mess on the anniversary of the action. Now they were going back for more, relieving a time-expired infantry battalion in the Northern Army command. Ogilvie halted the cab, waiting until the embarkation was complete. Behind the

Wiltshires went mixed drafts of cavalry, their horses being lifted aboard in slings and dropped down to the stable deck through hatches, a battery of the Royal Artillery, a detachment of the Army Medical Staff and Hospital Corps, plus unattached officers returning, like Ogilvie himself, from home leave. Ogilvie leaned through the cab window, glanced upwards: the Blue Peter was flying from the foretopmast head. The troopship would soon be away. As the main embarkation finished, Ogilvie watched his baggage hoisted in the baggage-nets, then climbed the gangway with the lance-*duffardar* behind him. His special accommodation had been arranged by the War Office ahead of his arrival: a steward escorted him to a stateroom with an off-leading, box-like cabin for the Indian cavalryman, who seemed quite unable to believe such splendid accommodation was being provided when white soldier-sahibs had to be content with the overcrowded troopdecks filled with hammocks and scrubbed mess tables and cursing, half-naked men.

At two p.m. the last lines were cast off and the *Jumna* moved off the jetty as the brass of the Portsmouth military command thundered out 'Auld Lang Syne'. Ogilvie smiled inwardly: as, so far as he could see, the only kilted officer aboard, he felt as though the tune was for himself alone, a graceful tribute to Scotland. *But seas between us braid hae roar'd* ... the music was drowned by a great outburst of cheering as the Wiltshire Regiment said its last goodbyes to England for seven years and the transport headed out for Spithead, past Fort Blockhouse to starboard and the old Sally Port steps to port, worn old steps from which Vice-Admiral Lord Nelson had left England for his great last battle off Cape Trafalgar, out past the gunner-manned sea forts that stood as extended guard for the garrison and town of Portsmouth, round St Catherine's Point and into the English Channel, turning westwards when south of the Isle of Wight to head for the Lizard, Ushant, Finisterre, Cape St Vincent and Gibraltar, first port of call on the long haul east.

After Gibraltar and a day spent on the filthy task of coaling ship came Malta, Port Said, the Suez Canal, Suez itself, the Red Sea, Aden beyond the Strait of Bab el Mandeb known to sailors as the Gates of Hell; the Arabian Sea and Bombay. With the Bombay pilot aboard they steamed slowly inwards for Prince's Dock, leaving behind them the Parsees' Towers of Silence on Malabar Hill. When the various reliefs had filed down the gangways to form up on the dockside and be marched to the railway station, James Ogilvie disembarked with the lance-*duffar-dar*. Immediately upon passing Kolaba Point Ogilvie had been enfolded into the aura of the sub-continent: it was almost as though his spell in England had never been. Now he was anxious only to have the long train journey over and done with and to be back with the Royal Strathspeys in cantonments in Peshawar, and to get to grips with the many urgent problems posed by Captain Soames of the Kohat Light Horse. But first there was that terrible railway journey: many days of heat and dust, of maimed and leprous beggars extending hands for alms at the halts, a long slow train crammed with soldiers not yet accustomed to the ways and climate of India – hot days, cold nights, with the heat sliding into intense twenty-four hour cold by the time they were as far north as Peshawar: for in India as in Britain, this was winter. Throughout that journey the meals would be frugal and never mind that ever-thoughtful authority had provided a kitchen coach for the officer sahibs...

It was just as he had left it months before: the trim gardens of the officers' bungalows, the compounds kept in first-class order by the *mali* and his boy assistants, the white-walled godowns occupied by the low-caste sweepers, the Royal Strathspeys' parade-ground alive, almost vibrating, with the diligent screams of the drill sergeants as they strove to keep up the perfection demanded by the Colonel, by the Regimental Sergeant-Major and by the Adjutant, Captain Black: Captain Black, who was crossing the parade-ground as Ogilvie got down from the transport sent to meet him from the train.

Black halted, swished his cane about his kilt.

'Ah, Ogilvie, it's you.'

'Indeed it is.' Trust Black to state the obvious.

'You look well, James.'

Ogilvie smiled. The 'James' indicated that Andrew Black was being friendly. It was a tradition in the 114th that officers, off parade, addressed one another, except in the case of the Colonel, by Christian names: but it was a tradition not always observed by the Adjutant, who was a man of moods. 'The English climate suits me, I think, Andrew.'

'And Scotland's?'

'And Scotland's.'

'Well, I'm glad to see you back. We've been short-handed, what with local leave and courses, always courses these days as

61

though we have not enough work to do in providing patrols.'

'Who's away at the moment?'

'Three captains, four subalterns. But I'll not detain you now, James.' Black's glance lingered, curiously. 'You appear to have attained some ... notoriety, is that the word, whilst on leave?'

'I hope not notoriety. Why?'

'Rape, and Dartmoor gaol.' There was something like a leer in Black's thin, dark face. 'Have you been muck-raking, James?'

Ogilvie's response was curtly angry. 'Is this common knowledge – what you speak of? I'd assumed a high degree of secrecy—'

'James, James! I am the Adjutant, am I not? I am not a common soldier.' The face grew darker. 'There is all the secrecy that is needed – it is all between you and me and the Colonel, I assure you. And the Major.'

Ogilvie apologised handsomely. 'You were sudden, that's all. I have the greatest respect for your discretion.' He smiled. 'It was a rotten train journey. I'm tired.'

'You have no right to be tired after long leave, Captain Ogilvie.' Friendliness had evaporated: Black swished his cane again, sending a draught around his bony legs beneath the kilt. 'Unless it was a mis-spent leave,' he added, with a sidelong look at Ogilvie.

Ogilvie stared. 'Is there some hidden meaning in that?'

'Oh, no, no, no. None at all. Should there be?' Black's face was innocent in a devilish kind of way. 'I'll not deny the grapevine's been at work. Major Archdale's widow ... in London, and coming out here to – where is it – Murree?'

'Yes. She has a cousin there.'

'Really – really?'

'As I'm quite sure the grapevine didn't fail to tell you. In any case, what has it to do with you?'

'It is of concern to the regiment, I think, Captain Ogilvie.' Swish, swish. 'I advise you to have a care. This is India.'

'Indeed it is. Has the Colonel asked to see me?'

'Lord Dornoch has gone over to Now-shera, and will not be back until tomorrow. When he wishes to see you, he will tell me. In the meantime, I'd be obliged if you would take over your company after breakfast tomorrow. There is a Brigadier-General's inspection the morning after. I trust I shall not see signs of slackness after leave, Captain Ogilvie.'

'I know you shall not, Captain Black.' It was back into harness with a vengeance. Black marched off and Ogilvie went into the ante-room; apart from Surgeon Major

Corton, the room was deserted. Corton was an old friend and a good brother officer, glad to see Ogilvie back. They talked of home, of Invermore and the regimental depot, and of London. Corton was anxious for a home posting: he had no wish to remain until retirement as a regimental surgeon, and to go higher meant additional qualifications obtainable only by study in England or Scotland. In the mess that night Major Hay, second-in-command, deputised for Lord Dornoch. Ogilvie looked pleasurably at the colourful scene of dress kilts, scarlet mess jackets, gleaming starch and buckled shoes, at the glitter of the hanging lamps on the regimental silver, the port standing like glasses of blood for the loyal toast. Dinner over, Major Hay buttonholed Ogilvie for brandy and a cigar in a corner of the ante-room. A group of subalterns approached the Major for permission to play the piano.

Hay nodded. 'Certainly, but try to keep the din down.' Hay was not a musical man, and in any case he knew subalterns. The music thumped and jangled and some of the officers sang. 'The Last Rose of Summer', 'Annie Laurie' ... Under song's embracing cover, Hay spoke of matters weighing upon the Colonel, but discreetly. 'How do you assess it, James? You've been close to the source, have you not?'

'Well, only the home end, John.' Ogilvie sipped the brandy in the big balloon glass. 'How do I assess it? I take it seriously, to start with. Trouble's on the way all right! As a matter of fact, I'm surprised ... haven't you noticed any straws in the wind out here?'

'Not really. They're not ready yet, I suppose. Of course there's always trouble of some sort in the damn Salt Department's territory – you know what I mean – forays and excursions, smuggling, the odd sepoy is found murdered – *thuggee*, or slit throat. The odd attack on the forts. But this is to be much bigger, I take it?'

'Much. Hasn't Fettleworth shown a reaction?'

Hay laughed. 'Poor old Bloody Francis is said to have been giving his Staff hell as a result of some anxieties – but for all I know his anxieties are more to do with matters of spit-and-polish than thoughts of war! You know how he loves massive parades ... there's a rumour that your esteemed father has put his foot down hard.'

'In what way?'

'More time should be spent on exercises in the field than on the parade-ground. Frankly, I agree with him – but bang goes Fettleworth's chief joy in life!'

Ogilvie grinned. 'Too bad!' He was about to signal a mess waiter to pour more brandy when the corporal in charge of mess servants approached the Major.

'Beg pardon, sir. There's an officer asking for Captain Ogilvie, sir.'

Hay turned to Ogilvie, eyebrows raised in a query, then spoke to the mess corporal. 'Ask him in, man! What's the delay?'

The NCO looked embarrassed. 'The officer, sir, 'e's not very well, sir.' The eyes looked away over the Major's head and the voice became even more stiffly formal. 'Sir! The officer's half seas over, and I—'

The NCO broke off: the officer was losing patience, and was coming into the ante-room. The face was belligerent and red, streaming with sweat; the two stars of a captain glittered from the shoulder chains of a cavalry tunic. The eyes glared above a thin jutting nose and a neatly trimmed black moustache, a pencil line of hair over a hard, thin mouth. Recognising Captain Soames, Ogilvie got to his feet.

'Which of you's Ogilvie?' Soames demanded, his voice and bearing truculent.

'I am. Major, may I introduce Captain Soames of the Kohat Light Horse?' Ogilvie did his best, so did Hay, who held out a friendly hand. The gesture was ignored; Soames went up close to Ogilvie, breathing hard. Ogilvie smelled brandy. The eyes were bloodshot, yellowish in the whites, unhealthy like the blotched skin of the face.

'So you're Ogilvie, eh?'

Ogilvie nodded. 'That's right. We have met—'

'Once, I think. Just – briefly. Stuck-up popinjay. Bloody General's son.' The ante-room had gone very silent; even the piano was at rest. The Major glanced around, a meaning look in his eye. Good manners took over once again, and the other occupants of the ante-room immersed themselves in their own conversations. At the piano a subaltern began playing again, something light and innocuous from Gilbert and Sullivan.

Soames sneered. 'Oh, awfully British. I'm beneath notice. All right, so I'm tight.' He lurched a little, steadied himself, and stood there swaying between Ogilvie and the Major. 'Got one of my men, one of my NCOs ... so I'm told.'

'Right. Lance-*Duffardar* Akhbar Mohammad Khan.'

'Why?'

Ogilvie met Hay's eye, a look that was seen by Soames. 'All right, Ogilvie, don't solicit instructions, let's have your own unaided answer.'

Ogilvie said, 'I'm sure you know what

happened.'

'Rape, wasn't it? The depot was told, of course. Why the interference? I want to know.'

'We believed he was not guilty, Soames.'

'Not guilty?'

'A case of mistaken identity. Wasn't your depot told that as well?'

Soames said, 'Yes. I tell you this much: my Colonel doesn't care for interference, Ogilvie. Especially from the British Army. We don't come under your lot, you know. Far as we're concerned ... the War House doesn't matter a fish's tit. We're Indian Army, not British Army in India, and I give you that information free, gratis and for nothing, Ogilvie.'

Ogilvie, well enough aware of the rivalries and jealousies in India, smiled slightly. 'In the circumstances as they were, Soames, mightn't your squadron have been consider-ed Indian Army in Britain, and as such answerable—'

'Answerable to no one in London,' Soames said loudly. 'Meanwhile, where's my NCO?'

Ogilvie considered the question and its implications; the lance-*duffardar*, met separately from the train in accordance with orders received in Bombay, had been taken to temporary accommodation at Brigade where he would be held available to report, with Ogilvie, as soon as summoned by the high command. The orders were that he was not to be returned to his unit until he had been cleared by the Political Department. At the same time, it was essential that Soames should have no suspicions aroused that he himself had had the finger pointed at him; a difficult tightrope to walk success-fully, but one that had naturally been ex-pected and prepared for.

Ogilvie answered the question. 'He's at Brigade,' he said. 'He'll be sent back to duty soon—'

'I want him now, this instant.'

'I'm sorry, Soames. He's under orders, and so am I.'

'Whose orders?'

'The War Office, but you'll find they've been confirmed by Sir George White's office in Calcutta. I'm sorry, Soames. I know he's yours and not ours, but the fact is, there are heads poised for the chopping-block in London. Unorthodox things were done, as you'll realise. There's a certain Major-General in the War House ... arrangements were made to get Akhbar Mohammad Khan out of England as soon as possible and beyond reach, but the Major-General's still there.'

'Worrying about his damn pension,'

Soames said with another sneer. 'Well, that's his bloody worry, not mine. I'm asking for that man back. You going to cough him up, or not, Ogilvie?'

'It's not my decision now. My part's done. I happened to be in London and available, and I got dragged in, that's all. I was glad to help.'

'Or interfere,' Soames snapped. The thin lips were drawn back tightly against the teeth. 'I'm his squadron commander. From now on, I'll do all the interfering that's necessary. I—'

'One moment, Captain Soames.' Hay, giving a quiet cough, interposed himself between Soames and Ogilvie. 'Captain Ogilvie, I think, has explained the situation in quite enough detail. I understand your views and your concern, of course, but any further representations must come from your Colonel and not yourself – and should be addressed to Brigade and not to Captain Ogilvie or anyone else of this regiment.' Hay looked Soames up and down, then added cuttingly, 'I think, sir, were you sober, you would understand this very well. And since you are not, then I must ask you to leave this ante-room and return to your own canton-ment.'

Soames's face suffused with blood, the blood of a reckless fury. 'You bloody old—'

'Unless you prefer to leave under escort.' Soames's breath hissed through his teeth. He glared around: by now three or four of the Scots officers had moved towards the group, casually. In their faces were looks of anticipation, and in their arms was a noticeable flexing of willing muscles. In the doorway stood the corporal of mess servants. Soames flicked his tongue around his lips; the situation was for a long moment one of touch and go. Then the cavalryman, without further words, swung round and went stiffly to the door, and disappeared. They heard lurching footsteps going down the corridor, then banging across the verandah to crunch away over the parade-ground towards the gate guard. In the ante-room nothing was said, the drunken intrusion shrugged off with raised eyebrows and sardonic looks. The piano softly played 'Come Where the Booze is Cheaper'.

'Disgraceful performance,' Lord Dornoch said next morning. He had arrived back from Nowshera a little after eleven o'clock and had sent for Ogilvie and Hay to come to his bungalow. They sat on chintz chair covers, drinking *chota pegs*. From the distance of the parade-ground came the tremendous voice of Regimental Sergeant-Major Cunningham. 'Doesn't endear one to the cavalry, that sort of thing. A bunch of loafers. Those that pass bottom out of Sandhurst always gravitate to the cavalry, but I'm not to be quoted on that!' He grinned across at Ogilvie. He had been delighted to welcome Ogilvie back, and for his part Ogilvie was glad to see him again and to relieve himself of his full, official report on the lance-*duffardar*. 'I wonder – drink apart – why he did it?'

Hay said, 'He seems to have regretted it, Colonel. Or perhaps, deep down, he's a sahib after all!'

'What d'you mean, John?'

'A runner came with a letter, just after breakfast. For me. Apologies to the mess and myself.'

Dornoch's eye gleamed. 'Abject?'

'Something short of that! But he wants to correct a bad impression, I think.'

'With an eye to his future? I'm still puzzled: why did he make an exhibition of himself in what he must have known was a useless effort? He knows the drill as well as anyone else. He *must* have had the word through his regiment that it had all been handed to Brigade, surely?'

Hay shrugged. 'As you suggested, Colonel: drink taken!'

'Perhaps. Or perhaps a case of the dog returning to his vomit! He had to confront

Ogilvie.'

'If guilty, Colonel. We can't be entirely certain.'

'Quite,' Dornoch said at once. 'I – all of us – must avoid seeming to prejudge him. But there have been so many unsavoury aspects, you'll agree. The action at Chakwal ... no proof, but the finger of suspicion was somewhat pointed. And the feller's wife, now. She was sick certainly, no deception there, but she recovered damn fast once Soames was back in India! A convincing malingery? Soames could have sent her an instruction by a cleverly worded cable.'

'That would suggest her involvement, would it not?'

'No, no, I don't suggest that,' Dornoch said with a touch of irritation. 'Just a way of getting the two of them together again is how *she* would have seen it. I don't condone it, but it's been known to happen before in India. Anyway, this visit of his. He's possibly the sort who dislikes inaction – and the cavalry have a reputation for being brash and impulsive.' He paused, then raised an eyebrow at Ogilvie. 'I'm sure you were properly circumspect, James, in your reaction?'

'Yes, Colonel.'

'Then we'll keep it that way. Not the smallest suspicion to be aroused that the lance-*duffardar* has talked.'

'Soames must be worrying about that already, Colonel.'

'It'll certainly have crossed his mind! But my view, and the Divisional Commander's view too incidentally, is that he'll still feel secure on account of his own inbuilt threat to the lance-*duffardar*. I don't need to stress how huge their white officers loom in the minds of the sepoys and sowars of the native regiments. Soames'll be nicely convinced that the man will be too damn scared of him to talk out of turn.'

'How's General Fettleworth taking it, Colonel?' Hay asked.

Dornoch grinned again. 'Anxiously! But he sees compensations. He's inflating fast. Tomorrow's inspection has been upgraded from a Brigadier-General's to an Army Commander's. Your father, James – he's already reached Nowshera from Murree, and there'll be much work for the Adjutant and all company officers, with the whole garrison on parade for inspection and march past. The Wiltshires look like being thrown in at the deep end of Bloody Francis's pool, poor beggars!'

Hay raised an eyebrow. 'Is there something behind this, Colonel?'

'Yes, there is. Sir George White will be present in person – it was considered safer for the mountain to come to Mahomet –

interests of security, according to the Political Officer at Division. You'll be smuggled in to see the Commander-in-Chief, James, after the parade, as will the lance-*duffardar*. Better than if the two of you were sent across by train to Calcutta, you see.'

'Yes, Colonel.' Ogilvie hesitated. 'There's a degree of real concern, then?'

The Colonel gave a short laugh. 'You could call it that. Well now, James, consider yourself briefed – and in the meantime, back to your ordinary duties. Let's have a smart turn-out tomorrow.' He clapped his hands, and a bearer entered the room instantly. 'A runner to the Adjutant sahib. My compliments, and I would like words with him.'

'At once, Colonel sahib.' The native bowed low, hands together, then backed away from the Colonel's presence.

Ogilvie had scarcely left the Colonel's bungalow, had only just passed Andrew Black hurrying to obey his summons, when a thunderclap occurred upon the parade-ground of the Royal Strathspeys, a human thunderclap that smashed boot-leather into the sandy surface as it halted in front of Ogilvie and dazzled his eyes with a shimmering salute and a pacestick held rigidly horizontal with the ground.

75

'Captain Ogilvie, sir! Good morning, sir! Welcome back, sir!'

'Thank you, Mr Cunningham. Glad to hear you in such good voice.'

'Aye, sir. And you look well, sir. Tell me, Captain Ogilvie, how was Scotland?'

'Bonnie enough,' Ogilvie answered seriously. He knew well Cunningham's love for Scotland, how the old warrant officer was torn between duty on the North-West Frontier and the mountains and glens and lochs of his beloved Speyside, scenes that seemed ever reflected in the deep piercing blue of Cunningham's level eyes. 'There were many at Invermore who asked to be remembered, both in the town and the depot. I told them the day would come when we'd be marching back into barracks off the train from Edinburgh – with you and your pace-stick keeping us all to the step!'

'Aye, sir, I'll be doing that. In the meantime, sir, there's the parade. They say the GOC's coming, sir.'

Ogilvie raised an eyebrow: the Indian bush telegraph was a most remarkable instrument. 'They do, do they, Sar'nt-Major? And anyone else?'

'Yes, Captain Ogilvie, the Commander-in-Chief in India.' There was not a flicker in Cunningham's expression. 'Will you be taking your company, sir?'

'Yes, I will.'

'Then with respect, sir, I suggest some drill. You'll have grown a little away from it on leave, sir. If you have nothing else to do at this moment, sir, I'll pass the word that you wish B Company on parade in drill order.'

Cunningham looked expectant: with the brass coming, he had no wish to be let down by officers sleek and fat from long leave. With as good a grace as possible, Ogilvie gave in. The bugle blew for B Company to fall in, and when they had doubled on parade Ogilvie did what he knew Cunningham expected him to do, and dismissed the drill sergeants. Under the personal and critical eye of Cunningham he wheeled and turned B Company, marched them up and down and back again, formed fours, formed two-deep, ordered arms, shouldered arms, presented arms, carried arms at the short trail, piled arms, double marched, turned into line and into column of route, sharpening to a fine point the voice of command that had become muted in talking to friends and elderly relatives, ghillies, tenants, and Mary Archdale. When the drill was over he felt he had a new liver, since he had not stood in one place for long himself, and was in no doubt at all that he had rejoined the regiment. And there was a word of praise from Cunningham: 'Not bad, Captain Ogilvie! Not bad. A touch more panache and we'll be back right where we were, sir.'

Five

The next day's parade was the usual magnificently stage-managed affair and never mind the short notice: the turn-out of the 114th Highlanders, The Queen's Own Royal Strathspeys, was impeccable. The scene was splendid and colourful. In a rising cloud of dust the dark blue, gold-frogged jackets of the Royal Horse Artillery moved past before the guns and limbers, to be followed by two squadrons of The Guides and two of the Kohat Light Horse, with Captain Soames commanding the lead squadron of his regiment. Behind them, dressed in review order, marched the infantry of the British Army – the Dorsetshires, the Middlesex, the newly-drafted Wiltshires, the 114th High-landers. Ogilvie, marching past the saluting base behind the pipes and drums, gave the eyes-left order to B Company: he was aware of his father, grave-faced and straight-backed, standing at the salute. A pace behind him swelled the pompous figure of Lieutenant-General Francis Fettleworth, commanding the First Division, eyes a trifle moist as he thought of Queen and Empire and sweated into his scarlet tunic beneath the drooping ostrich feathers of his cocked hat. The Scots moved on, and behind came the native regiments of the Indian Army with their mixture of Queen's Commissioned and Viceroy's Commissioned Officers. Colour and martial sound – the rumble of the limber wheels, the creak of harness, the rhythm of marching feet and the drums – the thin winter sunlight striking fire from the steel of bayonets and the brass of polished buttons, the white of pipeclay and the gleaming brown of leather equipment, and from the gaily coloured dresses of the ladies, wives and women of the Peshawar garrison: it was something to stir any heart, let alone Fettleworth's. Here in Peshawar the army was perched on the brink of Empire, the last defence line of the Raj: westerly lay the jagged peaks of Afghanistan beyond the lonely Khyber Pass, to the north the foothills of Himalaya rose to the everlasting snows; south and east lay the Salt Range with its seeds of rebellion. As the regiments marched away off parade behind their beating drums they seemed to leave a sense of forboding on the emptying *maidan*.

'I want the whole story from start to finish, Ogilvie,' Sir George White said. Ogilvie, who had been bidden to Brigade, was now seated while the Commander-in-Chief stood by a deep window looking out upon the Union Flag floating from its staff in the centre of a patch of brilliant green grass. With Sir George were Sir Iain Ogilvie and Fettleworth, the latter appearing to be highly frustrated at being forced to listen rather than speak his mind.

Ogilvie obeyed the order, giving the story concisely. Sir George pulled at one end of his drooping moustache. 'This man Zachary. Was Soames concerned in any way at his Court Martial?'

The question had been addressed to Fettleworth. 'He was not, sir,' the Divisional Commander answered.

'Never mentioned at all?'

'No, sir.'

'There's never been any imputation against Soames?'

Fettleworth scratched his jaw. 'Not in that connection, sir. And nothing *positive* at any time. There was the Chakwal massacre—'

'Chakwal. An Indian infantry battalion destroyed. And where, pray, did Soames come into that?'

'I don't know that he did, sir. It was not in

my view certain enough to make a report... at any rate, not at that time.'

'Then I suggest you make one now, and at once, General Fettleworth.'

Fettleworth sighed. 'Very well, sir.' He outlined the facts as known: Soames, then a staff officer attached to Brigade in Peshawar, was one of only two officers apart from Fettleworth himself and the Brigade Commander who had had advance knowledge of the relevant troop movement. The Wolf's men had been ready and the sepoys had marched straight into a trap. A tip-off had been suspected. In the meantime the other officer had died of a fever. Although Soames had been known to have ridden out alone from Peshawar a couple of days before the action, and had flown into a violent rage when his somewhat furtive return had been jokingly remarked upon, there was no proof whatsoever: the dead officer could have been guilty, if indeed anyone was. Since the dead officer had been of impeccable character, however, Fettleworth had taken the precaution of removing Captain Soames from the staff back to regimental duties. No further action had been taken.

'I see.' The Commander-in-Chief took a turn or two up and down the room, frowning. 'Nothing to go on, either then or now. Currently we have just the statements of two NCOs, one British and in gaol, the other Indian. What about this lance-*duffardar*, Fettleworth?'

'A man of first-class character, according to his Colonel's reports.'

'And rape wouldn't fit that character?'

'Rape's rape,' Fettleworth answered, 'and scarcely to be equated with military assessments – but I would doubt it fitting, I think.'

'Ogilvie?'

'I agree with General Fettleworth, sir. I formed the opinion at once that he wasn't guilty.'

'So you said indeed.' Sir George paused. 'In his middle thirties, long service, a medal for gallantry – yet he's no more than a lance-*duffardar*. Why?'

Fettleworth shrugged. 'A question of vacancies, I believe. They can't all be promoted.'

'True. Perhaps it's not important.' Again White paused, then went off on another track. 'This man they call the Wolf of the Salt Range ... he's been causing us trouble for years, but lately he's been quiescent, I'm told. Why's that?'

'Waiting to pounce!' Fettleworth answered belligerently. 'And I suppose that could be where Soames comes in. Soames passes him the information – disposition of our troops and so on – tells him when the time's ripe!

And I—'

'Ripe for what, General?'

Fettleworth thrust his chin forward. 'Why, sir, for bloody war – for revolt – for *mutiny*! It could all happen again – we must show eternal vigilance—'

'You believe this Wolf of the Salt Range to be capable of action on that kind of scale?'

'I do, Sir George. I do indeed! He could inflame all the border tribes, he could summon assistance from the Pathans inside Afghanistan, he could cause a rising in Waziristan, he could interrupt all the salt revenues – by God!'

'I don't disagree,' Sir George said mildly. 'I understand he's a man of influence in tribal circles.'

'And of power, sir. A man who'll stop at nothing, at no atrocity – a man whose hands are bloody with murder. And now, it seems, he has British officers in his pocket. It's disgraceful, scandalous!' Bloody Francis' eyes bulged from their sockets. 'We must act decisively, sir, and at once!'

'Yes. What would you propose, General?'

'I, sir? I would propose that we follow up the advantage of today's parade. That will have impressed 'em, by God! A show of strength, of British power and authority – we have the guns, the horses, the men!' Fettleworth's whole face shone with emotion, with faith in his lifelong panacea, a band-noisy muster of the visible power of the British Raj to put the fear of Queen Victoria into unruly natives. He repeated, 'We must follow up, Sir George. I suggest that Northern Command is reinforced as soon as possible with troops from Ootacamund – guns, cavalry, infantry and support columns – that all local leave be cancelled and all officers absent on courses be recalled. I suggest a strengthening of all our routine patrols and a doubling-up of the military and Salt Department garrisons of the outlying forts on the perimeter of the salt line – and a war footing along the Afghan border. We must alert the Border Military Police and the Khyber Rifles.' Fettleworth leaned forward robustly. 'We must find the Wolf, sir, we must cut him out before he has a chance to move!'

White nodded. 'And Soames?'

'Close arrest, sir, and a Court Martial. An example to be made of him!'

'And what would you charge him with?'

Fettleworth's mouth opened and shut again. He simmered. 'Are you suggesting we haven't enough evidence, sir?'

'We have untried evidence only. Hearsay, in effect. A clever defence could make mincemeat of any charge – and we have no right to assume that Zachary and the lance-

duffardar are speaking the truth, though on the face of it I incline to think they are. Captain Ogilvie's report was honest and convincing.'

'Then—'

'But we must be careful not to overplay our hands. We shall watch closely, and we shall be ready, but I shall not order such widespread counter-measures as you suggest, General Fettleworth.' White turned to Sir Iain Ogilvie. 'Has Northern Command the capability of containing the situation without reinforcement, Sir Iain?'

Sir Iain nodded. 'In my view, yes, short of a general rising. The moment that seems likely, if it does, then I shall ask for reinforcements as a matter of urgency.'

'Then I think we wait, gentlemen. And so does Captain Soames wait. I detest this as much as anyone, but it seems to me that a little more rope must be allowed. I'm sure you follow me.' The Commander-in-Chief pulled out a watch and glanced at it. 'Thank you, gentlemen. I'll see the lance-*duffardar* alone.' He smiled. 'So many generals ... a little off-putting, I fancy!'

There was time for a personal exchange in private between father and son, a somewhat stiff interview in which Sir Iain seemed ill-at-ease and to have matters of some embarrassment on his mind. James's mother, he said, sent her love. 'She wanted to come, but I considered this no occasion to have women treading on one's arse,' he said. 'In any case, I rather wanted a word with you alone. You know what your mother is.'

Warning bells sounded. 'In what way, father?'

'Oh, never mind.' Sir Iain pulled at his moustache: it was whiter, Ogilvie noticed, than when last they had met. 'How was Corriecraig?'

'Home!'

Their eyes met in mutual understanding: they shared a deep love of their background. Ogilvie expanded: he had done the rounds of the tenants and crofters. 'All's well, father, nothing that Uncle Rufus can't cope with. The odd leaking roof, one or two who can't muster the rent – Uncle Rufus tells them not to worry and sends down a hamper.'

'Good, good – times aren't easy for them, I know. Your Uncle Rufus never writes – probably can't for all I know. Illiterate lot, the navy.' Sir Iain cleared his throat noisily. 'And London? How was London? Have a good time, did you?'

'Yes, until the War Office nosed me out.'

'Quite.' Sir Iain brought out a handker-

chief and blew his nose. 'We understand –
your mother and I – that you met poor
Archdale's widow in London.'

'You *understand*, father?'

'There was a Mrs Major Babbit staying at
Brown's. You probably don't know her.
Babbitt was on the staff out here some years
ago – there's still a son in Murree, a
Civilian. She cabled him on his birthday.'

'And spent money on my affairs at the
same time?'

Sir Iain put a hand on his shoulder. 'I'm
sorry, James. You know what India's like,
and old habits die hard. Just be careful,
that's all I have to say – though your
mother's said a good deal more.' He paused.
'Is it right that she's coming out here –
Archdale's widow?'

Ogilvie ground his teeth in silent fury:
Mary, in his parents' eyes, would be stuck
for all time with the image of 'poor Tom
Archdale'. He asked, 'Mrs Major Babbitt
again?'

'No. The bush telegraph in Murree. Is
she?'

'Yes, she is. And I'm afraid it's outside my
control.'

'Of course. Well – I'll risk saying it again:
be careful, James. You're in a good regiment,
the best there is – and you're an Ogilvie of
Corriecraig.'

★ ★ ★

In a black mood, Ogilvie rode back to the Royal Strathspeys' cantonment. He felt no commitment towards Mary Archdale, and knew that she didn't expect him to, but any interference infuriated him – even to the point, he sometimes believed, when he might propose to her out of sheer dog-in-the-manger obstinacy and perversity. He enjoyed Mary's company; they laughed at the same things and she was very easy to be with, was not demanding and was full of understanding; and they had India in common, though she had always been inclined to take military life lightly and had no real interest in things regimental. Certainly she disliked, as much as he, the intrigues, the gossip, the reputation-shredding and the sillier social manifestations of wives and daughters with too little else to fill their days. He was not sure how the term 'love' fitted in with Mary Archdale: he was fond of her, but probably no more than that. And in any case, Murree was not Peshawar; in the normal course of events, they would not meet much. But Mary was perfectly capable of manipulating the course of events ... and Ogilvie knew it was not his parents alone with whom he had to walk warily: there had been occasions in the past when Andrew Black, full of regimental sanctimoniousness, had, taken him to task for his association with a Scarlet Woman – but that had been in the days when 'poor Tom Archdale', Brigade Major, had still been alive.

Ogilvie returned the salute of the Sergeant of the Guard as he came through the gate, and rode towards the stables where he handed his horse over to a salaaming *syce*. When he reached the ante-room on his way to his quarters, the mess corporal told him the Colonel wished to see him on his return, and he went at once to Lord Dornoch's office, where he made his report.

'As a matter of fact,' Dornoch said, 'a despatch has reached me ahead of you. The C-in-C's orders are confirmed – alertness but no panic is the basis of them. He doesn't refer to Soames in any way.'

'He's to be lulled, Colonel.'

'I rather thought so – a false sense of security. And closely watched, no doubt.'

'Yes, Colonel. What about the lance-*duffardar*?'

'Returned to his unit forthwith.' Dornoch shook his head. 'I don't like it.'

'It'll not be easy for him,' Ogilvie said in partial agreement. 'Soames will put pressure on. But it's the only way, Colonel. If anything else had been done, Soames would have been suspicious right away.'

'Yes, I realise that. It's still tricky, though, and a risk. There's another element that doesn't appeal to me in the least, and it won't have appealed to Sir George White either: the lance-*duffardar*'s going to be used as a spy – not that that's indicated in the orders, of course – a spy on a British officer!'

'A British officer who's asked for it, Colonel.'

'I realise that too, if he's guilty. It's still distasteful. I sometimes think we're no longer living the lives of gentlemen, James. Times are changing, and not for the better.' Dornoch gave a sigh and seemed to be looking back into past days, but then checked the drift of his mood, and smiled. 'I must be careful what I say, or I shall soon be thought too senile to command! I hold no brief for Captain Soames, certainly. Thank you for your report, James. I'll be having a word with the Adjutant shortly, and then battalion orders will be issued – we're required to provide more patrols for a start.' He nodded a dismissal; as Ogilvie saluted and turned about there came the sound of hurried footsteps outside and Andrew Black came in, saluted the Colonel, and handed him an envelope.

'Another despatch, Colonel, from Brigade.'

Dornoch slit the envelope, brought out a single sheet of paper, and read it quickly. He looked up, his face grim. 'Fort Gaza's been over-run – one of the forts along the perimeter of the Salt Range.'

'What happened, Colonel?'

Dornoch shrugged. 'No details beyond the bare ones: the whole garrison's been found with slit throats – Salt Department sowars. The Salt Department's asked for assistance, and Brigade's handing it to us.'

Black's eyebrows went up. 'A cavalry commitment, not—'

'Brigade says cavalry can't be spared. The Guides have been ordered out to the Afghan border and the Kohat Light Horse to Waziristan. I'm ordered to provide a detachment of half-company strength to act as mounted infantry and garrison Fort Gaza until a cavalry relief can be provided.'

Ogilvie, as the most experienced of the company commanders and by now a good horseman, was ordered by the Colonel to take command of a composite detachment of the best riders from all companies and to be ready to move out before dark. By the time the moon was up, coldly, to throw stark shadows streaming back towards the distant hills, Ogilvie was well on his way south and east with his makeshift detachment of mounted infantry, dressed in trews and sitting, uncomfortably for the most part, upon the backs of an assortment of horses and mules provided partly from regimental resources and partly by the Remount Depot. A number of mules were being led as transport animals, carrying heavy loads of stores, ammunition and equipment. With the half-company trundled a number of commissariat camels, also heavily weighed down by stores and water and more ammunition and arms, including a dismantled Maxim gun. In rear of the column rode Colour-Sergeant MacTrease like a sack of potatoes; and in the lead behind Ogilvie rode two pipers, their instruments currently and ignominiously laid between the humps of one of the commissariat camels until such time as, dismounted and in garrison at Fort Gaza, the pipers would come back into their own.

Riding with his senior subaltern, Ogilvie pondered on his orders and the information that had accompanied the despatch from Brigade: Captain Soames had gone with his regiment into the hills of Waziristan. It was anyone's guess what Soames' reaction might have been to that! Did it suit him to be sent into the Waziri hills, where he might make contact with other men in the pay of the Wolf of the Salt Range, or would he find it inconvenient and dangerous to be away from Peshawar at this juncture? Time might tell; for now it was Ogilvie's mission to establish a strong presence in Fort Gaza, to hold that area of the line for the Salt Department, to seek out and arrest the killers of the dead sowars and their officers – one of them British, a captain named Peterson on secondment from an Indian cavalry unit, and one a Viceroy's Commissioned Officer, a *risaldar*. Ogilvie was also under orders to assist the Political Department by finding out anything he could about the future plans of the Wolf. This might be possible by means of interrogation of any prisoners, but Ogilvie was sceptical as to the chances: bandits, brigands and rebels had never been noted as easy talkers, and if there was something big in the air they would have good reason to maintain clamps upon their tongues; the Wolf was a hard master, with the bloodiest hands in this part of India. Two years earlier his son, a boy of no more than twelve or thirteen years of age, had been taken by a British patrol and brought out from the Waziri hills to Peshawar. He had seemed to know little and a kindly Brigadier-General had ordered his release after some mild questioning. The boy got back into Waziristan where, according to the bush telegraph, his father the

Wolf, fearing he might have talked, had had him tortured. From there fact had taken over again from the bush telegraph: the boy had died and his body had been found by another British patrol, staked out in the hot sun of summer. There was little left of him and the remains were identified by an amulet. *Pour encourager les autres*, had been the theory in Peshawar. With the Wolf, business came first. Riding on through the moonlit night, the chilly winter night of northern India, glad enough not to be in the Khyber snows, Ogilvie talked to his subaltern about the Salt Department, so vital to India's wealth in its activities for the Inland Customs and in its armed maintenance of the customs line known as the hedge.

'We're outside the scope of the hedge around here, aren't we?' Anderson asked.

Ogilvie nodded. 'In a sense, in Fort Gaza, *we*'ll be the hedge. Us and the other outposts. We stand between the Wolf and what he regards, no doubt, as his rightful *cumshaw*.' Mentally Ogilvie reviewed the background of the sub-continent's money-spinning salt industry. The main centre was in the central and southern parts of the Khattack district, where the salt deposits were truly massive and were, in a geological context, thought to be an extension of the

Punjab deposits across the Indus, though there were certain differences of age and colour between those of the Punjab and those of the Kohat district. Something like one-fifth of the total area of Kohat was taken up by the salt workings; at Bahadur Khel hills and cliffs of salt rose some five to seven hundred feet, with, in some places, two-foot cappings of gypsum, the beds themselves containing salt of great purity – ninety-nine per cent sodium chloride or common salt. The bed of the Bahadur Khel gorge was pure rock salt, with a seam thickness of five hundred feet; and there was an exposed eight-mile seam running to a depth of almost a thousand feet. When the Punjab and other Sikh lands were annexed to the British after the Second Sikh War ending in 1850, the Kohat salt deposits came under British dominion; and as British rule was consolidated the Salt Department came into being and the salt became a dutiable product; as a natural result, smuggling grew up into a highly profitable business, and over the years there had been any number of bloody affrays against the British usurpers of the salt. The barrier-line of the embanked hedge had been constructed, and forts set up at strategic points along the hedge and in Kohat, with customs posts at the points where the roads crossed. Officers of the Inland Customs Department manned the line, took the duty, and dealt with smuggling. Of the forts, the majority were small outposts manned by fifteen sepoys of the Salt Department; but at more widely spaced intervals were larger ones such as Fort Gaza, manned by cavalry who had the responsibility of providing assistance to the smaller outposts as and when required; and since there was no other means of inter-communication, continual patrols were ridden out to keep in contact with the out-lying stations, patrols that came under some kind of attack more often than not; and it would be such patrols that the Royal Strathspey would be required to provide once in garrison at Fort Gaza...

They moved on, taking only two brief night halts to rest the animals. It was wild country, with the great jagged peaks seeming to press against the sky as though to puncture the heavens, and mainly overlaid with an intense silence broken occasionally by the cry of some nocturnal bird or beast of prey. After some thirty miles they forded the Sohan River east of Kalabagh; they had had to move at the speed of the laden commissariat and ammunition train, and never mind the Colonel's order for a fast ride; by the time they were across the Sohan

97

dawn was in the eastern sky. There was another fifty-mile ride ahead; but when the soldiers stiffly mounted again after the breakfast fall-out, they rode on in good spirits beneath a warming sun and clear skies, the hoofbeats sending up clouds of sandy dust below the hills covered with winter-withered acacia, a variety known to the local natives as palosa. Round here in due season would be wild olives, and large bushes with dark-green leaves, a kind of sloe berry known as gurgurra; and in the valley were trees of ber and shisham, trees whose wood was used for the building of houses. The country had its own peculiar beauty though largely it was barren now; it also seemed not to be hostile currently. The day's ride proved as peaceful as that of the night.

It was evening again when Ogilvie sighted Fort Gaza, defensively situated on rising ground that commanded a broad valley between great hills standing almost sheer along the sides, a place of extreme lone-liness and remoteness that the riders approached at right angles, dropping down from the north out of a mountain pass. The fort was surrounded by a thick, high wall of compacted mud, and from behind this wall rose a tall, battlemented watch-tower that would normally be manned day and night.

Now the fort stood desolate, with no guarding sentries visible. The gateway was closed, the flagstaff rose bare, with the trailing end of a cut halliard blowing in a cold breeze funnelling down the valley: a look of possible danger. Though the despatch to the Colonel had indicated a small holding force left behind by the Salt Department after finding the slaughter, it was always on the cards that there had been a second foray from the hills.

Ogilvie lifted his right hand, and the column came to a halt. Bringing his horse round, Ogilvie faced his mounted troop. 'Home,' he said, 'for God knows how long! We shall make the best of it, though I admit it looks like the end of the world! Colour MacTrease?'

MacTrease rode up and saluted. 'Sir!'

'We move in at a walk. There'll be watching eyes – and listening ears.' Ogilvie waved a hand around the hills. 'We shall let them know for certain that Fort Gaza's garrisoned again. Dismount the pipers, if you please, Colour, and send them ahead with the pipes.'

'Aye, sir.'

'We may need to break down the gate, so we'll have the pioneers ready with axes. And warn the men there could be a reception committee for all we know. Rifles at the ready, Colour.'

'They'll be that, sir.'

'And as soon as we're inside, I want the watch-tower manned. A lance-corporal and two privates.' Ogilvie looked all around the heights in the fading light, heights picked sharply out by the rays of a brilliant sunset. 'I fancy the fort's nicely placed to be out of range from the hills, but there's to be no lack of alertness.'

'Aye, sir.'

'Right, Colour MacTrease. Carry on, if you please.'

MacTrease saluted again and swung his horse away towards the column. His voice rang out sharply, echoing back from the dead-looking hills. As soon as he had reported, Ogilvie gave the order to walk march. Ahead of the mounted column the pipes, accompanied by the beat of a solitary drummer, burst savagely, triumphantly out, the stirring notes of 'The Campbells Are Coming' breaking harshly into the silence. There was something nostalgic about it: little imagination was needed to see Scotland's face in that remote spot, to change the Indian valley into Glen Etive by Glencoe, to see again Clan Campbell storming out from Inveraray to that same tune of war and glory and death. *Great Argyll, he goes before, he makes the cannon and guns to roar...*

Behind the pipes and the drumbeats the mounted column came down upon the fort, the pioneers, well covered by the rifles, now riding ahead towards the gates. But just as they came up close with their axes ready the gates swung open. In the aperture Ogilvie saw the native cavalry uniform and the three chevrons of a *duffardar*. Behind the *duffardar* were two sowars of the Salt Department.

The *duffardar* saluted smartly. 'Welcome, Captain sahib, to Fort Gaza.'

'Who are you?' Ogilvie asked, reining in his horse and halting the column again.

'*Duffardar* Abdul Qadir, sahib, of the detachment that found the slaughter.'

'And your officer?'

'Returned to make the report, sahib, leaving me and two sowars to hold the fort until relief came.'

Ogilvie smiled down at the *duffardar*. 'Nobly held! Did you come under attack?'

'No, sahib, all has been peace.'

'And your orders now?'

'Sahib, I and my sowars are ordered to remain here under your command.'

Ogilvie nodded and looked through the gateway: the fort was still in great disorder, so far as could be seen in what was now almost full dark. 'What's been done inside the fort?' he asked.

'All has been left as it was found, sahib.

101

Those were the orders of my *risaldar*, that whoever came as relief should see for themselves, and perhaps find indications as to who it was that did the killing.'

'And the dead?'

'Unburied, sahib. They are where they fell. Those, too, were the orders.'

Ogilvie felt a slight creeping of his flesh: true, it was winter, and cold enough for a high degree of preservation, but it was usual for burials in India to be carried out with the minimum of delay. Formally, his face stiff, he turned to his subaltern. 'Ride the column in, if you please, Mr Anderson, and walk the horses clear of the dead.'

Anderson saluted and passed the order. Ogilvie turned to the *duffardar*. 'You're from Kohat,' he said. 'Do you have any contact with the Kohat Light Horse?'

'Sometimes we meet, sahib.'

'You've heard, perhaps, of Captain Soames sahib?'

'By name I have heard of him, sahib. A much respected officer sahib, and brave.'

Ogilvie nodded. The *duffardar*'s face was only dimly visible and its expression could not be read; but the voice had been level, dispassionate enough, giving something like the expected answer, the reverence of a native NCO for a British officer of the Raj. It had been a shot in the dark, no more, and

102

it had produced nothing. Ogilvie said, 'Very well, *Duffardar* Abdul Qadir, you have done your duty. I take over now, and will be glad to have you and your sowars to reinforce the garrison.'

He returned the *duffardar*'s salute and rode through the gateway into Fort Gaza behind the rear files of the column. Inside the fort Anderson had split the half-company of riders into their two sections, one to the right, the other to the left, so that they formed a circle around the walls, avoiding what lay in the centre. By this time flares had been lit, and the terrible scene came up starkly, horrifyingly. Bodies lay everywhere, each with its throat slit from ear to ear, and the whole fort seemed red-brown with dried blood. Before the arrival of the *duffardar* and his men, the vultures had been at work: the bodies were badly ripped, indeed half eaten. Under one corpse lay a bloodstained Union Flag, cut down from the white-painted staff. More bodies lay in doorways, two leaned drunkenly from the battlements of the watch-tower, laid bare to the bone by the vultures, their blood staining the walls. There was an appalling stench in the enclosed space. In the stables the horses also lay with cut throats. War was war, and Ogilvie had seen more than enough of death in action during his years on the North-

West Frontier, but here, inside a garrisoned fort, a strong outpost of British power, it seemed to come home with greater impact. He rode his horse towards Anderson, and spoke in a low voice.

'There'll be more inside, David. Guard-room, armoury, living quarters. Take a corporal and two men. I'm sorry, but the bodies will all have to be searched. I'll see to the ones out here.'

'Right.' Anderson paused, seeming surprised. 'What'll we be looking for?'

'Anything that might be useful. I can't be precise. Letters, scraps of paper, personal things. It'd be best if you collect all their possessions together – contents of pockets and pouches – and we'll go through them later.'

'When do we bury the bodies?' the subaltern asked.

'At first light, assuming the search is finished by then. Then we'll clean the place up.' He looked sharply into Anderson's face in the light of the flares. 'What's up, David? Seeing ghosts?'

There was a shaky laugh. 'Oh ... just imagination!'

'About what happened here?'

'About what could happen again. If the bastards slaughtered one garrison, they can—'

'Cut it out, David. We have a job to do. We're going to do it. It's pretty plain there was slackness in the watch – the Salt Department only play at soldiers, after all. We're going to be a tougher proposition, and don't you forget it! All right?'

'Yes, of course.' The young officer's shoulders seemed to brace up again. He swung a leg over his horse's rump, dismounting and calling for a corporal. Just as he did so there was a shout from the watch-tower, already manned on the orders of Colour-Sergeant MacTrease.

'Captain Ogilvie, sir! Tribesmen, sir, attacking from the east along the valley! The buggers have sprung out of nowhere, sir!'

Ogilvie slid down from his horse, calling out for MacTrease. 'All men to the fire-step, fan out along the walls! Farriers to get the horses under cover and gun's crew to assemble the Maxim, fast as you can!' As he ran for the steps leading up inside the watch-tower, distant rifles spoke. He heard the impact of bullets thudding into the mud wall, heard the zing of others overhead, and then, a moment later, the much heavier sound, the roar of artillery.

Six

As the bullets flew, Ogilvie, sheltering as best he could in the lee of the merlons, looked out through field glasses. It was an attack in strength, what appeared to be upwards of a hundred tribesmen fanned out and advancing behind rifle-fire from the east – and another wave coming in now from the west. The artillery, just one single piece, Ogilvie thought, was firing from the eastern side. Gunsmoke drifted down on the fort, sharp and acrid, evil-smelling. The gunnery was poor; some shells flew over-head, others fell short, exploding to send showers of rock and debris over the fort. But the aim improved: a shell smacked into the top of the surrounding mud wall, breaching it for some three feet, and another shook the watch-tower itself. The first one left a gap in the ranks of the Royal Strathspeys: looking down, Ogilvie saw two of his highlanders lying in strange attitudes at the foot of the wall. Another man leapt down from the fire-step and ran towards them. Ogilvie turned to MacTrease at his side. 'That damn gun, MacTrease. It has to be silenced or it'll breach the wall low down and they'll pour in like the tide!'

'We'll get the crew with the Maxim, sir. I've ordered it to be brought up here, sir.'

'Good man!' Ogilvie turned back towards the native horde. They had advanced a fair distance, but they seemed halted now by the deadly rifle fire from the walls of the fort, and many had fallen. The element of surprise had gone, and the attackers were plainly shaken by the strength and ferocity of the defence. Curses and a sharp smell of body sweat heralded the crew of the Maxim, bringing their as yet dismantled gun to the top of the tower. Within moments it was assembled and in action, swinging its aim around the piece of artillery, which was still firing and blowing chunks off the walls and inner buildings of the fort. But that was not to last for much longer: Ogilvie was watching when there came a vast flash and an almighty roar and the gun seemed to erupt. There were shrieks from the tribesmen, who began running in all directions, and then came MacTrease's boisterous and happy shout: 'The bloody thing's blown up, sir! It's gone sky high, sir, and burst its bloody breech block!'

Ogilvie grinned tightly. 'The Maxim got

some vital part, did it?'

'I'd not be knowing, sir, but at a guess it blew itself up. It was probably last used in the Mutiny!' MacTrease wiped sweat from his face with a beefy hand. 'They're a daft lot of buggers anyway, sir, begging your pardon, who don't know how to maintain their weapons properly.'

Ogilvie grinned again. 'They obviously lack a good colour-sergeant!'

'Sir?'

'Never mind, Colour. Pass the order to cease firing – they're running hell for leather.' Ogilvie relaxed as MacTrease called the order down. 'First round to us!'

'Aye, sir. And they just may not be too anxious to try again.'

'We won't bank on that at all events. It looks to me as though someone means to obliterate Fort Gaza. I'm just wondering why!'

'It's the salt line, sir.'

'I know, but we're only one of many forts. Besides, all-out attacks, wholesale slaughter of garrisons – that's unusual. What we've come to expect is piecemeal stuff, isn't it?'

'Aye, that's true, sir.'

Ogilvie scanned the surrounding countryside closely through his glasses: the native attackers had faded right away already so far as he could make out. Nothing seemed to be stirring. Lowering his glasses he turned again to his colour-sergeant. 'Keep the men standing to until the moon's up, Colour MacTrease. When there's light enough to spot any attack while it's still distant, fall them out for supper and maintain a normal watch up here, and a gate guard. I'm to be informed at once if anything is seen moving.'

'Very good, sir.'

'And send a party to survey the damage, and make good where possible.' Returning MacTrease's salute, Ogilvie went down the spiral steps at the run, meeting Anderson at the bottom. He enquired about casualties: three men killed, two wounded but not seriously. He said, 'Get your search party together now, David, and go through the buildings. When the moon's up, we'll go out and take a look at the dead tribesmen out there.'

'Won't they take their dead with them, James?'

Ogilvie gave a short laugh. 'I fancy that's just what they haven't done! They didn't want to linger inside our range.' He turned away, found a sergeant and gave orders for men to be detailed to assist him in the search of the bodies lying in the open courtyard. The search was thorough, but nothing of interest was found on the dead: it had been a long shot and Ogilvie had not really expected to find gold; if any of the native garrison had been in Soames' pay – for instance – there would scarcely be documentary evidence, but the possibility could not have been overlooked. Anderson reported a similar lack of success inside the various compartments of the fort. The subaltern's face was white and drawn in the light of the guard lantern; he had not yet been long enough on the Frontier to have seen mass death on this scale. By now the moon was up, and the fort's surroundings were lit by silvery light, with deep dark shadows extending distantly from the hills. The night had grown cold, with a wind that seemed to come right down from the snows of Himalaya, penetrating shivering bodies with its icy fingers. Ogilvie heard MacTrease passing the orders for the men along the fire-step to stand down, heard him setting the watch at the top of the tower. A few moments later a dismounted detail marched smartly past the silent corpses on the ground to form the gate guard, a sergeant calling the step. MacTrease came up to report, and Ogilvie told him he was going out personally to examine the tribesmen killed in the recent attack.

'I'll take a corporal and six men,' he said, 'with rifles and side-arms. If there's trouble,

I'll want covering fire from the fort.'

'Aye, sir. Will I not come with you, sir?'

'No, Colour MacTrease. Detail the men at once, if you please. They must wait for their supper till they get back.' Ogilvie turned away with Anderson, who would be in charge in his absence. 'If we should come under attack, and I doubt very much if we will, there's to be no reinforcement from the fort, David.'

Anderson raised his eyebrows. 'But surely—'

'An order. It's to be obeyed. All I want is covering fire. The fort and its garrison's to remain as intact as possible. If we allow ourselves to be drawn, we'll be reduced by attrition. Understood?'

'Understood,' Anderson answered uneasily. 'But I don't like it.'

Ogilvie smiled. 'There's a lot to dislike on Indian service. Chin up, old man.'

They went out openly; there was no chance to do anything else under the strong light of the climbing moon. Behind them, the ready rifles of the tower detail and the muzzle of the Maxim provided some comfort. Corporal Williamson asked about burials.

'Of the tribesmen?'

'Yes, sir.'

Ogilvie said, 'No burials, Corporal. I

wouldn't risk lives, and in any case it won't be necessary. Use your eyes, man!'

Williamson looked ahead of the line of march, narrowing his eyes. There was a good deal of shadow ... but then he saw it: a kind of slow undulation, an up-and-down movement of a sea of black. He caught his breath, said in an awed voice, 'The vultures, sir!'

'Right! You've not been out here long, have you?'

'No, sir.'

'Watch this, then.' Ogilvie pulled his revolver from the holster on his Slade-Wallace equipment, and fired a round into the air above the seething, gobbling vultures. On the heels of it the black sea rose in an angry cloud, squawking furiously, spreading outwards, hovering, the odd bird swooping down again and then wheeling back into the sky, disturbed but watchful, ever ready to resume the interupted meal when the intruders had gone.

'The filthy bastards,' Williamson said in a low voice.

'You'll get used to it.' Ogilvie glanced sideways at the corporal's face. The man looked sick, greenish from the moon and his own disgust. He would have seen the horrible remains back in the fort, but remains were remains, and stood at one remove from a meal in progress. The party marched on, under the eyes of the hovering birds of prey, under God knew what other eyes, human eyes, that could be watching from the surrounding peaks. It was a naked, exposed feeling, and one that was not helped by their arrival among the dead. The vultures had had a fair start: the blood was fresh, the beak-rips gaped raw. Most of the already tattered, filthy clothing had been torn away to expose guts and entrails. The search was a thing of utter horror and beastliness: Ogilvie heard retching from the men and felt deathly sick himself. There was no interference from any living tribesmen, no shooting from the hillsides – Ogilvie believed they were in any case out of useful range – and, once again, the search to both east and west failed to produce the kind of evidence he was after. But it did produce evidence of a more or less expected kind: each corpse, where the relevant part had not been torn away by the vultures, showed a branded mark on the left side of the ribcage below the arm-pit – the head and the snarling jaws of a wolf, burned into the flesh.

At nine a.m. next morning a guard was paraded with the pipers and the drummer, and the Union Flag, a fresh one brought from Peshawar, was hoisted with proper ceremony to the head of the flagstaff: once again, Fort Gaza was manifestly a part of the Raj. As Ogilvie's and Anderson's hands came down from the salute, the rifles and fixed bayonets of the guard crashed from the Present to the Order, and the men were marched away with arms at the short trail. Next, the burial parties were detailed, the bodies of the three soldiers of the 114th and those of the former garrison were carried out of the fort on stretchers and in canvas tarpaulins found in the quartermaster's store, and to the sound of Last Post blown by the buglers, were laid in shallow graves covered with cairns of stones marked by small wooden crosses hastily constructed by the pioneers: all the dead had served the Raj, had died in the name of the Queen-Empress, and as such were honoured. Ogilvie, saluting the fallen, refused them only one thing: a firing party. In the days ahead they might well have a need of every round of ammunition, and the exigencies of the hurried march and the need to bring only essentials had provided them with no blanks.

Back inside the fort, Ogilvie made his rounds; already the fatigue parties had brought order and cleanliness, and the stores and ammunition had been properly stowed under the supervision of the Company Quartermaster-Sergeant and Colour-Sergeant MacTrease. The gate guard was smartly turned out with well-pressed trews, and polished leather bandoliers across the immaculate khaki tunics. Under the climbing sun the fort began to feel more like a British establishment, with the barrack-rooms cleanly swept and scrubbed and the tiny Officers' Mess, a room that served also as ante-room, as spruce as Ogilvie's bearer could make it.

Rounds finished, Ogilvie sank into a comfortable armchair and called for *chota pegs* for himself and Anderson. When the drinks had been brought Ogilvie dismissed the bearer, who salaamed his way out of the mess to his own pantry. 'Patrols, David,' Ogilvie said. 'I'd like you to detail two, to ride out shortly. Let's say a corporal and lance-corporal and six men for each patrol, with provisions, water and ammunition for twenty-four hours. I'll give them their orders myself when they're ready to go.'

'Communications?'

Ogilvie shrugged. 'As ever out here, David – none. And none with Peshawar. The Colonel raised the question of us laying down a field telegraph line, but the advice from Brigade was that in the Salt Range lines are always cut the moment the sappers are out of sight. Brigade's given up wasting

115

time and public money!' He drank whisky. 'We're absolutely on our own from now till we're relieved – and God knows when that'll be, old man!'

'Not too bloody long, I hope. I feel I've had enough already!'

'Someone has to do it. The Indian Empire rests on its ruddy salt!'

Anderson made a sarcastic sound. 'One would have thought some quarrying into the treasure chests of the native princes would pay off better. All those rubies and emeralds and diamonds. Not to mention the gold.'

Ogilvie wagged a finger in the subaltern's face. 'Politics, old man! That's not our job as soldiers.'

'I suppose not.' Anderson finished his whisky, got to his feet and moved across to the small, deep-set window that looked on to the courtyard and the flagstaff with its floating Union Flag. 'Soldiers of the Queen ... and all that! *For we're part of England's glory, lads...*'

'We're a damn sight more glorious than the politicians, at all events, David.' Ogilvie grinned suddenly. 'Have you ever met Blaise-Willoughby ... Political Officer at Division?'

'The major with the monkey? I've heard of him.'

'Marmoset, actually. Name of Wolseley.'

Anderson laughed. 'Does His Lordship know? Anyway – why d'you ask?'

'Oh, no reason really, except that he's my own personal picture of any man who wears the political label. And also because, sooner or later, he's going to crop up in this bloody business—' Ogilvie, who had been about to make indiscreet mention of Captain Soames, checked himself hastily. 'We'll have those patrols detailed and fallen in. See to it, there's a good chap.'

Anderson nodded, picked up his glengarry and Sam Browne, and left the Mess. Ogilvie heard him sending a runner for Colour-Sergeant MacTrease, and soon after heard the rattle of equipment and the stamp of the horses' hooves as the patrols made ready. The native *syces* held the horses; a snick of bolts told Ogilvie that Anderson was inspecting the rifles. As the men stood by their mounts the subaltern came into the mess to report; and Ogilvie went back with him for the briefing of the two corporals in command. He handed each of them a map of the area, and from his own duplicate map indicated the Salt Department outposts along a line running east and west of the fort.

'You'll see there's around ten miles on average between each, though, as it

117

happens, the next outpost to the west of us is about twenty miles off. After that one, the westerly line veers north-west to skirt a ridge of hills where a pass comes through, some miles above Bannu – between Bannu and Kohat. So the westerly patrol will find its next-but-one outpost on that northerly line. There's a hundred miles each way of us here before the next full-size fort like ours. Our responsibilities cover fifty miles east, fifty miles west – that is, five outposts to be visited in each direction. All right?'

'Yes, sir.'

'Good.' Ogilvie put his map back in its case. 'Corporal Mathieson, you'll ride east. Corporal Thompson, west. Make contact with each outpost and take their reports. Deal with anything you find along the way. You'll not under any circumstances reduce your strength by leaving men behind to replace any outpost casualties, but should an outpost come under attack while you're in the vicinity, you'll repel the natives before continuing the patrol. Any prisoners will be welcome. Any questions? No? Right. You'll find your directions by compass when necessary. The bearings from the fort are indicated on the maps. You'll return here to the fort by ten a.m. tomorrow. If you rest during the night, which you'll need to do unless you're under pressure, watch your

118

bivouacs. I don't need to remind you, the hills hold continuous danger. You must be on the alert throughout. All right?'

'Yes, sir.'

'And remember, if the opportunity arises we have to take the Wolf. We're not here only to garrison Fort Gaza and provide linking patrols. I doubt if the gentleman will manifest himself personally, in fact, but if you take prisoners you must interrogate them yourselves, in case they should get away before you bring them back to me. Try to find out the Wolf's whereabouts and movements. You needn't be too squeamish. You'll have my full backing afterwards.' Ogilvie looked along the line of waiting men, looked at a smart turn-out, at the polished leather of the Slade-Wallace equipment and the cartridge pouches, at the rifles and bayonet scabbards, at the glengarries that in winter replaced the Wolseley helmets and bore the blue-green flash of the Royal Strathspey. It was only too likely that not all the men would return; and for a moment Ogilvie felt a constriction at the back of his throat, as indeed he had felt when the dead had been buried earlier. Every regiment of the British Army was in a sense a family, but the 114th Highlanders were a clan regiment in a more positive sense than many others. Their recruiting area was geographically large but was small in population; very many of the men were related by blood or marriage, the vast majority of them had known each other and each other's families long before they had joined the Colours. Many of them were the sons of tenant farmers and crofters on the Corriecraig lands, lands that covered many of the hills and glens of Speyside from Strath Spey itself to the peaks of the Monadhliath Mountains and the 114th's regimental depot at Invermore. Ogilvie lifted a hand in a gesture of informality. 'Good luck to you all,' he said, then turned to his subaltern. 'Carry on, if you please, Mr Anderson.'

Anderson saluted and gave the order to mount. The two patrols rode out from the opened gateway at a walk, and parted upon their separate ways to east and west. From along the fire-step above the gates the pipes sounded out, playing the tune composed by Pipe-Major Ross when the regiment had first received orders for India – 'Farewell to Invermore'. Somehow it was like a knell; Ogilvie, with his recent thoughts in his mind, would have chosen any other tune than that.

The Sergeants' Mess was even smaller than the Officers' Mess: the Salt Department's garrison was thinner of *duffardars* than an infantry half-company of sergeants. Colour-Sergeant MacTrease had to share the small space with the Company Quartermaster-Sergeant, the Farrier-Sergeant, the Pioneer-Sergeant, and two section sergeants. It was a tight fit, and had it not been for the fact that at any given moment, day or night, at least two of the sergeants were on duty around the fort, the bunk space would have been short.

However, when MacTrease went into the Sergeants' Mess to slake a roaring thirst soon after the two patrols had left, he was alone. He was alone when the *duffardar* left behind by the Salt Department's patrol knocked politely at the open door and asked if he might come in.

MacTrease gave a somewhat surly nod; he was no lover of natives, whether or not they held NCO rank. Useful addition to the fort's defenders they might well be, but MacTrease would have as soon seen them ride back to their distant base. As it was, he was thankful enough that a cubby-hole sized apartment had been found for the accommodation of the three natives: none of the white soldiers would have tolerated their presence. Sourly he asked, 'Well, what do you want of me?'

The answer was a bombshell: 'Obedience, Colour-Sergeant sahib.'

MacTrease started, and stared in utter disbelief. '*What* did you say, you—' He broke off, very suddenly, having seen the muzzle of the heavy revolver looking him blankly in the face. 'By Christ! Now then, what's all this about, may I ask?' He lifted his voice high. '*Bearer!*'

The revolver moved closer. 'It is useless to call for the bearer, Colour-Sergeant sahib. He is dead.' With his free hand, the *duffardar* drew a line across his throat. 'My sowars are outside, also armed. You will now obey my orders. Sit down, please, Colour-Sergeant sahib.'

'I'm buggered if I will.'

'You wish, then, to die?'

'I won't die. You fire that thing, and the whole garrison'll come running.'

The *duffardar* smiled. 'The revolver is one thing, for use in emergency only – but do not mistake, Colour-Sergeant sahib, I shall use it if I must. The other thing is *thuggee*.' He drew a long, thin cord from his pocket. 'The garrotte, Colour-Sergeant sahib. I have only to call my sowars. Now, Colour-Sergeant sahib, please to sit down and keep very quiet.'

Seven

MacTrease was furiously angry; he was also flummoxed. In his view, the *duffardar* hadn't a hope in hell of getting away with whatever it was he intended doing. Any minute now, one of the sergeants would come in. Mac-Trease said as much, but the *duffardar* disagreed.

'No one will enter, Colour-Sergeant sahib. My sowars are guarding, and have orders to kill. They are concealed behind the pantry door, and are experts at *thuggee*.'

MacTrease swallowed. His soldier's eye had told him that the Sergeant's Mess could, under current circumstances, be considered a fine defensive position for the *duffardar*. The walls were thick, there was but the one door and one tiny window, too small to let a man in or out. The door led into a narrow passage, off which led the pantry, and another stout door at the end of the passage formed the sole exit to the courtyard. There was food and water in the pantry, he'd seen it stocked up with his own eyes, and all-in-all the mess could withstand a siege.

He stared coldly at the native NCO. 'What d'you want, you God-damn bugger?'

'I am taking possession of the fort, Colour-Sergeant sahib,' the *duffardar* answered politely. 'You are my hostage.'

'Why me? I'm not the officer.'

'Indeed not, Colour-Sergeant sahib, but you are an important sahib, and you are my lever. I have some knowledge of the British officer sahibs. They are careless of their own lives, but have a regard for those of their men in such circumstances as these.'

'You mean you're going to put pressure on the Captain sahib by threatening to kill me?'

'Just so, Colour-Sergeant sahib.'

MacTrease said scornfully, 'I think you underestimate the Captain sahib, and me too. There'll be no bloody surrender if that's what you believe.'

'We shall see, Colour-Sergeant sahib.' The revolver was aimed steadily at MacTrease's stomach now. The bullets were heavy ones, and would make a nasty mess. MacTrease read murder in the *duffardar*'s eyes, unmistakably: often enough, he had seen that look in close-quarter action. He thought about the *thuggee* that might be used instead, could almost begin to feel the tightening thin cord twisting into and cutting his flesh, squeezing his air passage shut. But – he was the hostage. You didn't kill hostages, thus depriving yourself of their services. *Or did you?* A hostage who refused to act as such might just as well be dead, he supposed. He swallowed again and asked, managing to keep his voice steady with an effort, 'Well, what's next in your bloody treachery, then?'

The *duffardar* smiled, showing a gleam of very white teeth. 'You will go to the window, Colour-Sergeant sahib. I shall be behind you. You will put out your head. Then you will call for a runner to fetch the Captain sahib, who is to approach the window outside. When the Captain sahib comes, you will tell him to remain a dozen feet away from the window, and you will tell him of your situation very precisely. You understand, Colour-Sergeant sahib?'

MacTrease nodded.

'Then please to go to the window.'

Slowly, MacTrease obeyed. He stuck his head through the opening and shouted for a messenger. A private came across at the double, halted, and stood at attention.

'Colour-Sar'nt?'

'Captain Ogilvie. My respects, and would he come at once.'

'The Captain, Colour-Sar'nt?' There was some incredulity in the voice: NCOs, how-

125

ever senior, didn't send for officers. 'D'you mean—'

'You heard, blast your eyes!' MacTrease snapped, relieving himself of some of his tension. 'Do as you're bloody well told, and at the double!'

The man turned about and went off fast. There was little delay. As Ogilvie came in sight MacTrease called out, 'Captain Ogilvie, sir, halt five paces from this window, if you please.'

Ogilvie came to a halt. 'What the devil's going on, Colour?'

'I'm held hostage, sir, by the Salt Department's natives. There's a gun in my back, and a threat of *thuggee*. The mess bearer's dead, sir. Murdered by that bloody *duffardar*, sir. The *duffardar* wants to talk to you.'

Ogilvie's face showed no expression. 'I see. I get the general idea.' He turned to the runner and spoke in a low voice. 'My compliments to Mr Anderson. I want all men except the gate guard and the tower sentries to fall in with rifles, out of sight from the Sergeants' Mess window and doorway. It's to be done as quietly as possible.' Ogilvie turned back to the window. 'I'll speak to the *duffardar*, Colour-Sar'nt.'

There was a pause, then MacTrease vanished and the brown-skinned face of the *duffardar* looked through. 'Please be careful,

126

Captain sahib. One of my sowars is guarding the Colour-Sergeant sahib, and will kill him if there is any difficulty.'

'What do you want?'

'I am taking possession of the fort. You will please order all your men to pile arms in the centre of the courtyard. They are then to go to their barrack-rooms, and you will lock the doors. That is what I demand. It is simple. But if it is not done, the Colour-Sergeant sahib dies. You have the choice, Captain sahib.'

Ogilvie managed to laugh, loudly. 'Not so fast, *Duffardar* Abdul Qadir. Before I can make my choice, I must ask questions. Is that not reasonable?'

'It is perhaps reasonable, but there must not be delay, Captain sahib. What are your questions?'

Ogilvie asked, 'If the Colour-Sergeant sahib dies, what becomes of you and your sowars? Is that not important to you? Do you wish to be shot to pieces by my soldiers?'

'My life is not important, Captain sahib. It is my mission that is important.'

'Your mission – for the Wolf of the Salt Range? What is it that your master wants?'

There was no direct answer to that. 'Whoever my master is, I am his most loyal servant. Death is acceptable.'

'But is failure acceptable?' From the corner of his eye Ogilvie saw the quiet muster of his half-company outside the Officers' Mess. 'If the Colour-Sergeant sahib dies, then you die. But you also fail in your mission for your master, *Duffardar* Abdul Qadir. Is this not plain to see?'

'It is a risk. All war, all endeavour, involves risk, Captain sahib. You will not wish your Colour-Sergeant sahib to die.'

So, Ogilvie thought, it comes to a game of poker. He called out, 'I, too, have loyalties. Loyalties – shared to the full by the Colour-Sergeant sahib – to Her Imperial Majesty Queen Victoria – my queen and your empress. The Raj is strong, *Duffardar* Abdul Qadir, and is vast, and does not fear the deaths of her soldiers. The Raj is bigger than I, bigger than His Excellency the Viceroy himself.' He paused, finding it hard to get the words out now. 'Bigger than the Colour-Sergeant sahib.'

'You play with words, Captain sahib.' The voice was sharper now. 'There is enough of talking, and the time for choosing has come. What is your choice?'

Ogilvie glanced along towards the men waiting with their rifles by the Officers' Mess, out of the *duffardar's* sight. The day was far from warm, but he felt the sweat soaking into the collar of his tunic and running down his back and chest. He called, 'You must give me one moment more, *Duffardar* Abdul Qadir, then I shall make my choice. I cannot accept the death of any of my men under threat.' Let the native, he thought, make what he chose of that! He turned away before the *duffardar* could react, moving out of sight towards the armed troops. As he went he heard MacTrease's shout: 'Dinna fret about me, Captain Ogilvie, sir. I'm no' a married man – and I'll no' see any surrender on my account.' Ogilvie took no notice; reaching the line of soldiers, he went into hurried conference with Anderson; without too much delay he then went back to his earlier place before the Sergeants' Mess window.

'Very well, Abdul Qadir,' he called out. 'My choice is made. I ask for the release of my Colour-Sergeant sahib.'

There was a moment's silence, a silence of much tension. Then the *duffardar* said, 'First, Captain sahib, the rifles in the court-yard. And the men in the barrack-rooms. Your own revolver to be thrown down first.'

Ogilvie drew his revolver from its holster and sent it spinning along the sandy ground: it lay there, in full view of the *duffardar*. He passed the order: 'All men to assemble opposite the Sergeants' Mess, and pile their arms.'

The order was obeyed; the men converged from their position in front of the Officers' Mess and began piling their rifles in the courtyard's centre – all except two: the Pioneer-Sergeant, an immense man built like a blacksmith, and a lance-corporal. As the courtyard muster proceeded these men, flattening their bodies against the wall, slid slowly and in silence towards the window. When the Pioneer-Sergeant was within arm's reach of the window, Ogilvie turned his head slightly towards the gate and seemed to stiffen. He called out loudly:

'Cavalry – some of ours!'

The *duffardar* was taken utterly by surprise: Ogilvie saw the startled reaction in the face as the native leaned a little way from the window, putting out his head and neck. As quick as a flash of lightning the vast hands of the Pioneer-Sergeant took the neck, gripped, wrenched, twisted. There was a high scream of agony and the lance-corporal dodged low beneath the window and ran for the outer door leading from the courtyard into the Sergeants' Mess passage. Finding it locked, he gave a shout for the pioneers. Two men went across at the double and swung their axes at the door. The wood was stout, but it splintered under repeated massive blows. As the door split down the middle, a revolver was fired from the passage. The bullet sang across the courtyard to embed in a barrack-room door opposite; and then a howl of pain came from inside. The lance-corporal and the two pioneers ran through the doorway. Inside was the Colour-Sergeant, a revolver in his hand covering the sowars.

'You all right, Colour-Sergeant?' the lance-corporal asked.

'I'm all right, lad.' MacTrease jerked a hand towards the mess behind him. 'You'd best go and take that *duffardar* from Sar'nt Chisholm before the bugger's strangled. You can leave these two to me.' He jabbed with the revolver. 'Outside, you!'

With the sowars ahead of him, MacTrease emerged into the open. Seconds later the *duffardar* came out rubbing his neck and howling, with the lance-corporal's rifle muzzle nudging his backbone. Ogilvie, much relieved, gave his orders: an armed escort was provided and the three native cavalrymen were searched and physically examined for brand markings and were then marched to the fort's tiny dungeon and securely locked in. In the orderly room Ogilvie took down MacTrease's report. He remarked on the fact that the examination of the natives had shown no wolf's-head brand.

'It's no proof either way, in my opinion, sir.'

'The *duffardar* made no mention of the Wolf, you said.'

'That's right, sir. But I reckon he didn't need to. It was plain enough to me, sir, brand or no.'

'The Wolf isn't the only bandit in the Salt Range, you know. Those three could be in someone else's pay, or they could be free-lancing.'

MacTrease nodded. 'That's true, sir, of course. But at this particular time ... well, with the Wolf said to be ready to go, ready to bring out the tribes, sir – it'd be chancy for anyone else to try to shove his oar in, would-n't it?'

'Perhaps.' Ogilvie frowned. 'It's odd, Colour. If they're the Wolf's men trying to take over the fort for the Wolf, then why didn't the Wolf leave a garrison behind when he murdered the Salt Department's troops? It doesn't make sense!'

MacTrease lifted a hand and scratched his face. 'No, sir. Unless the original killers were the someone else, sir. Not the Wolf at all. And Abdul Qadir and his sowars were then planted as an advance garrison – and then *we* turned up?'

'Well, we'll try to find out, but for now I'll make no assumptions, Colour. Nor will I question those natives just yet. It may do them good to reflect for a while and be kept guessing.' Ogilvie grinned. 'That dungeon doesn't look too comfortable.'

'It's not, sir. No light, for one thing. And plenty of livestock, not that they'll be worried over that.'

'Well, they can stay for a while. And we'll keep them without food and water in the meantime. I'll let you know when I'm ready to see them, Colour.' Ogilvie got to his feet, took up his glengarry and walked out into the courtyard. Pulling his tunic straight as he came into the open, he smelt cooking smells coming from the fort's kitchen. There would in fact be little improvement on the rations provided on the march by any regiment's field kitchens, but at least the result could be eaten in a moderate degree of comfort, and Ogilvie realised he was hungry. His watch showed eleven forty-five. He climbed the spiral staircase to the watch-tower, returned the salutes of the men on lookout duty. 'All quiet?' he asked.

'Yes, sir.'

'Nothing been moving on the peaks?'

'Not a thing, sir.' The man coughed into his hand and ventured an opinion. 'I reckon we taught 'em a lesson last night, sir.'

Ogilvie repeated what he had said to MacTrease the night before: 'We won't bank on it, Prescott. We must expect another attempt, but probably not till after dark.'

'Aye, sir.'

'Full vigilance, Prescott.'

'There'll be that, sir.'

Ogilvie stood in silence for a while, looking along the broad valley and the surrounding hills. The sun was bright and brought some warmth to the cold northern day, but a wind was already getting up to chill exposed men to the marrow. India was all or nothing: you froze or you melted in a pool of sweat, or in due season and depending where you were stationed you drowned in continual rain. While his professional soldier's eye scanned the hills, standing light brown beneath the sun, gaunt and daunting in their extreme loneliness, his thoughts moved to the softer delights of Simla and the feverish round of socialising that took place when the Viceroy moved his court and government from Calcutta's stinks and suffocating closeness. Simla meant racing at Annandale, Simla like Peshawar had once meant nights passed in Mary Archdale's bungalow, Simla meant the exercise of all a man's wits to keep one jump ahead of gossip, of the prod-nose ladies endlessly and unproductively waiting for Staff husbands to come home, or carrying on affairs of their own with regimental officers on leave from the northern garrisons at Murree, Rawalpindi, Nowshera and Peshawar. To talk intriguingly about other people's peccadilloes averted attention from one's own, although in all conscience such ladies as Mrs Colonel Bates of the Supply and Transport were unlikely enough to have the opportunity ... in their case, jealousy was the root. Acid tongues, sharp eyes and facial hair were no more conducive to lovemaking in Simla than anywhere else on God's earth...

Ogilvie was brought back to Fort Gaza, so stark and innocent of women, by the bugle summoning the officers to their luncheon, the rank and file to dinner. The notes rang out loud and clear in the still air, almost an act of defiance to the ears that would be listening from the cover of the jagged peaks to right and left. During the meal, served by the bearers in white gloves and with all the ceremony of the mess in cantonments, Ogilvie carried on a desultory conversation with his subaltern, his mind occupied now by the more weighty consideration of the *duffardar* and the two sowars, yet to be questioned. After the meal there was coffee, and Ogilvie and Anderson smoked cigars before the subaltern left the mess to make his rounds of the fort. Ogilvie flipped through some dog-eared magazines left behind by some previous white officer in command: there was *Punch*, the *Tatler*, the

135

Illustrated London News; society, far removed from war and rebellion and death except by virtue of sons serving Her Majesty overseas, had been keeping its traditional round of balls and weddings, hunts and shooting parties or merely staying as guests in the stately homes of the great. Ogilvie was in fact dozing off when he was unceremoniously roused out by a messenger from the watch-tower.

'Cavalry, sir, approaching from the north.'

Ogilvie grabbed for his glengarry and Sam Browne belt. 'Who are they?'

'Don't know yet, sir – they're still some five miles off, sir.'

'Right!' Ogilvie went at the double to the top of the tower, taking the steps two at a time. A look-out indicated the dust-cloud to the north: little could be seen through that cloud, but at all events it was certain that it was not moving fast. Ogilvie lowered his field glasses. 'I doubt if it's an attack, but we won't take any chances. Sound the alarm.'

As the bugle blew for action, the fort came alive with men running to the fire-step along the mud walls, carrying rifles. On the tower the Maxim was already swung to bear upon the approaching horsemen.

Eight

Ogilvie made his identification within the next fifteen minutes, and passed the word for the men to stand down. In a sense it was anti-climax, yet the advent of one of the riders in particular gave food for thought. Ogilvie leaned over the watch-tower's parapet.

'Mr Anderson!'

The subaltern looked up from the fire-step. 'Sir?'

'Talk of the devil,' Ogilvie said, grinning. 'As we did this morning – remember?' He waved an arm towards the riders. 'Name of Wolseley, but not the Commander-in-Chief in Whitehall!'

'Major Blaise-Willoughby?'

'Correct! With a troop of Probyn's Horse from Nowshera and Wolseley clinging like a leech.'

Anderson grinned back and asked, 'Do we turn out the guard?'

'We'd better,' Ogilvie said.

★ ★ ★

Major Blaise-Willoughby returned the salutes as his escorting troop rode beneath the gateway into the fort, the gates being shut again behind the last man through. The Political Officer was looking pale and ill; he was no horseman, and neither was Wolseley. Blaise-Willoughby's rumpled cream-coloured jacket of tussore silk bore traces of the marmoset's vomit. Blaise-Willoughby almost tumbled from the saddle, to Wolseley's chattering alarm, and reached ground on one knee. Ogilvie, keeping a straight face, helped him up.

'Welcome to Fort Gaza, Major,' he said, and added, 'I thought there was a shortage of cavalry?'

'There is!' Blaise-Willoughby said snappishly. 'I happen to be one of their commitments. I'm entitled to an escort, as if you didn't know.'

'Sorry,' Ogilvie said. 'To what do we owe this sudden visit, Major?'

'Where's your office?'

Ogilvie pointed.

'When we get there, I'll tell you.' For a moment a smirk appeared on the Political Officer's sallow, liverish face. 'I expect you hoped we were your relief, didn't you, Ogilvie?'

'Not really. We've only just got here. It would have been too much to hope for.' He led the way to the orderly room while Anderson, after giving orders for the troop and their horses to be refreshed, ushered the *jemadar* in command of the escort to the mess. Ogilvie sat Blaise-Willoughby in a rickety basketwork chair, going himself behind the desk. 'Now, Major. Do you bring orders?'

'Not precisely.' Blaise-Willoughby shifted uncomfortably, one hand stroking Wolseley, who stared with unblinking black eyes at Ogilvie. 'God, how I loathe horses! It's like being at sea.'

'You're lucky you weren't given camels. I noticed you weren't travelling very fast.'

Blaise-Willoughby ignored the remark. 'I've got a backside like raw steak. I could do with some lanolin.'

'I'll get the Farrier-Sergeant to fix you up with some horse rub.'

'Don't try to be funny. All you damn regimental people are the same. You wouldn't get far without us politicals let me tell you!' Blaise-Willoughby waved a hand towards the regions whence he had come. 'I could tell *you* a thing or two, you know, Ogilvie. I've done my regimental soldiering. You haven't got any pickets out, out there, have you?'

'No.'

'Why not? I'd have thought—'

'I know my job, Major. Pickets are not necessary. We have perfectly adequate distance between us and the hills. Also, I don't propose to reduce the strength of the fort by sending out small parties that can easily be picked off. Is there anything else, Major?'

Blaise-Willoughby went on wriggling. 'You wanted to know why I've come. I'll tell you.' He looked around, carefully, probingly. 'I hope we can't be overheard?'

'No, we can't. Why the mysterious air?'

Blaise-Willoughby flushed angrily and leaned forward to speak in a low voice. 'It's about Soames – that's why! I've been doing some detective work.'

'If you'd done it earlier, you'd have been saved a nasty journey.'

'It all took time!' Blaise-Willoughby snapped. 'I've been working on Soames ever since the first despatch came through from the War House at home.'

'Well?'

The Political Officer's voice dropped even more, and his eyes flickered around the small room. 'No precise links with Zachary or that lance-*duffardar*. None leading to the Wolf either. Note that I say *precise*.'

'Noted. Can you be imprecise, then?'

Blaise-Willoughby scowled. 'I don't think you take your duties seriously enough, and I hate flippancy. I have no intention of being imprecise. I prefer to say that what I have found out is circumstantial evidence rather than concrete. *Pointers*, don't you know.'

'Go on, Major.'

'Soames is in a good regiment, and it's not easy to afford *any* cavalry regiment if you're not a wealthy man, especially when you're a married one. Soames is not wealthy. He has around two hundred and fifty a year private means to supplement his pay. It's not enough by a very long chalk indeed. He'd need ten times as much to keep up with his tastes.'

'And they are?'

Blaise-Willoughby's tone was disdainful. 'Whisky. Women – one feels damn sorry for his wife. Horses. Sport – polo, mainly, but he also hunts and shoots. And he's a first-class pig-sticker, very keen.' He paused meaningly. 'He's in deep water financially.' The next pause was even more pregnant. 'Or was.'

Ogilvie lifted an eyebrow.

'My – er – investigations have gone pretty deep I can tell you. Banks, solicitors, what-have-you. Don't ask me how, that's *my* business. Three years ago he had a large overdraft – more than four thousand. His father guaranteed it, but was threatening to turn the tap off since it was getting to the point where it was going to outrun his own

141

resources. In the nick of time a sufficient sum of money was paid into Soames' account – five thousand sterling in rupees, paid via a Calcutta bank. Similar payments, some smaller and some larger, have continued to be paid in at irregular intervals since.'

'Tying up with salt smuggling or forays – with the Wolf?'

Blaise-Willoughby shook his head, looking regretful. 'I can't say that, no. Not *tying up*.'

'Retainers?'

'Possibly. Or a degree of circumspection. I don't suppose Soames is a complete fool. He may call upon funds when he wants them, keeping the payment dates clear of the dates of his – er – activities.'

'I suppose you've checked these credits against any legitimate funds he's in possession of?'

'Yes, of course, my dear fellow! As I've already said, his resources are pretty damn slender. On a couple of occasions he's sold out stock, nothing very much in the way of capital value, and the proceeds appear to have been paid into his account in London.'

'Any outpayments, regular ones?' Ogilvie was thinking of Major-General Feathe-stonehaugh's remark in London, that Soames may have been paying out silence money. 'Anything that could link, say, with

142

Sar'nt Zachary?'

Blaise-Willoughby shook his head. 'I'd thought of that one, but no, I couldn't pin anything down. One or two payments were rather ... unaccountable's the word I think. But nothing positive. Nothing regular, either. Anyway, as I was saying: the proceeds of realised stock have gone into his London account and from time to time he's bought other stock through his brokers, but on the whole he doesn't appear to be building up his capital. It's mostly going on current expenses – as already detailed.' Blaise-Willoughby sniffed. 'Officers with expensive tastes are a bloody nuisance, and don't do the army any good.'

Ogilvie made no comment, but smiled to himself at the Political Officer's baldly dogmatic statement. Certainly Blaise-Willoughby had no such tastes; Wolseley was perhaps his sole extravagance and indulgence. Once, Ogilvie had been bidden on duty to Blaise-Willoughby's bachelor bungalow. There had been a degree of slovenliness, an indication that Blaise-Willoughby's head was too high in the clouds to allow him to take proper charge of his native servants. The place had been seedy and threadbare and oddly there had been an overall aroma of cheese ... Remembering something else that had been in evidence that day, and never mind that

143

the commodity had just been listed as one of Soames's sinful excesses, Ogilvie asked, 'Would you care for a whisky, Major?'

Blaise-Willoughby pursed his lips and gave a high-pitched giggle. 'It's early, isn't it? However, I've had a *beastly* journey.'

'Quite. Shall we go along to the mess?'

'Is it safe?'

'Absolutely. I'll send the bearers away.'

'What about your subaltern?'

'I can hardly keep him in the dark, Major.'

'No, I suppose not ... I suppose not.' Blaise-Willoughby got to his feet, broodingly. 'There must be the fullest possible discretion, though. Not just on account of stopping bush telegraphy. An officer's career is at stake. I hope you'll do all you can to keep it from the men.'

'Naturally.' Ogilvie led the way to the mess. 'Until such time as it has to come out. That time may come, you know.'

'Well, yes, in the end. If he's guilty it certainly can't be hushed up.' Blaise-Willoughby looked uneasy and sad; he was a scruffy little man with greasy skin and a rotund figure, and he had poor manners, but he was a notorious snob, and Soames came of a good family. 'There just may be ways and means, though. It depends a lot on your father as a matter of fact. If Soames merely sent in his papers and quietly disappeared the GOC might be satisfied. But that would be conditional on the *very fullest* secrecy in the meantime.'

Once again Ogilvie made no response; Blaise-Willoughby was always made worse by argument, but Ogilvie saw the ultimate preservation of secrecy as virtually impossible. He also saw it as undesirable, and knew his father would too: if Soames was guilty, he was guilty of the worst crime in Queen's Regulations. Reaching the mess, Ogilvie ordered a *chota peg* for the Political Officer and when it had been brought, ordered the bearer to make himself scarce; currently, Anderson was not present.

Ogilvie said, 'You've given me news, Major. Now I have news for you.'

'Oh?'

'*Duffardar* Abdul Qadir, of the Salt—'

'I know all about him, my dear chap.'

'You *know*?' Ogilvie raised his eyebrows in astonishment. 'Don't tell me you're psychic, Major!'

'Psychic? I don't understand. It's largely because of Abdul Qadir that I've come – not *only* to tell you the result of my enquiries into Soames.' Blaise-Willoughby fixed Ogilvie with a hard stare and drank some whisky. 'Mean to say something's happened?'

Ogilvie told the Political Officer the story

145

of MacTrease's seizure as a hostage: Blaise-Willoughby appeared totally unsurprised. He said, 'Well, you did all right, Ogilvie. Abdul Qadir is a tough nut. It's because he'd volunteered to stay behind – I learned that when his patrol rode back into Kohat – that I came along.'

'You know him?'

'I know of him. He's in the pay of our friend the Wolf. I've been watching him.'

'But you didn't tell his Commanding Officer?'

'No, I—'

'Foolish, wasn't it?'

Blaise-Willoughby scowled. 'I don't need you to tell me my job, Ogilvie. I have my methods. The fewer who know these things, the better.'

'Until the spy lands up in Fort Gaza and tries to take it.'

'I told you, I've come—'

'A little late. And another journey that needn't have taken place.' Ogilvie was white with anger. 'If you'd taken the man's C.O. into your confidence, you wouldn't have had to bounce your way on horseback all the way from Kohat, would you, Major?'

'I don't think anything's been lost as it's turned out,' Blaise-Willoughby said in a frigid tone. 'Abdul Qadir seems to have shown his hand and he hasn't succeeded, has he? I suppose you've interrogated him? What's the result?'

'I'm leaving him to stew for a while—'

'Yes, that's sometimes sensible.' Blaise-Willoughby gave a cough. 'As a matter of fact, now I'm here, I suggest I interrogate the man myself. With your permission, of course?'

Ogilvie spread his hands. 'Gladly, Major! It's not a job I want in the very least. And I've no doubt you're much better at it than I.'

Blaise-Willoughby reached up a white-fingered hand and stroked Wolseley's fur. 'I guarantee results at all events,' he said, and gave his high-pitched giggle.

Blaise-Willoughby had the three men separated, the *duffardar* being left alone in the cell and the two sowars being incarcerated in minute compartments leading off the quartermaster's stores. This done, he left them for just under an hour, during which time he sat in the mess, drank another *chota peg*, and chatted about garrison life in Nowshera, talking disparagingly about Bloody Francis Fettleworth's methods of native impressment. 'We don't need all that jingoism, Ogilvie. A little *intellect* goes much further. One of these days we'll have a proper system of military intelligence.'

'Where,' Ogilvie asked mischievously, 'will Fettleworth fit then?'

Blaise-Willoughby reached up and pressed Wolseley close to the side of his face. 'Fettleworth's an anachronism already, but don't quote me on that, there's a good chap.'

When he fancied the three natives had stewed alone for long enough, the Political Officer took himself off to his interrogation duties. He was absent for a considerable time and came back with a long face to find Ogilvie and Anderson conferring on the next day's orders. None of the men, it seemed, had uttered; Blaise-Willoughby's threats and promises had fallen upon very stony ground and he was no better off than before he had started.

'What d'you make of it?' Ogilvie asked.

'Oh, for God's sake, what *can* I make of it?' Blaise-Willoughby said disagreeably.

'Well, for one thing, that someone else's pressures are rather stronger than yours!'

'That's obvious. And that does give a pointer.'

'To the Wolf?'

'Yes. His edict runs, unfortunately, Raj or no Raj.' Blaise-Willoughby frowned and added, 'However, I've not got to the end of my particular rope, not by a long chalk.'

'You're going to try again?'

'Of course I am, but not here. At Division. Division's an impressive place! All brass, and spit-and-polish. That can help.'

'Aren't you being a shade Bloody Francisish, Major?'

There was a chuckle. 'I never said there wasn't a time and a place for everything, did I?' Blaise-Willoughby paused. 'Would it be very inconvenient if I stayed overnight, Ogilvie? I don't fancy a ride back without a decent rest first.'

Ogilvie caught his subaltern's eye: Anderson was first in the line of fire, as it were, for the giving up of accommodation. Anderson sighed but said nothing, and Ogilvie nodded. 'We'll be glad of your company, Major. I'll have arrangements made for your escort, though I'm bound to point out that they'll have to rough it. The fort's overcrowded already.'

'Yes.' Blaise-Willoughby glanced at the clock hanging from the wall of the mess. 'As they say at sea, the sun's over the fore yard, I think.'

'*Chota peg*, Major?'

'Well, that's very kind.'

Ogilvie raised his voice for the bearer. It began to seem that the whisky supply was not destined to last.

One of his reasons for staying, Blaise-

Willoughby said after another *chota peg*, was that he would have an opportunity of hearing the reports of Ogilvie's two mounted patrols when they rode in. Ogilvie raised the question of the security of the three prisoners during the ride back to Nowshera; they would, he said, be at considerable risk of attack. 'The Wolf's going to want those natives safe, where they can't talk. I doubt if he relies a hundred per cent on his personal magic.'

'For all he knows, they could have talked already.' Blaise-Willoughby took a mouthful of whisky. 'Still, I do take your point – they're available to give evidence, while alive. As a matter of fact, I've already been having second thoughts.' He paused, then asked, 'How are you placed for providing an additional escort, Ogilvie?'

The answer was prompt: 'I'm not. Sorry, Major, but I have the responsibility of the fort, and I've been given what was considered the minimum strength necessary to hold out and at the same time provide patrols. I simply can't spare anyone.'

Blaise-Willoughby's small eyes were fixed on Ogilvie's face. 'You could be overruled, you know.'

'Yes. But not by you.'

Blaise-Willoughby flushed. 'I have the rank.'

'But not the military authority. The Political Department doesn't take precedence over combatant arms yet. I'm sorry, Major.'

'Oh, all right, all right.' Blaise-Willioughby shifted irritably in his chair, his eyes snapping. 'You're not very co-operative, Ogilvie, which is a pity. You take a narrow view. That's not the proper attribute for a commander.'

'Then you'd better report it at Division,' Ogilvie said calmly, 'and it'll go on my papers.' He added, 'Let's stick to the essentials, shall we? You mentioned second thoughts. What are you going to do about those natives? Take 'em or leave 'em?'

Blaise-Willoughby jiggled the whisky remaining in his tumbler, staring out into the short Indian twilight. He said, 'I'll have another go at interrogation later. Then I'll make my decision in the morning.'

Ogilvie woke suddenly: it was still dark, and the fort was silent, but he had been brought awake by some isolated noise in the night.

He sat up in the bed, feeling for the revolver in its holster on a low table beside his pillow. Swinging his feet down, he stood up and pulled on tunic and trews over his pyjamas and went to the door giving on to the courtyard. The two men on sentry duty at the tight-shut gate were staring inwards towards the far end of the fort.

'Did I hear something?' Ogilvie called.

'Aye, sir, a cry. A scream, sir.'

'Where from?'

'The dungeon, sir.'

'I see. Is Major Blaise-Willoughby there, by any chance?'

'Aye, he is, sir.'

Ogilvie nodded and moved fast towards the block that housed the dungeon. As he went, there was another scream, a sound of agony, animal-like, hoarse, pitiful. From the Sergeants' Mess came two figures – MacTrease and one of the section sergeants, half dressed like Ogilvie.

'Did you hear that, sir?'

'Yes, Colour. I'll handle this.'

'Alone, Captain Ogilvie, sir? The guard—'

'No – this is domestic, nothing outside.'

MacTrease stared, his face puzzled in the moonlight. Then he ticked over. 'Ah – the prisoners, sir. I understand. The officer from Division, sir?'

'I think so, Colour.'

'He'll know his business, sir. Those bastards—'

'All right, Colour MacTrease. I'd be obliged if you and Sar'nt MacNab would turn in again.' Ogilvie held the Colour-Sergeant's eye; after a moment MacTrease shrugged and turned away, and MacNab followed him back inside the building. If MacTrease approved torture, Ogilvie did not; and his was the responsibility, Political Officers notwithstanding. His face hard, he went on towards the dungeon. The door was closed; he looked through the spyhole. In the yellow light of a guard lantern he saw Blaise-Willoughby, with two sowars of Probyn's Horse. On the dirty floor of the dungeon lay *Duffardar* Abdul Quadir, each of the sowars pinning him down with a booted foot; they were holding cavalry sabres within an inch of his head, while Blaise-Willoughby was occupying himself with a canister of water. Hearing a small sound behind him, Ogilvie whirled round: two more sowars stood there, faces sombre, even apologetic, but there was no mistaking the threat of the sabre held poised by one of them, nor the tremendous strength in the arm that the other placed around Ogilvie's chest.

Nine

The screams had continued for a little longer and had then been replaced by different sounds: gasping and gurgling, and a thrashing of frantic limbs. Ogilvie, recognising the very obvious fact that the sowars were acting under the orders of the Political Officer, forebore to bring about a scene that would have caused havoc in the fort. A reckoning later with Blaise-Willoughby would be more dignified.

After a while the gasping and gurgling stopped, and was replaced by the sound of broken weeping. This was followed by talk that Ogilvie was unable to follow, and then Blaise-Willoughby, with the marmoset still grinning and chattering from his shoulder, came briskly out of the dungeon followed by his sowars with their sabres, one of which was red with congealing blood.

'I'm sorry, Ogilvie,' Blaise-Willoughby said, and sounded perfunctory. 'I had to do my job without interference, and I had a feeling you might come along.'

'To put a stop to torture – yes, you were

damn right, Major!'

Blaise-Willoughby's expression was sour; he had the aspect of a man suffering from a severe bout of indigestion. 'My dear chap, did you or did you not tell me that you'd given your patrols *carte blanche* if they had to question prisoners?'

'There wouldn't have been torture of your sort.'

'No?' Blaise-Willoughby raised an eyebrow. 'You regimental officers ... damn it, you can convince yourselves of anything, can't you, when it suits! What the eye doesn't see ... you can't have two standards, Ogilvie.'

Ogilvie flushed with annoyance; there was more truth in Blaise-Willoughby's utterance than he cared to admit. He said coldly, 'You'll have some explaining to do now, Major. It's hardly constitutional to use your sowars to inhibit an officer in military command—'

'Oh, balls,' Blaise-Willoughby snapped. 'I admit the technical point, but there's damn-all you can do about it. Success brings its own immunity, as if you didn't know. The same applies to my methods.'

'What did you do to him, Major?'

'The water treatment.' Blaise-Willoughby moved out into the courtyard; Ogilvie followed. 'A gag on the mouth, and water dripped into the nostrils while the head's tilted backwards. It doesn't sound much, but it's bloody hell to endure. It gives the feel of drowning. I've never known it fail.'

'You mean Abdul Qadir talked?'

Blaise-Willoughby nodded. 'Yes. A most valuable witness, Ogilvie. He'll have to be got back to Division soonest possible, and in safety.'

'What did he say?'

'I'm not telling you out here.'

Ogilvie shrugged, and led the way across the moonlit courtyard to the mess, under the eyes of the watchful sentries on the tower and at the gate. Snores came from the pantry, where the native bearers lay curled on the floor. Ogilvie lit a guard lantern; in its yellow light Blaise-Willoughby's face looked like that of a flabby, seedy devil.

'Well, Major?'

Blaise-Willoughby spoke in a whisper. 'The Wolf is ready to attack. He has all the support he needs from Waziristan and across the Afghan border – the tribes are ready to ride out in strength.'

'When does the attack come?' Ogilvie asked.

'Three days from next midnight.'

'And his objective?'

'Widespread,' Blaise-Willoughby answered, giving a look over his shoulder. 'First, to take all the forts and outposts in the Salt Range and seize control of the salt workings, the quarries. That's with his own what you might call domestic tribesmen. From there it spreads with the assistance of all the others from points north and west.' He added, 'He means to take Fort Gaza first. It's his lynch-pin—'

'Then why didn't he hang on to it after the massacre, for God's sake, Major?'

'Ah, but that wasn't him, Ogilvie! At that time he wasn't ready. An independent tribe out of the Waziri hills was responsible for that, and the Wolf, who knew damn well we'd send in a fresh garrison, brought up his warriors just after you'd got here. Too late – but he'd made his preparations to cover all eventualities—'

'He planted Abdul Qadir, you mean?'

'Right! Following orders received on the bush telegraph, Abdul Qadir stepped forward when his Salt Department officer asked for volunteers to remain and hold the fort till your arrival.' Blaise-Willoughby added, 'Simple but effective, my dear Ogilvie.'

'Evidently not effective enough,' Olgivie said sourly, then asked his next question with much meaning. 'Anything else, Major?'

'Yes, there is,' Blaise-Willoughby answered. 'Our friend has no names, and I believe him, but a white officer has been seen in the Wolf's company, and there's a rumour that this officer's intention is to cause some interference with the British defence of the area.'

'What sort of interference?'

'Nature unspecified – not known.'

'So what's the next move?'

Blaise-Willoughby said disparagingly, 'Well, obviously, Division has to be informed – fast!' He coughed. 'There's something else, too.'

'Well?'

'We must expect attack, Ogilvie. I told you, the Wolf's ready now. Abdul Qadir was to hoist a signal from the tower once he'd taken possession. This signal was to be the head of the officer commanding ... I'm awfully sorry to be blunt, my dear chap. By now, the Wolf will know something's gone wrong. Which means your head's still somewhat unsteady.'

There was no knowing when the attack might come; Blaise-Willoughby gave urgent advice in which there was sound common sense: the first and most vital consideration was to get word back to Divisional HQ at Nowshera, but both Ogilvie and Blaise-Willoughby agreed that to send a single rider, or even two riders, with a despatch would be highly unlikely of success. The area was surely teeming with the Wolf's men, and the one hope would lie in a force strong enough to beat off the attacks as and when they came. Very forcefully, the Political Officer put the point that to inform Division was in fact more important now than to hold Fort Gaza, however large the fort might loom in the defensive line and in the Wolf's reckoning. If the full attack struck an unexpectant Raj, the whole line and more was likely to go; the Raj itself was in danger, and in any case, said Blaise-Willoughby with a high degree of truth, the absence of Ogilvie's head on the tower was undoubtedly going to lead to an attack in such strength that the garrison would be unlikely to win through.

'You're suggesting I abandon the fort and ride you to Division with my whole garrison?'

'Correct. And with Abdul Qadir. We mustn't lose him, Ogilvie. In my view the choice is plain.' He added, 'But the decision must be yours, of course. And it must be made at once.'

'You're forgetting one thing, Major: I have two patrols out still. Two corporals, two lance-corporals, twelve privates.'

'Yes – a pity. But we have no alternative but to accept the reduction, have we?'

Ogilvie gave a hard laugh. 'You've missed the point. I'm not riding out and abandoning those patrols, perhaps to drop smack into a trap!'

'There are much bigger matters at stake, Ogilvie.'

'To the Political Department, no doubt. But as you've said several times, Major, I'm a regimental officer. I'm not abandoning those men.' He looked at the clock. 'They're due back in six hours. Until then, I'm making no firm decision.'

There was bluster and bad temper from Blaise-Willoughby but Ogilvie remained adamant. He left Blaise-Willoughby to his protests and made rounds of the sentries, warning them to be extra vigilant. Then, there being nothing else to do, he turned in again. Sleep was hard to come by, but in the end he fell into the unease of nightmare in which he was floating in the air above Fort Gaza, looking down upon his own head impaled on a stake above the watch-tower while Blaise-Willoughby bargained for his own personal immunity with the Wolf of the Salt Range. He dragged himself from such unpleasant scenes, waking to the sound of the stables being mucked out by the *syces*, and lay in bed thinking, planning, wondering what would be Division's reaction to his abandoning his post. Regimental officers were expected to obey the last order; on the other hand, a failure to use initiative and to react properly to changed circumstances could also be considered a dereliction of duty. The dividing line, as ever, was unclear, and would ultimately be drawn for him by the judgment of other men who would have had many easy days in which to think about it in the safe comfort of Division.

Ogilvie got up, called for his bearer to bring water, and washed and shaved. Dressed, he sent for Anderson and told him of the night's events.

Anderson asked, 'What's your decision, James?'

'The inevitable one. We ride out for Nowshera once the patrols are back.'

'Isn't a fort a better defensive position than a body of men in the open?'

'Not always. In a backs-to-the-wall situation it's a nice feeling, but forts have a habit of succumbing to sieges – the advantage usually lies with the attack rather than the defence.'

'Sieges can be lifted.'

'Yes, but in this case, only if the situation's known in Peshawar or Nowshera.' Ogilvie swatted at a fly. 'In the open you have a better chance – even if it's only speed in running away! Anyhow, that's not the point this time, is it?'

161

'I suppose not.'

'You'd better tell MacTrease. I want the half-company and the troopers from Probyn's Horse ready to ride out by ten o'clock, with a strong close-escort for the prisoners under a sergeant and corporal.'

After this there was nothing to be done but wait. The morning sun showed empty terrain all around, the peaks of the light-brown hills innocent of any tribesmen with the inevitable snaky-bayoneted, long-barrelled *jezails*, many of them ancient relics of mutiny and pre-mutiny days. The watching eyes would of course be there in concealment, awaiting the grisly message from Abdul Qadir. Perhaps they wouldn't be unduly worried after all: Abdul Qadir would have had to wait his chance, and the Wolf would be well aware of this. Perhaps the garrison would be crossing its bridges too soon ... yet the first requirement remained, the message to Division. And about this Blaise-Willoughby nagged continually, anxious to be on his way, taking all possible advantage of daylight hours when an attack could not materialise unheralded from the night darkness of the surrounding hills.

At five minutes to ten the eastern patrol was reported from the tower, and the gates were swung open to admit the weary, dust-covered riders. The corporal's report was brief: all outposts intact, no tribesmen encountered. Blaise-Willoughby was not surprised: this was the lull before the storm, the time when the tribes gathered for the kill. The western patrol came in late, after much fingernail-biting by the Political Officer: it was almost eleven o'clock before their dust-cloud was reported by the sentries. Their report was similar: no trouble anywhere. Ogilvie was much relieved that there had been no casualties. To Blaise-Willoughby's annoyance and dismay, Ogilvie insisted upon resting the patrols. One hour's rest for men and horses, he said, and refreshment. They would move out at noon. Blaise-Willoughby had to make the best of it.

'It's likely enough we'll come under immediate attack,' Ogilvie said, addressing the ranks. 'It would have come in any case sooner or later. We're bringing the danger closer, not initiating it.' In a few words, and without breaking security as the Political Officer put it, he outlined the situation. 'We have important intelligence to take through to Division, along with the prisoners and Major Blaise-Willoughby. That's our job. It's straightforward, and we shall do it successfully. It's twenty-five miles to Kohat – that's all. From then on, there's nothing to worry about. Colour-Sar'nt?'

'Sir!'

'For extra security we'll divide into two troops, riding half a mile apart laterally. I'll take one, Major Blaise-Willoughby the other. Abdul Qadir will ride with my troop, with the close-escort as detailed.'

'Very good, sir.'

'If one troop is attacked, the other will ride on and not join in. In any case, it'll split the enemy. The ride will be fast once we're well clear of the fort. At first, any tribesmen watching will be puzzled, and to puzzle them still more we ride slow and hope they put it down to exercise or manoeuvres, or just plain British idiocy. All right, Colour?'

'Yes, sir.'

'Then carry on, if you please.'

A swinging salute, and MacTrease turned his horse towards the ranks of horsemen. He gave his orders; the front rank turned and rode out, forming A Troop; the rear rank followed, forming B Troop. Ogilvie and the prisoners, the latter bound hand and foot and lashed securely to their led horses, rode with A Troop. In the interest of speed the commissariat camels were being left behind with all the food stores, but the ammunition had been distributed among the men, none being left behind; and the Maxim, dismantled, was also distributed among the horses and mules of A Troop. A close watch was kept on the peaks to left and right, but still nothing was seen. When the two columns of mixed cavalry and mounted infantry were a little over three miles from the empty fort, Ogilvie passed the word to break into a canter. Heavy clouds of dust rose in the still air, and soon Fort Gaza was little more than a speck behind them. Ogilvie looked across at B Troop: such was the dust that he was unable to make out any individuals beneath it, but he guessed that Blaise-Willoughby and Wolseley would be feeling the strain of a cavalry canter; by the time they reached Kohat, let alone Nowshera, the Political Officer's backside would be stuck firmly to the saddle, or at any rate his *jodhpurs*, by its red rawness.

After some nine miles, they came to the place of greatest danger, the obvious reason why no attack had materialised in the open valley behind them: no need for the enemy to take risks when the British riders had to pass through a narrow defile between high hills, a defile that ran for some four miles before it spilled into open country at its northern end. Had he been marching through with infantry, Ogilvie would automatically have ordered pickets out. But cavalry was a different proposition and its speed was a better insurance than pickets, who would cause lengthy delay while they scrambled up the hillsides to seek out and kill any lurking tribesmen waiting to fire down into the defile. As they neared the cleft in the hills Ogilvie raised an arm and indicated that Blaise-Willoughby's troop should close and ride in behind him. B Troop swung left in obedience, and A Troop rode in between the enclosing peaks, hills with almost sheer sides that would in fact have made hard going for any pickets. Once inside the day dimmed, the hills taking away the light so that the men seemed to be riding into an open tunnel. Ogilvie was forced to bring down the pace of the advance: obstructions of rock and boulders lay liberally sprinkled in their path; but there was an air of desertion and nothing hostile could be seen above them. Ogilvie began to feel easier, to feel that God was definitely on the side of the Raj. A mile inside by his reckoning: three to go, and success was very much on the cards. Once out of the defile, Kohat was within good striking distance and they were likely enough to meet British patrols too. But Ogilvie's happy thoughts took a tumble when the crack of a *jezail* sounded like a thunderclap in the enclosed, rocky defile and behind him a man toppled from his mount. The single shot had been a signal: hard on its heels a hailstorm of bullets came down, and as Ogilvie turned in the saddle and lifted a hand to halt the column and send the men dismounted into cover, a heavy native body, naked and oiled to an intense slipperiness, seemed to drop from nowhere and cling like a leech to his back.

Ten

Falling from his horse, Ogilvie came down hard on the rocky ground, knocking all the breath from his body. He struggled furiously as the native's hands went round his throat, squeezing. Blood drummed in his ears, and over it he heard the sounds of the rifles in action on both sides. A furious battle raged in the defile as men and bullets poured down from the heights. But the shouts of men and the screams of horses in agony, and the rifle fire, faded into the background as Ogilvie fought his personal battle for his life.

The man who had landed on him so squarely was strong, wiry and impossible to grip and hold. Ogilvie's fingers slid from the man's wrists as he tried to loosen the pressure on his windpipe. He lashed out with booted feet, tried to slam a knee into the native's groin. All he managed to achieve was a reversal of their positions, so that the oiled body lay beneath him, but the grip didn't slacken. There was a greyness in front of his eyes now and he felt the beginning of a slide into unconsciousness. Fighting it, fighting back with all his reserves, he let go of his attacker's wrists and seized the head, lifting it as far as he was able and then slamming it down on to the ground. The head seemed made of iron: all that happened was that the grip on Ogilvie's throat tightened even more. The last thing he was aware of was a rider coming for him at the gallop, his horse's hooves striking sparks from the scattered rock.

The place was a shambles: broken bodies – men, horses, mules lying everywhere. There were moans and cries from the wounded, from the obviously dying. Nine men of the Royal Strathspeys were dead, twenty more wounded in varying degrees. Nevertheless, the attack had been well fought off: Colour-Sergeant MacTrease reported a count of seventy-four native dead and wounded and the rest fled.

'Disciplined fire, sir,' he said. 'That's what always routs the buggers! You look sick, if I may say so, sir.'

Ogilvie rubbed tenderly at his throat. 'I feel it, Colour, but I'll survive. I'm not quite sure what happened in the end.'

'A sowar of Probyn's Horse, sir. He used his sabre like a lance, to do a little pig sticking. The man who attacked you has a head split in half like a cut apple, sir.'

Breath hissed through Ogilvie's teeth. 'It sounds bloody, but I'm more than grateful! I'll have a word with the sowar soon. Give me a hand up, will you, Colour.'

'Sir!' MacTrease bent and helped Ogilvie to his feet. 'Are you all right, sir? Are you fit to ride?'

'Yes. The sooner we clear the defile the better. There may be another wave coming in.'

'I'd doubt that, sir, but you're right about moving on quickly, of course. I'll have the wounded secured to the mules as comfortably as possible, and the dead too. I take it you'll not want to delay for burials, sir.' MacTrease coughed: he had news to impart. 'Major Blaise-Willoughby, sir—'

'Is he all right?'

'Major Blaise-Willoughby is very well indeed, sir. He hid behind a rock, a big one. And now he's gone, sir.'

'Gone?'

'Gone, sir, with escort and bloody monkey, sir. With the three prisoners too, sir.' MacTrease's face was wooden. 'He said he could not afford delay and that he must reach Division whatever happened to us.'

Ogilvie nodded. 'He's right, Colour. His despatch is vital. So long as he gets that and the prisoners through...'

'We can be dispensed with, sir?'

'Something like that.'

'Well, sir, I understand well enough. It's all in the day's work.' MacTrease tweaked at his moustache. 'Permission to carry on, sir, please?'

Ogilvie nodded. The Colour-Sergeant gave a swinging salute, turned about and crunched away down the pass, calling his orders. In double quick time the wounded men and the dead were lashed to spare mules, the wounded being made as easy as possible. Ogilvie rode down the line, having a word with each man. One of the minor casualties was his subaltern, Anderson, recovering nicely from a blow to the head. Ogilvie looked also at the native corpses; in each case the flesh showed the brand of the Wolf. The sadly shortened column was reformed and ridden out with the minimum of delay, Anderson riding alongside Ogilvic. No further attack came, and soon they were out into the open plain with little distance to go to reach Kohat. And when they were still some five miles from the town, Ogilvie saw the dust-cloud ahead and a little later made out a body of infantry, a force of company strength marching out towards them. When the two groups closed Ogilvie recognised the badges of a light infantry regiment of the Indian Army; and the Company Commander told him that Major Blaise-Willoughby had made contact a little earlier, had reported the situation, and had ridden on to Nowshera.

'Does he mean to report ahead on the telegraph?' Ogilvie asked.

'No. And he left word that you were not to use it either. Very insistent, he was!'

'Then his will be done!' Ogilvie said in a sardonic tone. 'As for us, we'll follow on after I've seen to my wounded.'

'I'll take them over,' the infantry captain offered. 'I've brought *doolies* – they'll be a damn sight more comfortable and I'll see they're taken straight to hospital.'

'Thank you,' Ogilvie said, much relieved. 'And the dead?'

'I'll take them over too. Everything will be done – don't worry.'

'I won't, and I'm grateful. I'll leave my pipers. They'd appreciate that.' His face stiff, Ogilvie turned his horse and rode down the line for another brief word with each man who was to be left behind in Kohat. When they had all been removed from the mules and laid in the *doolies* Ogilvie rode on with Anderson and the remnant of his mounted infantrymen. They would, he told MacTrease, not now deviate into Kohat but make straight for Division at Nowshera.

'We'll not rejoin the regiment in cantonments, sir?'

'Not yet, Colour. Division may have a need of us – if Major Blaise-Willoughby doesn't get through.'

'For your report, you mean, sir?'

'That's right, Colour.'

With no further trouble along the rest of the route, which was well patrolled by British and Indian units, they rode into Nowshera late that evening: and they rode in with Blaise-Willoughby, whom they had overtaken along the track north of Kohat with his escort of Probyn's Horse. The Political Officer, still accompanied by his marmoset, had looked sick from his long ride and had confessed as much.

'I'm bloody tired, Ogilvie.'

'Not far to go now.' Ogilvie gave him a sidelong look. 'You were lucky to get through to Kohat.'

'There wasn't far to go, and I had my cavalrymen,' Blaise-Willoughby said.

'I still say you were damn lucky.' Blaise-Willoughby, Ogilvie fancied, seemed a little on the defensive, as well he might after his headlong dash from the fight in the pass. 'Are you going to report direct to

General Fettleworth?'

'Of course.'

'I'll come with you, Major.'

'I don't think that's at all necessary.'

'Then I take a different view. I commanded at Fort Gaza, remember.'

Blaise-Willoughby seemed about to pro-
test further, but evidently decided against it
and said disagreeably, 'Oh, very well.'

As later they entered the city they passed
through sleazy outskirts, with closely built,
ramshackle dwellings alongside the inevitable open drain with its appalling stench
and its rats and flies and incipient diseases.
Vague shadows flitted, mostly keeping out
of the way of the British soldiers; pariah
dogs lurked with long, yellow, fang-like
teeth bared in cringing snarls. Ogilvie had
always found the Indian cities meanly
unpleasant, a sad contrast with the British
cantonments outside, an even sadder contrast with the rich splendour of the great
palaces of the princes of India – the Maha-
rajahs, the Nawabs, the Gaekwars – with
their magnificent grounds and fountain-
spattered courtyards and pillared halls; and
he was unable to escape the reflection that
the great princes were in fact splendidly
buttressed by the power of the British Raj
itself...

Reaching Divisional Headquarters in the

cantonment area on the other side of the city, they were halted by the Sergeant of the Guard. Blaise-Willoughby, who was known to the sergeant, gave orders for a runner to be sent at once to a Staff Major. 'Whereabouts is General Fettle-worth?' he asked.

'I dare say he'll be still in the mess, sir. He was being dined by the Staff tonight, sir.'

'Was he by God!' Blaise-Willoughby said, and turned to Ogilvie. 'He'll not be pleased at our interruption.'

Ogilvie shrugged but said nothing. They waited for the Staff Major; after some five minutes a portly figure was seen coming from the Headquarters Mess, the starched white shirt front gleaming in the light from a guard lantern. Blaise-Willoughby rode his horse forward impatiently.

'Take your damn time, don't you, Peter? This is Ogilvie, of the 114th. Major Dunlop. We have to see the General immediately, Peter.'

'Important?'

'Vital. You'd better buttonhole the ADC. And I've some prisoners for safe custody...' Blaise-Willoughby made his arrangements and saw the prisoners taken over by a strong guard; then he and Ogilvie dismounted, handed their horses over to the *syces* roused out from the stables, and, leaving Anderson

175

in charge of the detachment, accompanied the Staff Major to the Divisional Commander's quarters, where, in an ante-room, they were left to kick their heels while Fettleworth was prised loose from his after-dinner brandy-glass. He came, in fact, fairly quickly, heralded within ten minutes by his ADC and accompanied by his Chief of Staff, Brigadier-General Lakenham. He was red in the face, a colour to match his mess jacket, and sweating like a pig into his dress shirt. With a clink of decorations and campaign medals, in miniature as appropriate to his mess dress, Bloody Francis came to a halt in front of the Political Officer.

'I expected you back before this,' he said huffily. 'Why have you brought young Ogilvie – hey? Ogilvie, I thought you'd been sent to garrison Fort Gaza?'

'Yes, sir. I've evacuated.'

Fettleworth's face was a study: his jaw dropped, his eyebrows went up. He couldn't believe his ears. 'Evacuated did yer say?'

'Yes, sir. I—'

'Upon whose orders, may I ask?'

'My own initiative, sir. I—'

'Don't answer me back, blast you! I'm *talking* to you! I've never heard of such a thing in all my life, damned if I have! Evacuating without orders – leaving a whole damn sector of the salt line undefended! Whatever next? I'll damn well tell you: you'll be under arrest, my dear sir, and facing Court Martial!'

'Don't take any notice of him,' Blaise-Willoughby said fairly loudly to Ogilvie.

'What was that?' Fettleworth demanded.

'Nothing, sir.'

'Nothing? I distinctly heard ... it's that bloody monkey again! I won't have it! Filthy little brute. Come into my office – and leave that damn monkey outside. Give it to my ADC.'

Fettleworth swept in through the door held open by the ADC. As Blaise-Willoughby went past he grudgingly broke Wolseley's grip on his shoulder and handed the animal to the ADC. Wolseley chattered amiably: the ADC was his customary resting place when master attended upon his General. Fettleworth sat himself behind his desk, waved the others to seats.

'Now what's all this?' he demanded. 'I want to know in detail why Captain Ogilvie decided to abandon his post.'

Blaise-Willoughby said, 'On my advice, sir. In the circumstances, it was the only sensible thing to do. Events have moved a long way beyond Fort Gaza, sir, as you shall see.' Quietly, with determination, he made his points.

'All right, all right!' Fettleworth broke in angrily when he had heard enough. 'I understand the position. It's possible that Ogilvie acted correctly. I'd be obliged if you'd give me the substance of your report, Major.'

'I'm about to,' Blaise-Willoughby said in a grim voice. 'It's not pleasant and I have no doubt that we shall all want it kept strictly within these four walls until such time as it has to come out. I refer to Captain Soames.'

'Ah! Then kindly go on and don't waste time, Major.'

Blaise-Willoughby scowled but did as he was told. He stressed that the *duffardar*, when broken down, had named no names; all the evidence against Soames was, even now, no more than circumstantial, but things looked, in his view, as black as night. If Soames was not guilty, then there was an unacceptable degree of coincidence around; nevertheless, in all fairness – as well as on grounds of security – the affair must be kept quiet to the best of everyone's ability.

'So you've said already,' Fettleworth put in. 'The feller *sounds* guilty to me. Damn blackguard! We've come to a pretty pass when we have to suffer bounders like that.'

'Not a bounder, sir.'

'Not?'

'On a point of pedantry, sir. He comes of

178

a good family. A landed family, well represented on the bench, in the army, and on the hunting field. *Not* a bounder.'

'Pity. Don't like having to hound gentry, never did. Still, there we are. Sores – filth – must be eradicated and will be.' Fettleworth's tone was gravely pompous: he would face an unpleasant duty like a man. 'Thing is, what do we *do*? Hey? Lakenham?'

'I would let the Political Officer finish, sir. It seems to me that what is yet to come is linked with what has gone before.'

Blaise-Willoughby nodded. 'Quite right, it is. And because that's so, we must not be precipitate.' He turned back to Fettleworth. 'We face trouble, sir, military trouble – a rising on a large scale. My information is precise. In three days' time the tribes will rise, from Dir to Jammu by way of Waziristan and all along the Salt Range.'

Fettleworth stared glassily, then put his head in his hands and groaned. 'I *told* Sir Iain Ogilvie – I *told* Sir George White – I haven't the troops to cope! Nor has Murree. A wholesale rising!' He turned to the Chief of Staff. 'This means mutiny, Lakenham!'

'Close enough to it, I agree, if Blaise-Willoughby's information is to be believed—'

'And that blackguard Soames giving comfort to the enemy!'

'A British officer, unnamed, sir. We should

179

stick to the facts.'

'Of course it's Soames!' Fettleworth almost shouted, his face now a mottled red and purple. 'Blaise-Willoughby, we can't take any risks now – Soames must be arrested at once and—'

'No, sir.' Blaise-Willoughby, who in fact had scant respect for Fettleworth, spoke with firm insistence. 'He still needs rope, and to arrest him now would be to tell the Wolf his plans are out. This still needs very careful handling. We have three days in hand, three only, and they must be used to the fullest advantage. And one of the things we shall need to find out is this: in what way is Captain Soames – or whoever the officer may be,' he added as he saw the triumphant look on the General's face, 'in what way is he expected to help the enemy?'

'How do we find *that* out?' Fettleworth demanded.

'There are ways and means, sir,' Blaise-Willoughby said with a smile. 'I shall work upon them, you may be sure, and I may ask for Captain Ogilvie's assistance. But first, sir, let us consider the military situation. I take it you would yourself be inclined to send troop formations hither and thither to impress the Wolf with our strength and mobility?'

'I think that was rudely put,' Fettleworth

snapped, carrying out a violent scratching motion in the region of his stomach: the woollen cummerbund customarily worn beneath the clothing to keep out the night chills brought, even in winter, a degree of prickly heat to the General's portly body. 'I do not send troops hither and thither. When they are sent, they are sent to a plan.'

'I apologise, sir. But I don't consider this an occasion for the movement of troops and guns. We should be circumspect—'

'This *duffardar*,' Fettleworth interrupted. 'You seem to suggest that the Wolf will not be expecting him to have given away information – that the bugger will think we're still in ignorance as to the rising. I find that hard to credit, Major Blaise-Willoughby. The Wolf is not a child.'

'I agree, sir. But he can't be certain either way. In any case, that's not my point at this moment—'

'Then, for God's sake, Major, what *is*?'

'That our troop concentrations are at present *already* in the right places to meet trouble. Also that reinforcements from Southern Command couldn't possibly reach us in time in any case—'

'Murree can reinforce my Division speedily enough, my dear Blaise-Willoughby—'

'Undoubtedly, sir. But to denude Murree before replacements come up from Ootacamund would be unwise. I have no doubt Sir Iain Ogilvie would agree with that.'

Fettleworth thumped his desk. 'Then what do you suggest?'

'Circumspection, sir. Deviousness.'

'I dislike deviousness.'

'We have a devious enemy to fight, sir. And deviousness happens to be my job as Political Officer.' Blaise-Willoughby leaned forward, reaching up in an automatic gesture to stroke the absent Wolseley. 'I would like to see the very minimum of offensive, or even defensive, movement. I would like the Wolf to remain as lulled as possible—'

'But we have only three days left according to you! *Three days!*'

Blaise-Willoughby nodded. 'That is so, sir. If I may repeat myself, we are as ready as possible without further overt movement. And there is another thing to be considered, someone else to be lulled.'

'Soames?'

'The white officer, sir, which is all we can say with assurance at the moment—'

'Don't beat about the bush!' Fettleworth's eyes bulged from a furious face. *'Soames!'*

'Oh, very well, sir, Soames. He is the Wolf's link, it seems, in a sense his military adviser. I suggest he be left with no advice to tender! That is – with no *helpful* advice. I'm sure you understand me.'

Reflectively, his eye moved towards Ogilvie. For a moment nothing more was said. The eyes of the Divisional Commander and his Chief of Staff met; then they, too, were turned upon Ogilvie.

Eleven

Soames, Blaise-Willoughby insisted, had yet to commit himself; more importantly for the Raj at the moment, Soames could in the meantime be of use.

'Be precise,' Fettleworth said.

'Very well, sir. I understand Captain Soames is at present with his regiment inside Waziristan. I would like to know exactly where.'

Fettleworth raised his eyebrows at his Chief of Staff, and Lakenham answered the question: 'The Kohat Light Horse is in camp by the Tochi River, twenty miles east of Miran Shah.'

'Sending out patrols?'

'Yes.'

'And their specific orders?'

'The same as for all other extended units deployed since we were alerted – to watch for any signs of trouble and to report immediately.'

'And to apprehend the Wolf if possible?'

Lakenham laughed shortly. 'Of course!

But we regard the possibility as remote.'

'Unless we can be *led* to the Wolf, sir,' Blaise-Willoughby said.

'D'you mean by Soames?' Fettleworth asked, taking the point with surprising readiness.

'I do, sir. And by Captain Ogilvie.'

'How, by Ogilvie?'

'Deviousness again, sir. I suggest Ogilvie be used to provoke catalysis—'

'Provoke *what*?'

'A chemical term, sir. Certain chemical reactions occur at greatly increased rates when in the company of a third substance – or in this case, a third person. Ogilvie shall be a catalytic agent to provoke a reaction between Captain Soames and the Wolf of the Salt Range. If he is successful I would expect the reaction to be a somewhat decisive one – but you'll no doubt agree that as from now speed, sheer speed, is of the essence.'

Much discussion took place, and to most of it Ogilvie was a mere listener, the helpless inhabitant of a body that was entirely at the disposal of the Lieutenant-General Commanding Her Majesty's First Division in Nowshera and Peshawar, who, as Blaise-Willoughby expounded, slid into obvious agreement with the Political Officer's

185

strategic deviousness. Ogilvie was to rejoin his regiment immediately, and Lord Dornoch would be ordered to turn out the 114th Highlanders for a forced march towards the Tochi River: Ogilvie himself would carry the relevant despatch to his Colonel. At the same time orders would be sent by telegraph to Kohat that a rider was to be sent post-haste to the Lieutenant-Colonel commanding the Kohat Light Horse that they were to strike camp, withdraw from the Tochi, and fall back upon Kohat. On the assumption that the 114th Highlanders would move out at dawn from Peshawar, it could be expected that they would encounter the northbound cavalry at about midnight next day. Since each would be using the same track through the hills, they could scarcely miss each other. Lord Dornoch would then pass fresh orders from Division to the effect that the combined infantry and cavalry force was to halt and go into bivouacs as an advanced guard to contain any out-thrust of the Waziri tribes towards Kohat and Peshawar. If this was a subterfuge to bring Soames and himself into innocent contact, Ogilvie thought, it was cumbersome but foolproof: militarily, it made sense in the present situation. From Soames's viewpoint, it would cause confusion; and it could be assumed he would wish to pass information back to the Wolf of the Salt Range to the effect that the British were ready for any movement against them. As for Ogilvie himself, his task would be to make the earliest possible contact with Soames, to be friendly but watchful, pursuing his catalytic role to panic Soames into some precipitate action.

He asked, 'What about the Colonel of the Kohat Light Horse, Major? Will he be fully informed?'

It was Brigadier-General Lakenham who answered that: 'Colonel Keeley is already in possession of the facts, Ogilvie – that is, the suspicions in regard to Soames. He's under orders not to let it show.'

'And the lance-*duffardar*, sir – Akhbar Mohammad Khan—'

'The man from London. He's been returned to his unit, I think you know that. Well, that's one of the reasons Colonel Keeley had to be informed. The lance-*duffardar* is as well protected as is possible, you may be sure.'

'Does that mean—'

'It means,' Fettleworth interrupted briskly, 'that the man's in some obvious danger, but so are we all on the North-West Frontier – aren't we? Hey? The Raj comes first, you know. And Her Majesty.' For a moment Fettleworth paused and a look of reverence came into his eyes: they began very slightly to water. Those eyes – and each of his audience knew it well – had suddenly ceased to see the walls of his office at Division in far Nowshera; instead they saw the battlemented walls of Windsor Castle and the Royal Standard flying nobly out above the keep and above the rotund figure of the old lady in deepest black, the imperious widow who ruled the greatest, most widespread empire the world had ever seen, the autocratic figure with the bun and the lace cap who was more powerful than Caesar, Charlemagne, Attila the Hun, Alexander the Great and Napoleon all rolled into one national flag ... Fettleworth, almost beating time to God Save The Queen, gave himself a shake. 'Now, Captain Ogilvie, you shall lose no time! Muster your mounted infantry and ride with all speed to Peshawar! Lakenham, the despatch – quickly. And draft a telegram to Sir Iain in Murree. He's to be kept informed, of course – and it would do no harm to jog his memory about reinforcements. If this rising comes about, it'll not be settled quickly and Ootacamund may as well be ready for drafting troops by the railway.' He eased the bulk of his stomach, resplendent in its tightly-fitting mess jacket, and roared out: 'Bearer!'

At the end of the room the great doors

opened and an Indian bearer came in, approached humbly, and salaamed. 'General sahib?'

'*Chota pegs.*'

'At once, General sahib.'

'It had better be, or you'll feel the weight of the ADC sahib's boot up your backside.' Fettleworth gave a belch.

'What the devil...' Andrew Black sat up in bed, looking sourly furious. 'Good God, it's you!'

'Yes—'

'You're supposed to be in Fort Gaza. What's going on?'

'Orders from Division, and they're urgent, Andrew—'

'Can't they wait till morning, blast you?'

'By morning, the regiment's to be on the move. I have despatches and need to see the Colonel at once. Get out of bed, Andrew.'

The Adjutant grumbled himself to full wakefulness. Within ten minutes Lord Dornoch had been wakened and informed and the bugles had blown to rouse out the men from their barrack-rooms. Thereafter the Royal Strathspeys' cantonment was a scene of apparent chaos, but of chaos under full ultimate control. The transport and commissariat sections were mustered and the horses, mules and camels were checked by the farriers and the Veterinary Officer, while the Regimental Quartermaster-Sergeant, in kilt and vest, supervised the stores and herded the miserable bunch of camp followers who would inevitably trail along in rear of the advance and be a confounded nuisance to good fighting men, the cross that every infantry formation had to bear when on the move. Surgeon Major Corton and his medical orderlies stocked the oxen-drawn wagon that would form the first aid post and field dressing station for the march, always assuming its wheels would last; the colour-sergeants checked rifles and ammunition-belts as the men mustered by companies in the light of the guard lanterns, grumbling, cursing, joking. MacTrease and the other ranks from the erstwhile mounted detachment thankfully exchanged trews for the kilt. In the windows of the married quarters lamps shone; inside the bungalows hasty goodbyes were said: so far no one knew the orders for sure, but rumours flew and it was certain enough that the battalion was about to march into action. By the time the dawn came up, green and blue and violet from the east, the Royal Strathspeys were drawn up ready on parade, with the pipes and drums on the right of the line, the men's kilts blowing coldly around their knees in a wind off the

Himalayan foothills in the north. All the reports were made: section sergeants to colour-sergeants, colour-sergeants to company commanders, company commanders to the Adjutant, Adjutant to the Second-in-Command.

Major Hay turned his horse and rode towards the Colonel. 'Battalion ready to move out, Colonel.'

'Thank you, Major.' Lord Dornoch, as spruce beneath his highland bonnet as if he'd paraded normally after a full night's sleep, returned the Major's salute. 'Move out in column of route to the right, if you please.'

'The pipes and drums, Colonel?'

'Certainly!'

Hay turned and passed the order. Captain Black repeated it in a loud shout. 'Queen's Own Royal Strathspeys will advance to the right in column of route ... right *turn*!' There was a rattle of side-arms and sloped rifles, a crash of boot-leather and swirl of dust around the tartan of the kilts. 'By the right ... quick – *march*!'

Bosom Cunningham, Regimental Sergeant-Major, eagle-eyed as ever, busied himself with his pace-stick, marching briskly beside the troops as the regiment moved out, using his tremendous voice to call the step. 'Left ... left ... left, right, left ... you

191

there, that man *you*, hold that perishing rifle *straight*. Left ... left...' As the drums beat out the pipes wailed into life, coming out strongly and nostalgically with the brave notes of 'Blue Bonnets Over The Border'. Ogilvie, riding ahead of B Company, felt, as he always felt when the whole regiment moved out of cantonments, a heady sense of what in other moments he called Fettleworthism: that portly General's sentiments were at times perfectly understandable. The army was a splendid institution, doing a splendid job in all corners of the world; often it was cumbersome, often it was slow, always the proper routines and procedures as laid down in Queen's Regulations had to be observed, and always there was a degree of contrived drama and show with pomposity lurking somewhere in the wings of the least staid and stuffy of regiments. One day, far into the dimness of some future that none of them marching out this morning would see, the army might shed its fat and in becoming leaner become faster and less concerned with tradition and procedure; but in so doing, Ogilvie felt, it would lose much of what made men join the Colours, much of that indefinable quality that swelled men's hearts and lightened their step on long marches, and sustained them in action when the bullets sang through the ranks and the thunder of the artillery drowned the tormented screams of the wounded and the dying.

Luncheon lay at the mercies of the field kitchen; for this meal Lord Dornoch halted the column after a forced-march south of some fifteen miles that took the regiment down towards the Parachinar-Khushalgarh railway line a little to the west of Kohat. Before dispersing the men he addressed the column from horseback as the companies gathered round him in a circle. He told them the ostensible orders: merely that they were to rendezvous with the Kohat Light Horse by midnight and hold the line against a likely rising.

'The whole Frontier's under threat,' he said. 'We're entrusted with this part of it. By now, no doubt, the bush telegraph will have seen to it that the Wazaris know we're coming. We must expect action, but it won't be for the first time for many of you. Action's something we expect from the time we set foot in India. I know I can rely upon every man to hold the line to the last. That's all.' As Lord Dornoch nodded to the Adjutant to fall the men out, there was a burst of cheering: it was utterly spontaneous and it seemed to catch the Colonel off his guard. He smiled wryly, and took off his bonnet, waving it in acknowledgment. There was another cheer, then the men dispersed along the track under the watchful eyes of the pickets ahead and on the flanks. Dornoch caught the eye of the Adjutant.

'A jingoistic little speech,' he said quietly, 'but what else could I do?'

'What else indeed, Colonel? I think the cheering showed it was well enough received.'

'Perhaps. Certainly they're keen enough for action ... it's better than the boredom of cantonments, I don't doubt! That is, until it comes.'

'Colonel?'

Dornoch laughed. 'Oh, I'm not showing a yellow streak! But we're going to have casualties. We've lost so many of the original draft we came out with, Andrew. It's very noticeable on parade.' He added, 'More so, in church.'

'In *church*, Colonel?'

'Yes. The lessons, you know ... when I'm at the lectern. The padre's remarked on it too, very often. One looks for faces ... when they're all staring at you – and thinking of beer in the canteen.'

'I'd never thought of it,' Black said after a pause.

'The old faces go, the old friends with experience and shared hardships, the ones who understand what it's all about. You see the green ones, the expectant ones who have it all yet to undergo. They're so ... dependent. I don't know if you follow, Andrew.'

'I think I do, Colonel.'

Dornoch sighed. 'You will for a certainty when you command a battalion in India. I often wonder why the devil they don't see through us!'

Black raised his eyebrows. 'See through us?'

'See that no colonel is really God Almighty ... whatever their NCOs tell them.' Suddenly Dornoch swung his horse away and spoke over his shoulder. 'I'd like a word with Captain Ogilvie, if you please.'

Black saluted the Colonel's back and rode away muttering to himself. The Colonel, he fancied, could be showing his age – or his long spell of Indian service. It was not good to command too long in India, in Black's view: the vision became distorted though at the same time the arteries of the mind, if there were such things, hardened and became static. Not that the Colonel was showing signs of being static ... soft was a better word. In Black's opinion the men were there to obey, to fight, to die. They were paid for that, and there were always recruits joining the home depot to be sent out after training. To Black, one face was indistinguishable from another, a mere smudge beneath a highland bonnet or a Wolseley helmet: it was not the face but the arm or shoulder that gave the distinction. Chevrons or the lack of them, the crossed flags of a colour-sergeant, the Royal Arms of the Regimental Sergeant-Major, the stars and crowns of God's annointed commissioned officers – that was where men differed, not in the face that could end up as an unidentifiable mask of blood and shattered bone and flesh ... Scowling now with his thoughts, Black snapped at a private to run and find Captain Ogilvie and then, dismounting from his horse, walked towards the trestle tables that were being set up under a canvas screen for the officers' luncheon. The day was a cold one, and now that the sweat of the ride from Peshawar was evaporating, Black felt decidedly chilly. Under cover of his water-bottle and a turned back, the Adjutant took a private *chota peg* from his whisky flask.

'Ah, James. Sit down.'
'Thank you, Colonel.' Ogilvie sat on a camp stool, one of a rather special pair belonging personally to Lord Dornoch; constructed entirely of wood that slatted neatly together when folded and formed a seat with bowed arms when set up, they had

been used at the Crimea by a distaff-side forebear who had served in the cavalry under Lord Lucan and had charged the Russian guns with the Light Brigade. Blown to fragments himself, his camp stools had survived.

'A word about your orders, your personal orders.'

'Yes, Colonel?'

Dornoch paused, pulling at his moustache. 'I don't know how forthcoming you're able to be, taking into account the involvement of Blaise-Willoughby, from whom God preserve me. You must be your own judge of that. But I'd like to know what you're supposed to do when we make contact with Soames.'

'Watch him, Colonel.'

'And precipitate him into some overt act of disloyalty – so much I know, James. But after that, d'you see? If he leaves the column, which we must assume he will in order to contact the Wolf, is he to be followed?'

'The General was no precise, Colonel, but—'

'A failing of generals, in case events turn against them! But go on, James.'

'I gathered it was to be left to me, Colonel.'

'To you – alone? How deeply – if at all –

was the regiment to be involved?'

Ogilvie's answer was indirect. 'Colonel, nothing was said to the effect that I shouldn't ask you for assistance.'

'More imprecision?' Dornoch's eyes gleamed.

'Yes, Colonel.'

Dornoch nodded. 'Then I think some precision is called for, James, to redress the balance! I'll not interfere with your orders from Division, but I shall ask you to keep me closely informed – and you may rely upon me for all assistance when you need it.'

'Thank you, Colonel.'

Dornoch got to his feet; Ogilvie followed suit. The Colonel said rather heavily, 'According to regulations, I must consider you as detached from my command for the time being. But I want you to remember you're still a Royal Strathspey. That's all, James. Off you go to your luncheon.'

As soon as the field kitchens had cleared away, the bugles blew the fall-in; no time was being lost. The Regimental Sergeant-Major and the colour-sergeants chased the companies into column and in the van the Colonel gave the order to advance. The pipes and drums began with 'The Muckin' O' Geordie's Byre', a lively six-eight march, and the men stepped out with a will. Here in the hills there was never any point in attempting to advance silently, except when on the march at night. During the day there were always the invisibly watching eyes, sharp behind the *jezails* and the long snaky bayonets, behind the knives and the thin cords of *thuggee*. Riding his horse ahead of B Company Ogilvie thought about the Colonel's closing words: 'Remember you're still a Royal Strathspey.' Lord Dornoch was the most honourable of men; there could have been a hint of his distaste for what amounted to a spying mission upon a brother officer. Distasteful it was to be sure, and never mind what Soames had done, was doing, and intended to go on doing: Ogilvie had no doubt at all in his mind as to Soames's guilt. His mission, his orders, still stank; his whole upbringing from the nursery to Sandhurst and beyond made him detest it more with every hour that passed. There was, as Blaise-Willoughby himself had stressed back in Fort Gaza, a clear cleavage between regimental officers and the Political Department. It needed a particular type of officer to volunteer for the Political side; it was suited to men who, at school, had been swots and sneaks, always ready to drop someone else beneath the swiping cane of a housemaster or who, as

Gentlemen Cadets at Sandhurst, had taken pains to keep on the right side of their Cadet Sergeant, to remain in the good books of the Junior Under-Officer of their company. Such a man Blaise-Willoughby would have been, sharpening his wits and his diplomacy for future intrigue. And even Blaise-Willoughby had expressed reservations about this business, albeit ones based upon snobbery. It had been the robust, outgoing Bloody Francis, the least sneaky, least swottish officer imaginable, but also a snob, who had drooled for a spy to be set upon Soames. Human nature was certainly unaccountable, Ogilvie thought with a hard smile. Or perhaps it was all attributable to the degree of command held by the person concerned!

Ogilvie's thoughts were broken into by Anderson, moving up beside his horse. 'This is very similar country to Fort Gaza, James.'

Ogilvie looked around at the starkness of the light-brown hills with their withered palosa, darkening ahead where the track led through a defile. 'Yes. It's not surprising. We're not all that far as the crow flies – or the vulture!'

'I suppose not.' Anderson shielded his eyes against the sun. 'What ... fifty miles?'

'Give or take a little.'

'A fairish distance.'

'Not in India.'

They moved on behind the advanced scouting party, passing into the dim light of the defile, and out again in safety, covered by the busy pickets climbing the hillsides on either flank, doubling down again at breakneck speed when relieved by the next detail, shepherding the column through against any lurking bandits. Some four miles clear of the pass, the order came down the column for the men to fall out for a brief rest. They threw themselves down beside the track, easing their feet in their boots, relaxing away for half an hour the strains of a long march over appalling surfaces. Ogilvie, smoking a pipe and walking around to relieve saddle-stiffness, was approached by the Regimental Sergeant-Major who swung a hand to the salute, pace-stick rigidly horizontal beneath his left arm, boots striking sparks from rock as he halted with paradeground precision, kilt swinging around thighs like tree-trunks.

'Sir! A word, if I may?'

'Of course, Mr Cunningham. But first – may I forestall you?'

'Sir?'

'Rumour is circulating – right?'

Cunningham nodded. 'Aye, Captain Ogilvie, it is.'

'And it says?'

'This, sir: we're expected to be in action after nightfall. If that's to be the case, then the men would like to know.'

'I can understand that. But action's always likely, Sar'nt-Major, you know that. If the Colonel had definite information, he'd not keep it to himself. Further than that, I can't answer for him.'

'No, sir. Of course not. But I just wondered what the chances were.' Cunningham hesitated. 'I'm sorry to have bothered you, sir.'

'You never bother me, Mr Cunningham.' Ogilvie smiled. 'You're a rock in a world of shifting sands! As to action, just tell the men to be ready and alert, that's all. I have an idea something else is bothering you, isn't it?'

'Aye, it is that, sir.' The RSM's eyes stared over Ogilvie's head, woodenly, expressionless. 'There's talk of treachery, sir.'

Ogilvie started. 'On whose part, Sar'nt-Major?'

'Rumour doesn't go that far, sir. But there's talk we may be marching into a trap.'

'I'd advise you to check that sort of talk, Sar'nt-Major, and firmly. To my knowledge, we expect no trap, although it's always possible for movement orders to leak out ahead to the tribes.'

'Yes, sir. And the treachery?' This time, Cunningham's eyes looked directly into Ogilvie's – very blue eyes, and honest, and now troubled. 'Can you set my mind at rest on that, Captain Ogilvie?'

The day was growing colder, but Ogilvie felt the sweat break out on his body. Mentally he cursed the omniscience of the wretched bush telegraph, the lightning-speed vehicle that operated no one knew how, a process almost of magic or of some sixth sense. Cunningham had come to him, genuinely, for advice; Cunningham's whole concern, like the Colonel's, was for the regiment and the men who made it. Cunningham had immense trust in him, Ogilvie; so, as Ogilvie knew, had the rank and file. That went not only for his own company but for all; detesting the Adjutant, they had come to regard him as their link, along with the RSM, with the Colonel. This was something that Ogilvie found humbling, found himself totally unworthy of. Meanwhile some answer had to be found for Cunningham. Cunningham was a man to be wholeheartedly trusted, and sooner or later Cunningham would have to know the truth. He might have to know it very soon, if Soames showed his hand. Ogilvie made up his mind. He said, 'I can set your mind at rest that treachery will be dealt with.

Division is fully aware of what may be going on. I can't say more for now, Mr Cunningham, except this: it would help if you were to play down the rumours. Let the men know all's well. I'm sure you'll find the right formula.'

'I'll try, sir. And thank you, sir.'

Ogilvie nodded. 'Then carry on, if you please, Sar'nt-Major.'

Riding on again as the sun went down the sky to leave long shadows extending back from the western hills, Ogilvie knew he had not satisfied Cunningham. He had been guilty of an officer's cardinal sin: he had temporised, and left it to the warrant officer to make what he could of it and act accordingly; in short, he had shirked the issue. It was not a happy feeling to ride with, but it could not now be rectified, and at least he had not denied the undeniable. When events came to their fruition, Cunningham would understand. The march continued, the pipes and drums silent as the swift darkness came down upon the column. Lord Dornoch had passed the word that the night's bivouacs would not be entered until contact had been made around midnight with the Kohat Light Horse advancing from the south. There had been a halt for supper, and later there would be another brief period of rest for men and horses, and that was all. The rest period was called from the van at a little after nine thirty. Strong pickets were posted, and a mounted subaltern was sent ahead to halt the advanced scouting party and to remain with them until the march was resumed, which would be in half an hour's time from the halt order. No lamps were lit, and the word was passed for silence and no smoking. It was a time for eeriness, for imagination to run riot. The only sounds were a sighing of wind, a cold wind, and an occasional dry scuttle of some disturbed rock-dwelling creature. All else was still, but stillness was not to last. Orders were about to be passed for the march to be resumed when the unmistakable boom and roar of gunfire came from ahead, the raw metallic voice of heavy artillery in the south.

Twelve

'Remain where you are – all men, keep in cover but stand to your rifles!'

The Colonel's voice came loudly, and the order was repeated along the column. The next order was for all company commanders to join the Colonel. Lord Dornoch stood with Major Hay and the Adjutant, in the centre of a small circle, only dimly and spasmodically seen as the moon peered fitfully from behind heavy cloud.

'We don't know what's going on,' he said. 'It's a reasonable assumption that the cavalry is engaged, but they're a long way ahead if so, judging from the sound of the guns. I intend to wait for a report from the scouts before advancing. I dare say it'll not be long. I don't propose to run into a trap in the meantime.'

'Are we not wasting time, Colonel?' The voice, coming from the darkness, was impatient, and belonged to Angus Seymour, commanding E Company.

'We are here to hold the line,' Lord

Dornoch answered calmly. 'We shall not hold it by throwing ourselves away in a trap. We may need to stand in the place of the Light Horse.'

'But assistance, Colonel—'

'Will be given, depending upon the report from the scouts. They're there for a purpose, Captain Seymour, and I shall respect that purpose.' He paused. 'I hear a rider now.'

So did they all: they waited as the galloping horse came nearer. The rider was the subaltern sent ahead to join the scouts.

'Well?' Dornoch asked.

'Gunfire, Colonel—'

'We know,' Dornoch said drily. 'Who's engaged? The moon was showing for a while, was it not?'

'Yes, Colonel. I think it's the Kohat Light Horse, engaged by native artillery, about three miles ahead of the scouts.'

'And the ground? I take it it's clear between the regiment and the scouts. What about the ground ahead?'

'Clear so far as could be seen, Colonel.'

'No obvious trap?'

'None, Colonel.'

'Very well.' Crisply the Colonel gave his orders. 'Ride back to the scouts, Mr Phillips, and tell them to wait for us. Major, fall in the regiment in column, if you please, and advance immediately to the south. Hold the camp followers where they are – detail a guard. Captain Black, the pace is to be kept as fast as possible and we shall double in when the enemy's in sight, and then extend.'

'Very good, Colonel.'

'And full silence so far as possible, until we're seen.'

Black saluted and hurried away. No bugles were blown; the orders were passed by the NCOs and the men were quickly fallen in and the advance began through the night under the still fitful moon. The going was terrible; men stumbled and fell over jags of rock, cursing savagely as knees and elbows were grazed or faces smacked into ironhard earth. The ranks moved almost at the double already, urged on by the sergeants and corporals whose verbal lashings were no less unkind for being uttered in low voices. The distance closed: the scouts were overtaken and carried on with the main advance. Another report to the Colonel indicated the cavalry as holding their own nicely so far as could be seen, with at least two of the enemy guns having been blown up by fire from the Kohat Light Horse's attached battery. The native attackers, however, appeared to be standing fast across the track, effectively, as yet, blocking the cavalry's advance to the north.

Half an hour after overtaking the extended

scouts, the battle could be seen ahead. For some while the gun-flashes had flickered across the night sky; now the whole panorama could be seen: the blinding explosions as the shells landed, the orange flame from the mouths of the guns as they fired again and again, the smaller but more widespread flashes as the carbines of the Indian cavalry kept up a sustained fire.

Ahead of the regiment, Lord Dornoch stood in his stirrups, waving his drawn sword above his head. 'Royal Strathspeys will fix bayonets! Extend to right and left! Advance at the double!'

With the moonlight glinting off the naked steel of the bayonets, the Scots ran ahead behind the Colonel, charging the exposed and so-far unsuspecting rear of the tribal artillery. As soon as they were near enough, Lord Dornoch shouted the action order to the bugles: the notes blew strong and vibrant and were overtaken by the crash of the Scots rifles as the now extended front opened. Lord Dornoch's voice was heard again: *'Pipes and drums!'*

Pipe-Major Ross filled his bag with air, his chest swelling to the next indrawn breath. Loud and stirring, the notes of the action tune of the Royal Strathspeys, 'Cock O' The North', blew along the rising wind. Ahead of the running Scots there was consternation: natives dashed here and there, many of them leaving their guns. The cavalry's attached artillery battery was now silent, no doubt so as to avoid any possibility of dropping shells over into the infantry advance, but after the first panic the native guns were turned upon the Scots. There were explosions that left deep craters in the rocky ground and caused many casualties; but then the swiftly advancing line was upon the natives, engaging them hand-to-hand, and the advantage of the guns was lost. The fighting was furious and bloody: Ogilvie's horse was hacked from under him by scimitar-like blades, and fell screaming with its stomach split. As Ogilvie picked himself up and fired a shot from his revolver to put the animal out of its pain, he was attacked by a heavily bearded man wielding another blade that glinted silver in the moon's light. As the blade swung for him in a great slicing arc, he ducked beneath it and fired point-blank into a dirty-robed stomach. The body fell almost on top of him and as he struggled clear he saw Andrew Black riding past, dragging a body that had become caught up on his stirrup. Black bent, and hacked downwards with his sword, trying to free it. As it fell, it screamed: it was not quite dead. Running feet, both Scots and native, trampled it into the ground. Gunsmoke drifted chokingly. By this time Ogilvie had taken temporary cover behind a sizeable jag of rock, where he was joined by a private of his own company. Firing from this cover, they brought down a number of the native force. The battle was becoming more and more confused and it was more and more difficult to isolate any point of aim. The Scots' bayonets were having a good effect: the frontier tribes had never been anxious to face cold British steel. Already they were running to the flanks. As Ogilvie reloaded his revolver in the lee of the rock, there were blood-chilling shouts and yells from the south, where the artillery was still silent.

'What's that, sir?' the private asked.

'The cavalry's coming in. Stay where you are, Meldrum.' Dangerously, Ogilvie jumped up and shouted at the nearer Scots, ordering them off the track to give the cavalry a clearer field. In the moonbeams and the rifle flashes he saw the Regimental Sergeant-Major and the Adjutant, apparently shouting similar orders, then he saw Black go down from his horse clutching at a shoulder. Now the drumming of horses' hooves was loud, a sound like thunder on the hard ground. The moon showed a splendid sight – the Kohat Light Horse with pennons flying out from the van, and the sabres drawn to be whirled over the riders' heads with a sheerly savage intent, charging at full gallop along the Indian valley, the men shouting, yelling, whooping above the pounding hooves. There was a crackle of fire from the *jezails* and one or two riders fell before the Scots rifles spoke again and silenced the native fire. From then on it was a case of panic and precipitate flight, the natives beating it into the hillsides where the cavalry could not follow. They were pursued by the Scots until the order came from the Colonel for the bugles to sound Retire; the Scots straggled back. The cavalry, at the full pitch of their charge, stormed through to the rear before their Colonel halted them and turned them about, and rode them back at a walk towards the highland line.

Dornoch approached the cavalry Colonel. 'Lord Dornoch, is it not?' the latter asked, breathing hard, his face shiny with sweat beneath the turban of the Indian Army. 'Keeley, of the Kohat Light Horse – we've met, I fancy? And well met again!'

Salutes and handshakes were exchanged. Keeley said, 'You and your men saved the day. Or the night, I should say! We're grateful, Colonel. What brought you here?'

'Orders,' Dornoch answered briefly. 'For you.'

'More orders?' Keeley sounded immensely surprised. 'I've only just had the last lot –

to ride back to Kohat—'

'Superseded,' Dornoch broke in. 'We were to march south and meet you and pass the fresh orders.' He looked around: infantry and cavalry officers were coming together, exchanging congratulations, and Black was shouting orders for the pickets. By now the enemy was nowhere to be seen, only the abandoned native guns and the dead of both sides bearing witness to a bloody fight. 'I have orders from Division to remain here with your regiment, and to make camp, and to hold the line to Kohat.'

'Bloody Francis, Colonel?'

'Bloody Francis himself.'

'I see. Well, orders are orders, though I could have done with the comparative comforts of Kohat.' Keeley, Dornoch fancied, was a man to appreciate comfort; he was well-fleshed, and in daylight his cheeks would be florid with much past whisky, and there was, somehow, a hint of the lecher. 'What's in the air, d'you know?'

Dornoch, after another look around, spoke loudly. He had spotted Ogilvie, had exchanged glances, and Ogilvie, with a slight movement of his head, had indicated one of the cavalry officers sitting his horse beside him: *Soames*, that inclination of the head had said clearly. 'Division, I believe, intends to reinforce Kohat city as a main defensive base. I know not why! But strong forces are on their way, and you and I, Colonel, will form the extended defence line.'

Keeley shrugged, then gave a laugh. 'So be it – Bloody Francis has spoken. We have a fair strength – infantry, cavalry, and what's left of the guns, and there's a brigade down at Bannu to give distant cover to our southern flank...'

The camp followers were retrieved and for the remainder of the night the joined units went into bivouacs, being woken early to turn out stiff and cold and dirty to bury the dead and make proper camp for an indefinite period of duty in the wilds. A ditch was dug around the perimeter, backed by an earth rampart, and protected by a double apron of barbed wire; every hundred yards was a make-shift bastion for the perimeter pickets. By day only a few of these bastions would be manned, each of them with a solitary sentry; but from nightfall to dawn all the pickets would be guarding against any sudden rush from the hills. If such came, the perimeter could be manned in seconds from the infantry lines where every man would sleep with his rifle by his side. The guns were positioned along the perimeter, with the horses and camels, mules and oxen protected in the centre. During the preceding night not all the men had slept: the gunners had stripped their guns and had effected refurbishments and inspected the abandoned native pieces for any use that might be made of them; and the medical details under Surgeon Major Corton and the cavalry's Medical Officer had attended to the wounded, sorting them out from the dead and making them as comfortable as possible. Many were bandaged, many lay in stretchers, grey-faced with pain in the dawn's light. In point of fact the casualties were not as bad as might have been expected: the Royal Strathspeys had lost nineteen dead and forty-three wounded, the latter figure including Black's wounded shoulder from which Corton had extracted a bullet during the night, to the accompaniment of a good deal of fuss and complaint from the Adjutant – the bullet had not in fact gone very deep. The cavalry had lost thirty-one dead and sixty-seven wounded, also a number of horses had had to be shot. Of the artillery, two guns had been put out of action badly enough to need refit by the ordnance at Brigade.

Of the ambushing natives: 'Christ, there's bloody mountains of 'em!' MacTrease said in some awe to a section sergeant. 'Worse than a slaughterhouse, is this!'

215

'Aye, an' a bloody good lesson it'll teach the other buggers, Colour-Sar'nt.'

MacTrease gave a grisly laugh. 'Us, too!'

'Why us, then?'

'They'll stink, soon.' This was a fact well recognised by Corton and the Colonel. Once the bodies had been closely examined – and each was found to carry the brand mark of the Wolf – burial details were organised and the massive task began, the bodies being carried some distance from the encampment lines and respectfully clear of the stone cairns marking the shallow graves of the dead of the British and Indian Armies, over which Last Post had been sounded as the sun blazed up from eastward.

'You look fed up, Ogilvie.' Soames smiled, teeth white in the sunburned face. He was a good-looking man – too good-looking by half, Ogilvie thought, not with jealousy but with deep mistrust. All the circumstantial evidence quite apart, Soames did not exude trustworthiness. Another thing had been ground into Ogilvie by his upbringing and his army life: anything that went to extremes must be viewed with suspicion. Looks that were just too good, clothes that were just too smart, too good a command of a foreign tongue, a manner of speech that was just too precise ... all these could be the hallmarks of the bounder but they could also be the hallmarks of the untrustworthy, of the cad; and as Blaise-Willoughby had remarked, Soames, whatever his crimes, was not a bounder.

Ogilvie responded to the greeting, coolly. 'Not fed up, Soames.' He waved an arm towards the fresh burial ground. 'I've just come back from out there.'

'I know. So have I.'

'I just don't like it, that's all. Men one's served with ... and the letters to be written to wives and mothers.' Ogilvie looked at Soames with curiosity. 'It doesn't affect you, does it?'

Soames shrugged, tapped his silver-topped cane against his polished cavalry boots. Action or no, he could have stepped straight out of a band-box. 'I know what you mean, but ... no, it doesn't really *affect* me. What's death, anyway?'

'Something pretty final.'

Soames laughed. 'How the devil do you know? Not that I'm any sort of a Holy Joe myself. I leave that to the damn padre. What I meant was ... out here, death's part of life. Something we all have to face. Those out there – they've faced it already, that's all. It could be our turn next. Will it make any damn difference if we're wept over?'

Ogilvie made no answer. Soames went on as they walked past the end of the cavalry lines, 'Talking of weeping, old man.'

'Well?'

There was a chuckle. 'Wouldn't you like to know!'

'Oh, for God's sake!' Ogilvie said irritably. 'Don't let's behave like children or old women—'

'Ah! And talking of old women ... all right, Ogilvie, I'll put you out of your misery. A chap called Alderson brought our last-but-one lot of orders through from the depot – from Kohat. D'you know him?'

'No.'

'Captain, Indian Staff Corps. Good chap – Alderson. Knows the right people, don't you know.' There was a pause. 'He knows a chap called Babbitt, a Civilian in Murree. Babbitt's had a letter from mum, a second one I gather. Want to know what was in it, Ogilvie?'

Mrs Major Babbitt, in Brown's Hotel during that last week of leave ... Ogilvie ground his teeth. He was reluctant but he had to know. 'All right, Soames. Get on with your gossip.'

Soames, grinning, began to hum: *'I saw a ship a-sailing, a-sailing on the sea* ... She couldn't wait, Ogilvie, you lucky bugger! One of the B.I. ships left Tilbury not long

218

after you sailed from Portsmouth. It was quicker than waiting for the next P & O. You can guess the rest.'

'Can I?'

Soames said, 'Depending how long we're left out here like watchdogs, old man, she may well be in Murree before you.' He added, 'I just thought you'd like to know.'

'Thank you. A kind thought,' Ogilvie snapped.

'Don't mention it,' Soames said, a gleam in his eye. 'It's something to sustain you, isn't it, while we're marooned out here.' He paused, halted as they reached his regimental lines, and slapped again at his boots. 'Funny thing, rumour. The bush telegraph. Alderson knew about your Mrs Archdale, but he evidently didn't have an inkling that we were due for yet more orders to contradict those he'd brought. Odd, that.'

'Not really. Division changed its mind, that's all. You know what Fettleworth's like, surely?'

'I've a fair idea! Look, what's in the wind, Ogilvie? Haven't you brought any rumours from Peshawar?'

'You can't trust rumour, Soames.'

'Probably not, but it's usually interesting. Come on, old man – give! One good turn deserves another, doesn't it?'

Ogilvie yawned, having no need to act to

produce the motion. 'Oh, vaguish stuff. There's talk of a rising, and Fettleworth's said to be having a general post of his troops.'

'Oh?'

'That's really all I know. Nothing definite, and God knows where the rising's supposed to be coming from. But whatever it's all about, I assume we're part of it or we wouldn't be here. Mind you, I'm pretty sure my Colonel knows something the rest of us don't.' Ogilvie brought out his watch. 'I must go, Soames. There's any amount to be done before the regiment's bedded down.'

Soames nodded absently as Ogilvie walked away towards the Scots lines, where the tents were going up and the Regimental Sergeant-Major, with the RQMS and the colour-sergeants, was checking the distances between them with his usual diligence before Adjutant's Inspection. Bending to tie up a bootlace, Ogilvie took a quick glance behind: Soames was where he had left him, slapping his boot with his cane and looking highly thoughtful as he stared towards the Royal Strathspeys' lines. Something, Ogilvie knew, had been planted. So far, so good; he busied himself around his company lines, together with his subalterns, and after a while Soames vanished. Ogilvie waited until the bugles and the cavalry trumpets blew for luncheon, then went to the Colonel's tent.

It was well handled by Lord Dornoch, if with reluctance. Major Hay and Captain Black were sent for during the afternoon, and duly briefed; and subsequently Black was openly indiscreet. He sent runners to all company commanders with the word that the Colonel required their presence in his tent at nine p.m., by which time it would be full dark. A conference was to be held, said the order. In his conversations later, Black was again indiscreet: he talked of orders, hitherto secret, about to be divulged. Very important orders, Black said, sounding important and knowledgeable himself. This spread fast; there were no old women in the lines, no Mrs Colonel Bates, no Mrs Major Babbitt to embroider the story, but the bush telegraph, always strong in camp and under active-service conditions where tension acted in a way similar to the boredom in cantonments, did its work well and quickly. In no time word had penetrated to the artillery and cavalry lines; in no time the ears of Captain Soames were attuned to the news that the Colonel of the 114th Highlanders was about to break startling information. Thereafter Soames walked alone, pacing the iron-hard ground of the remote, lonely valley, puffing clouds of smoke from his pipe, tapping cane against polished leather boot, obviously deep in thought.

'A word in your ear, Mr Cunningham.'

'Sir!' The customary thunderclap of Cunningham's halt took place.

'Between ourselves, Mr Cunningham, very strictly – except in so far as you will expressly need to issue orders. I want you to produce me the most trustworthy private you know of, and the one with the closest mouth. Suggestions?'

The RSM said at once, 'Private MacArthur, sir. He has my personal guarantee.'

'Right,' Ogilvie said. He would have given the same name himself. He knew MacArthur as an old sweat, a private soldier nearing forty, single in his state, single in his devotions: booze and any woman he could find in the bazaars when out of barracks, but strictly the regiment when inside. Booze or not, MacArthur consistently did his duty, was never absent over leave, always marched straight when coming back blotto through the barrack gate. Over the years of service he had earned and retained three good-conduct stripes and a resplendent row of four medals. He would do. Ogilvie went on, 'I want Private MacArthur to take over sentry duty on the Colonel's tent from eight to ten p.m. tonight. Can you alter the rosters?'

'I can, sir.'

'Without it looking suspicious?'

'You can rely upon me, Captain Ogilvie.'

'I know, Bosom,' Ogilvie said, using the RSM's nickname: Cunningham had a massively out-thrust chest. 'MacArthur is to have special orders, very special ones. They'll not be easy to follow, but a lot depends on his success in carrying them out convincingly.'

'Sir?'

'I have reason to believe,' Ogilvie said in a low voice, 'that during the Colonel's conference tonight, an officer of the Kohat Light Horse may ... saunter into our lines. Do I make myself clear, Bosom?'

There was a silence, broken only by the RSM's heavy breathing. Then Cunningham said in a formal voice, 'Treachery was mentioned yesterday, Captain Ogilvie. Yes, I think you are clear.'

'Good. This officer is to be allowed to approach the Colonel's tent. MacArthur is not to chase him away.'

Cunningham blew up the waxed ends of his moustache. 'A tall order, sir! A sentry, to be in dereliction of his *duty*!'

'It's vitally important, Mr Cunningham. I'm sure you'll find a way. I need hardly add that no action will be taken subsequently against MacArthur.'

'But this officer, Captain Ogilvie. He'll know the Colonel's tent will have a sentry posted outside. How does he imagine he'll be permitted to eavesdrop, sir?'

Ogilvie shrugged. 'I can't answer that, I admit. But I suggest he may saunter past—'

'A recce, sir?'

'Exactly. He must be shown that the way's clear for him. If he finds it a trifle coincidental – well, that's a risk we must take. I could be wrong in any case, and he may not come. But I think he will. Can you manage, Bosom?'

Cunningham said, 'Something will be done. Have no fear about that, Captain Ogilvie.'

As the RSM marched away towards the Sergeants' Mess tent, Ogilvie found little reassurance in his words. There was much doubt in his mind, for plenty could go sadly astray if Soames should make his getaway – as Ogilvie felt certain he would after listening to Lord Dornoch – before he could be discreetly followed. Then the fat might be in the fire. For if Lord Dornoch's falsification of the overall planning should just happen to coincide with any genuine movements of Division – and to convince Soames it all had to come reasonably near likely fact and truth – then when it was known to have reached the ears of the Wolf there would be much trouble that would reverberate from Calcutta to Whitehall and back again.

Thirteen

At sundown the bugles and trumpets had sounded Retreat, the signal for all men to stand-to so as to ensure that all personnel knew their alarm posts for the dark hours. Checked by company officers and colour-sergeants, they were fallen out again, leaving only the duty pickets around the perimeter and on the overlooking hills. At nine p.m. sharp the officers as detailed reported to the Colonel's tent. Black was already in attendance at Lord Dornoch's side as the latter sat behind a trestle table under the light of a guard lantern. The Major sat smoking a cigar as the company commanders filed in and stood in a semi-circle before Lord Dornoch. Outside, Private MacArthur marched his post, stolidly, reflecting on his strange orders from the RSM: sergeant-majors did funny things from time to time, as bad as officers they were, but Private MacArthur had been in the Queen's service long enough to realise that everything had its reason, no matter how daft it might seem to

226

the rank and file.

From the cover of the armourer's tent, Cunningham was keeping a watching brief: he had a fair view of the regimental lines, also of the adjacent cavalry lines. Not many men were stirring; rest and sleep were of more value than an aimless peramble in the darkness of a hostile valley, and though there was a feeling of security in the camp behind the watchful eyes of the pickets, no man could ever know when a sniper's bullet might shatter the peace and find its mark: the moon was up, and men could stand out well enough for a good aim to be taken. Nevertheless there was some movement in the cavalry lines: the horses seemed to be restive, and there was a coming and going of the *syces,* and of one of the white troop officers accompanied by the Squadron *Duffardar*-Major. Cunningham sucked at his teeth and went on watching, and after a while, from his cover, he saw the lone approach of the officer from the lines of the Kohat Light Horse. Slow, casual, all the time in the world for a stroll before turning in – and no reason why he shouldn't walk down into the infantry lines, none at all. A glance at a watch, its face lit by a small pocket torch, and a directing of steps to take him past the Colonel's tent.

This, then, was the recce.

The officer, smartly dressed in overalls and tunic with the two stars of a captain glinting from his shoulder chains, drifted past the Colonel's sentry smoking a cigar. From Private MacArthur, no butt-salute upon his rifle: MacArthur remained impolitely at ease, swaying a little, and had the cavalry captain been close enough – and maybe he was – he would have smelt the strong blast of just enough of the Officers' Mess whisky to make Private MacArthur highly appreciative of his strange orders without rendering him genuinely incapable of carrying them out.

Staring as MacArthur belched loudly, the officer went on past, keeping his eyes open to right and left. Some twenty yards past the Colonel's tent, he turned and looked back, whereupon Private MacArthur very convincingly slid to the ground and lay there in a motionless huddle of drunk sentry, dead to the world. Cunningham saw the officer drop his cigar and stamp on it. The officer turned back, still not hurrying, and disappeared behind the tent: the officer did not reappear.

Inside his tent, the Colonel had been playing for time, talking what he knew was a degree of nonsense – a kind of sermon for officers whose keenness and devotion to duty was never in question, an unnecesary sermon about rifle inspections, physical fitness of the men who needed to be kept fully occupied during a period of waiting, the question of Divine Service should they remain in camp over a Sunday, and so on. Black and the Major, and Ogilvie, who all knew the facts of that night's conference, kept their faces blank; the other officers politely suppressed yawns and tried not to shift their feet too much. The Colonel was well liked and respected, but tonight he appeared to be dithering. It was the lecture of an old woman, of a commander weighed down into triviality by the strains and stresses of the very nature of command. Not surprising, perhaps; the Old Man had commanded longer than most lieutenant-colonels, and on the North-West Frontier at that – but still!

Dornoch dithered on, progressing from the orderly splitinch straightness so essential for the lines of tents to the conscientious polishing of brass buttons and equipment and the need to keep feet washed and socks darned...

Into all this fell a sound, the rifle-rattle of total collapse. It was not a loud sound, and it meant little to those who were not expecting it: no more than a passing butt salute. Standing just inside the tent flaps, Ogilvie lifted a hand, catching the Colonel's eye in the middle of a dissertation on the proper ironing of kilt pleats, and at once Lord Dornoch moved smoothly on.

'...and so now, gentlemen, we come to the real nub of what I've been saying, to why it is so important to maintain full efficiency and alertness.' He paused. 'There has been rumour which I'm quite sure you've all heard – rumour of a Frontier rising, and one that is not expected to be confined to the Frontier itself. Now I shall give you the facts: it's known beyond doubt that within the next forty-eight hours the Raj will be in total action against the man known as the Wolf of the Salt Range. I think this will not surprise you, except perhaps as to the short-ness of the time left to us. Now as to the disposition of troops from the First Divi-sion...'

It was a concise, reasoned statement of apparent General Orders from Division, and it was uttered in clear, loud tones. He, Lord Dornoch, was, with the cavalry and artillery, under orders to hold the route out of Waziristan. Within the next twenty-four hours a brigadier-general with two more infantry battalions, a cavalry regiment, and field and horse artillery would join them, the present encampment being well sited for use as an extended base from which all the routes in and out of Waziristan could be watched and defended by strong patrols connected to the camp by field telegraph lines by means of which reinforcements could be asked for instantly when required. More formations, similarly constituted, were already on the move south from Murree and Rawalpindi to contain the whole area of the Salt Range on its northern and eastern flank, while the Maharajah of Kashmir was moving his own army in from Jammu to take care of the southern extension. From Peshawar and Nowshera General Fettleworth was moving cavalry and guns to contain the mouth of the Khyber while units from Mardan would similarly contain the other passes to the north. Constant patrols would be maintained; and in support the sappers would be using their new-fangled balloon sections which, from their commanding positions in the sky itself, could spot any movement of the tribes for many miles around and direct the ground forces quickly to their destruction.

The Wolf of the Salt Range was to have his levies totally and finally destroyed, his person was to be taken, alive or dead, and if alive he would be tried by a military court and hanged for his crimes against his own people and against the Raj.

As Lord Dornoch ended, he said, 'A moment, if you please, gentlemen, before you leave. I have no more to say on action matters, but there are certain regimental affairs ... Captain Ogilvie, I understand you have company duties, and you may carry on.'

Ogilvie saluted and left the tent. Outside, he saw Soames, still sauntering, moving away down the Scots' lines, and he called to him. 'I say, Soames. Care for a stroll?'

Soames turned and moved towards him, grinning. 'Want more news of Mrs Archdale? Sorry – I've told you all. By the way, I suppose you've seen your sentry? Drunk as a lord.'

'That's being dealt with.' It was; Cunningham, in person and alone, was lifting MacArthur to his feet. MacArthur and his whisky-laden breath would be relieved by another sentry before the rest of the officers emerged. 'Let's hope we get a nice, quiet night.'

Soames looked him up and down. 'D'you suppose we might not, Ogilvie?'

'You never know out here, do you?'

'I suppose not.' Soames paused. 'Just in case we don't, I'm for bed. Sorry to be unsociable. Good night, Ogilvie.'

'Good night. And sleep tight.' Before Ogilvie turned away he added, 'I never asked you ... did you get that lance-*duffardar* of yours back?'

'I did.'

'No more troubles?'

Soames said, 'Not that I'm aware of. Should there be?'

'I don't know, I was only enquiring – I had an interest, you know.'

'Very kind of you.' There was a sneer in the cavalry officer's voice. 'I'm sure he was grateful.'

'He seemed a good man. I never believed he was guilty of rape. Is he still in your squadron?'

'As a matter of fact, he's not.' Soames walked away towards his own lines. Moved to another squadron by order of Brigade, Ogilvie guessed – and lucky for the lance-*duffardar* that he had! When Soames had gone, Ogilvie went quickly to the Royal Strathspeys' horse lines and made sure his replacement horse was ready to ride out: for his money, Soames would leave camp that night. If he was truly in the pay of the Wolf of the Salt Range, he would have the most urgent news to report and it was undoubtedly in his interest that the Wolf should not be taken. Having seen his horse ready with heavily muffled hooves, Ogilvie reported back to the Colonel's tent.

'All right, James?'

'Yes, Colonel.'

'Good! I'll go across to talk to Colonel Keeley immediately. You'd better make sure that MacTrease and the others are ready.'

'Very good, Colonel.'

'I doubt if Soames'll go while the moon's up. There's cloud about, but it won't give him darkness for a while yet – the wind's dropped. All the same, keep on watch, James.'

Ogilvie saluted and left the tent. Keeley, already informed of the doubts about Soames, would now be given information as to the subterfuge; and Ogilvie had no doubt that he would co-operate in what Lord Dornoch was about to ask. And co-operate he did; when the Colonel returned from the cavalry lines he sent for Ogilvie and told him the lance-*duffardar* would report the moment Soames had ridden out and would himself join the discreetly-distant pursuit. In the meantime it was a question of waiting. Lord Dornoch said, 'Colonel Keeley's worried about the same point that worried us: will Soames throw everything to the wind by in effect deserting his regiment? I told him our view – that he has no choice left. He'll simply go native – in the interest of avoiding a firing squad!'

'And Colonel Keeley?'

Dornoch stuffed tobacco into a pipe, and

shrugged. 'Well, he agreed but at the same time differed. Soames, it seems, has always been something of a law unto himself – they're like that in the cavalry. Devilment, high spirits, occasional flamboyant disregard of orders – they've the money to get away with it, of course. In Keeley's view, Soames could get away with it yet.'

'How, Colonel?'

'It could be easy! Throw off the pursuit if he spots it – which he could, as we're aware – reach the Wolf, pass his message, ride back into camp and say he went out on a lone patrol. Against orders, perhaps – but better than going native if the latter's avoidable. And who's ever to say afterwards he was not speaking the truth?' Dornoch lit his pipe and puffed a cloud of smoke. 'It's up to you now, James. Do your best – and don't get killed!'

It was almost midnight when heavy cloud began to slide across the moon. The long shadows shortened, changed their direction, and finally disappeared. The night was as black as pitch, cold and eerie and filled with vague menaces both real and imagined. In the care of the pickets and sentries, the camp slept and there was an over-all silence. Ogilvie stood ready in the horse lines with his Colour-Sergeant and six riders, all with their horses' hooves muffled like his own, and carrying plenty of spare muffling material with their other equipment, and all of them, including Ogilvie, now wearing a strange and smelly assortment of native clothing obtained from the *syces*. All exposed areas of skin had been darkened with boot-polish, and each man carried spare tins of polish: they had no idea how long they would be in pursuit, and the disguise might need to last. As they waited, Ogilvie ran through the orders again.

'The lance-*duffardar* will be in the lead – he knows the territory better than any of us. I ride a safe distance behind, keeping him in sight. Then you, Colour – another safe distance depending on the visibility, keeping *me* in sight. The five privates follow you at proper intervals, and Corporal Stainton brings up the rear. Full silence, full cover at all times – that shouldn't be too difficult in the passes, which are full of bends. The hardest part's the start.'

'And maybe farther on too, sir,' Mac-Trease said, 'since we don't know where he'll be leading us.'

'We'll cross that bridge when we come to it. If he spots the leader, the leader goes to ground for a while. If anyone gets killed, the next man takes over as leader. As soon as he gets to where he's going, each man passes the word back. Everyone stays in position except the last two, who ride back here and report. What happens then is up to the Colonel, but at least we'll know we won't be on our own.' He looked over the assembled men. 'Has anyone anything they want to ask?'

There was a shaking of heads; Ogilvie was about to wish them all good luck when, from the cavalry lines, they heard faint sounds, sounds that could have been hoof-beats. Tensely, they waited. The sounds faded into the distance, and then, just a moment later, a man was seen coming at the double from the cavalry lines. Ogilvie step-ped out into his path. As expected, it was the lance-*duffardar*, also dressed, not in his uniform of the Kohat Light Horse, but in the rags and tatters of a tribesman of the frontier.

'Captain Ogilvie sahib—'

'Yes, Akhbar Mohammad Khan. The sounds – were they Soames sahib?'

'Yes, sahib. He rides to the east, openly. He walked his horse past the sentries, then mounted. He will be passing through the picket line shortly, sahib.'

'Right!' Turning to his weird-looking troop, Ogilvie gave the order to mount. The lance-*duffardar* swung himself on to the horse provided for him from the Scots' stable. Ogilvie said, 'Good luck, Akhbar Mohammad Khan. Keep safe – and don't lose Soames sahib!'

'I shall not lose him, Captain sahib, this I promise.'

There was quiet determination mixed with a deep hate in the lance-*duffardar*'s voice. Ogilvie warned, 'And don't kill him either. He's still an officer of the Raj. Until he commits himself, his death will be murder, and punishable by the rope.'

The lance-*duffardar* saluted and rode towards the camp's perimeter. Ogilvie, waiting his turn to follow, found his mind filled with a single thought: a British officer's character and loyalty had now been finally impugned before common soldiers and one native. Blaise-Willoughby back at Division would be most upset, since Soames was not a bounder! Blaise-Willoughby, and never mind his pettishness, his self-interest and his bloody monkey, had influence. For the sake of his own career if nothing else, Ogilvie knew he had to bring this business to a successful end.

Fourteen

Akhbar Mohammad Khan was a first-class hillman, born and bred for the very job he had to do. He allowed Soames to get nicely clear at the start; no suspicions could be afforded and Soames would be watching his rear until he was well away. Nevertheless, and despite the total dark of the moonless night, the lance-*duffardar* picked up the trail with no delay once he had ridden out; like a mounted ghost he flitted through the picket lines, already warned by Keeley that men would be riding out at intervals. The difficulty lay with the British soldiers, Ogilvie included: it was, in the event, a good deal harder than Ogilvie had thought to keep the lance-*duffardar* in view. Invisible to Soames, he was almost equally invisible to Ogilvie, though each of the British soldiers was given confidence by the knowledge that he was one of a chain.

Soames appeared to be heading consistently east; it seemed he might be riding straight for the Salt Range. Once he entered the hills, his direction seemed confirmed in the light of the maps that Ogilvie had studied before riding out: the pass led east, though there were other passes crossing it farther on. Extra vigilance would be needed when those intersections were reached; but Ogilvie felt he could rely on the lance-*duffardar* not to lose his quarry.

The moon had reached the edge of the heavy obscuring cloud and was just starting to sail out and bathe the barren peaks of the hills in its silver light when Ogilvie saw the native figure riding fast towards him out of the east. About to dismount and dive for cover, he realised he had heard no hoof-beats: the rider must be Akhbar Moham-mad Khan. And it was; the lance-*duffardar* pulled up his horse and turned alongside Ogilvie.

'Well?'

'Soames sahib has stopped, and is talking to a man, sahib.'

'What man?'

'A hillman, sahib, a Waziri – a Mahsud, mounted on a horse.'

'Have you been seen?'

The lance-*duffardar* shook his head. 'No, Captain sahib. I am sure of that.'

'Right! It looks as if Soames sahib may have had a prepared rendezvous, a contact

240

point in case of need. Ride back, Akhbar Mohammad Khan, and watch – and remain out of sight.'

'And you, Captain sahib, and your soldiers?'

'When Soames sahib has passed his message, I think he'll ride back to camp. When he's passed me, I'll come on and join you, and we follow the man he spoke to. In the mean-time, I shall ride to the rear and warn my soldiers. Do not lose the man, Akhbar Mohammad Khan.'

'I shall not, Captain sahib.' The lance-*duffardar* rode away as fast as possible, the muffled hooves making scarcely any sound. Ogilvie turned and rode down his extended line. calling softly to the men as he went along; the moon was bright but they had all found good cover for themselves and their horses behind the proliferating rocks and craggy out-croppings of the desolate hills. He ordered MacTrease and the others to remain in cover until Soames had passed by, then to resume their separated advance as carefully and quietly as before. Riding back, cursing the moon that had chosen this particular time to make its reappearance, he took up his own position in the lead again; and had only just made cover himself when he heard the horseman coming down openly and fast from ahead.

He watched: it was Soames, Soames in uniform with his dark face devilish as it was outlined in the hard light of the moon, the mouth grimly set. This was a time for lightning decision: should he after all shout his men out from cover now, and arrest Soames, state in evidence that he had been seen by the lance-*duffardar* in conversation with a native who could – if caught – doubtless be identified as one of the Wolf's tribesmen? It was a strong temptation, but Ogilvie let it go: Soames would keep a while yet. It seemed certain enough he was riding back to camp and in the morning would do as Lord Dornoch had suggested: make up a story about a lone patrol, an attempt, perhaps, to take a prisoner and gain information. There would be nothing concrete against him, just the word of a lance-*duffardar* with a well-known grievance against a Raj that, in London, had cast him into a cell.

Soames would have no difficulty in wriggling his way out of that!

As soon as the British officer was safely gone to the rear, Ogilvie rode on. He passed the first of the intersections, saw the lance-*duffardar* waiting ahead to give him his direction along the main pass, waited in his turn to wave back to MacTrease behind him. Keeping the lance-*duffardar* just in

242

sight from time to time, he advanced east-erly: two more intersections were passed. The pursuers rode on. Ogilvie was only too well aware that the wretched moon was jeopardising their security against any hidden watchers along the crests reaching heavenward from the pass; but to such eyes they would seem only a line of natives moving on behind the man contacted by Soames: suspicions would not necessarily be aroused – and in point of fact they might not be all that visible. The pass was deep, and largely in shadow even now. But the route seemed endless, and as the moon faded into the first light of dawn the dangers increased, the dangers of being seen and reported ahead to some waiting reception committee. They rode on and on, weary now, sore from the saddles, hungry and thirsty but conserving the precious contents of their water-bottles against greater need, lonely, isolated in their separated positions. It was well beyond the dawn when Ogilvie saw the lance-*duffardar* riding back towards him.

He pulled up his horse.

'Captain sahib,' the lance-*duffardar* said, 'the Mahsud has left the pass ahead—'

'Then why have you left him?' Ogilvie demanded.

'Sahib, he is riding down into the valley of

the Salt Range, and can be kept in full view through field glasses.'

'Yes, I understand. Is he still alone?'

'Yes, Captain sahib.'

'No one's made contact with him?'

'No one, sahib.'

Ogilvie nodded, and spurred his horse. 'We'll go ahead and look, Akhbar Mohammad Khan.' They rode on together under the climbing sun; a little warmth stole gradually into Ogilvie's bones. Soon he would begin to sweat, and his filthy garments would begin to smell much more positively than hitherto. About a mile ahead they reached the end of the mountain pass, and from cover looked down into a broad, deep valley that seemed to run to the ends of the earth. The lance-*duffardar* pointed. 'There, Captain sahib. There is the Mahsud on his horse.'

Ogilvie brought up his field glasses and swept the area; he could see the rider plainly, riding fast now towards the east. Also in his glasses Ogilvie could see a small fort, an outpost standing to the north side of the valley, and, farther on, much farther on, another fort, very distant. It must, he thought, be all of twenty miles from where he watched, but was fully distinguishable in the clear air and from his superior height. And, though he was viewing the valley now

244

from the end opposite to that of his earlier experience at Fort Gaza, he had picked up the bearings that his maps had told him he should expect to find: the outpost ahead was the one that lay twenty miles from Fort Gaza and a little to the west of it the defensive line began its turn north-west to skirt the mountains through which he had just come.

He spoke to the lance-*duffardar*. 'The distant fort, Akhbar Mohammad Khan. It's Fort Gaza.'

'Yes, sahib.'

'And that Mahsud could be heading there – past the other fort, the outpost. Or maybe he'll go to that one ... I think we can assume it's no longer held by the Raj!'

'Yes, sahib. Nor Fort Gaza.'

'Exactly so.' Ogilvie went on staring through his glasses. 'Now, Akhbar Mohammad Khan, I want you to ride back to the Colour-Sergeant sahib. My compliments to him, and I wish the men to close me here.'

'Yes, sahib.' The lance-*duffardar* mounted his horse and rode away. Within the next fifteen minutes all the men had ridden in and had taken cover with Ogilvie, who indicated the lie of the land. 'The Mahsud looks as though he's heading for Fort Gaza – I've got him in constant view. Colour MacTrease?'

245

'Sir?'

'What does it suggest to you?'

'I think, sir, that the Wolf himself may well be in Fort Gaza.'

'So do I!' Ogilvie gave a tight smile, more of a grimace of lips stretched against teeth. 'Still looking for my head, perhaps!'

'Perhaps, sir. Do you mean to deliver it to him, sir?'

'Not if I can help it, Colour!'

'Then what do we do now, sir?'

'Wait. I want to be sure of that Mahsud's destination first.'

They waited as it seemed interminably; but in fact the messenger below in the valley was riding fast, and once he had passed the nearer fort Ogilvie decided to delay no longer. Turning to MacTrease he said, 'I'm going to assume he's making for Fort Gaza, Colour. And I'm going to act on that assumption of ours that the Wolf's there, or at any rate in the vicinity.'

'Aye, sir.'

'Two men, Colour – the two best horsemen. They're to unmuffle hooves and ride like the devil for the regiment. A personal report to the Colonel, giving him the facts.'

'Are you asking for the regiment to march, sir?'

'That must be for the Colonel to decide. In the meantime, we wait where we are – at any rate till after dark.'

MacTrease looked at him curiously. 'And after that, Captain Ogilvie, sir?'

'I don't know yet, Colour.'

As the day moved towards evening, a shot rang from the picket line guarding the encampment. This was followed by a series of oaths in broad Scots, heard by the extended picket who had opened fire upon an apparent native, but unheard by the camp sentries.

The swearing man pulled up his horse. 'Christ, ye bluidy lunatic!'

'Who the hell are you, then?'

'Private Bell, of B Company—'

'I don't see how I was to know.' The picket spat.

'Wi' a message for the Colonel in person.' As if instinctively Bell lowered his voice as the sound of bugles and trumpets came from the alerted camp. 'An' I don't want the bluidy cavalry to know, nor does Captain Ogilvie. So ye'll run me in as a prisoner, all right?'

Ten minutes later Private Bell, relieved of the rifle in his back, was in the guard tent, alone with Lord Dornoch and the Adjutant. Bell made his report; he had started out with Corporal Stainton, who had been shot down and killed back along the pass. Bell himself had two bullet wounds, one in the arm, the other in the flesh of his backside, presented fair and square to the tribesman's *jezail*. The rest of the ride had clearly been painful, but nobly executed.

'There'll be a mention for you, Bell,' the Colonel said. 'You've acted bravely.'

'Sir!'

'You'll go to the medical tent at once, but under guard until you reach it. I know you'll understand why, and that it's not to be talked about.'

'Aye, sir.'

When Bell had been removed between a corporal's escort Lord Dornoch caught Black's eye. 'If Ogilvie's right, we have the Wolf in our sights, Andrew!'

'Rather distantly, Colonel.'

'That distance can be closed, however.'

Black pursed his lips. 'Are you thinking of moving the battalion out, Colonel?'

'I don't know yet. At the least, we owe Ogilvie some support.' Dornoch got to his feet. 'I'm going over to the cavalry lines for a word with Keeley. I'll see you in my tent with the Major when I get back.'

'Very good, Colonel. With respect, I think you should bear it in mind that Fort Gaza's all of two days' forced marching from here, and word will go ahead of us for a certainty – and we shall lose the Wolf.'

Dornoch nodded. 'I take the point, Andrew, but the same can be said of any advance of any force in the hills, can it not?'

Keeley's view was similar to Black's. 'The bastard'll simply up sticks and away, Dornoch. We'll find an empty fort.'

'Not necessarily.' Dornoch's tone was patient, even conciliatory: the cavalry never welcomed the views of the infantry, and vice versa. The British and Indian Armies, too, were divided by professional rivalries. 'Of course, I appreciate that you Indian fellows know the country better than us ... but you'll agree with me, I'm sure, that if we take the view that the Wolf will always know our movements in advance, he'll never be caught. I say risks must be taken.' He added, 'In any case, he may decide to hold Fort Gaza as a strongpoint.'

'Never!' Keeley gave a contemptuous laugh. 'He'll not allow himself to be holed up in a trap, where every unit in Northern Command can be deployed against him! Wouldn't make any sort of sense, would it?'

'But we have to act upon the situation as it's known to be at any given moment, Keeley. There he is, in Fort Gaza – I believe that's fairly to be relied upon. If not in it, near it. We know that Blaise-Willoughby had information that the Wolf meant to take it, realising its potential as a strongpoint.'

Cautiously the cavalryman said, 'Well, I'll agree to this extent, Dornoch – he may be using it as his HQ base. But even that's doubtful. The hill tribes prefer to be based where they're best equipped to be – in the hills! They aren't fort minded. Forts are vulnerable things – especially to a hillman!'

'Then perhaps it would be the last place he'd expect us to look for him.'

Keeley gnawed at a fingernail. 'Too subtle. Oh – they're devious all right, Blaise-Willoughby's bloody monkey has nothing on them! But I repeat, and I'll go on repeating it, the hillmen stay in the hills.' He wagged a finger in Dornoch's face, his heavy, jowl-hung face accusing. 'You're working on a hunch. It's just not good enough, it really isn't. All we can do at this stage is to send a runner back to my Brigade HQ at Kohat and get a message through to Bloody Francis indicating your suspicions – in all conscience, my dear fellow, they're no more than that!'

Dornoch stood in his tent, his back ramrod-straight, his face hard with anger. 'Keeley will not move out,' he said to Hay and Black. 'Not even in support, with a pincer movement from the south of Fort Gaza. The man's immovable!'

'He may well be right,' Black said mournfully. 'I have indicated my views, Colonel.'

'Major?'

Hay said, 'I dislike leaving Ogilvie and his men in the lurch, Colonel—'

'And so do I!' Dornoch blazed. 'So do I! Reading between the lines of his message, Ogilvie's relying upon us. We mustn't forget that blackguard Soames either.'

'Did you raise that with Colonel Keeley?' Hay asked.

Dornoch nodded. 'Of course. Soames has been told the lance-*duffardar* deserted in his absence – he'll scarcely find that surprising, if all our suspicions are correct. Soames himself will be kept under surveillance. It'll be discreetly done, but naturally the time may come when some overt action'll have to be taken. For instance – no more lone patrols. I gather that's already been forcibly borne in upon him, as a matter of fact. If he disobeys, then that in itself may give Keeley the excuse to place him in open arrest with no other reason given – but we shall see. That must be left to Keeley. We, however, are no concern of the Kohat Light Horse, gentlemen!'

Hay lifted a bushy eyebrow, quizzically.

'The battalion will move out in one hour from now, Major. Captain Black, make your arrangements, if you please. No bugles, and as much silence as possible.' Dornoch brought out his watch and held it to face the two officers. 'In not much more than twenty-four hours, the Wolf is due to rise against the Raj. I am convinced he means to direct the rising from Fort Gaza – that fact alone will have immense impact upon the minds of the tribesmen – a British strongpoint, used to command against the Raj! We'll not get there within the time, I know, but even if the word of us flushes the Wolf out, it may act to upset his plans in advance.'

When the day's hot sun had faded into night and all appeared peaceful, Ogilvie had passed final orders to MacTrease. After pondering throughout the daylight hours he had determined on what could prove a disastrous mission but which, if successful, could be of great value to the Raj: an attempt would be made to take the nearer and smaller outpost down in the valley. With any luck, they should have the advantage of complete surprise in their favour, and in Ogilvie's view his small force of one colour-sergeant, one lance-*duffardar* and four privates, all mounted, should be enough to give a warrantable hope of bringing it off. To have that outpost in British hands just before the rising was planned to start would be to thrust an inconvenient and dangerous thorn into the Wolf's hide at an awkward moment. And if it could be done in something approaching silence, then so much the better.

'No firing unless it's inevitable, Colour,' he said. 'Attack from out of the dark and try to take the gate guard by hand-to-hand fighting.'

'How do we get the buggers to open up the gate in the first place, sir?'

'We're all dressed as natives, Colour. And my Pushtu's passable. I think a little bluff should do the trick.'

MacTrease gave a sigh and rubbed a hand across his boot-polish-darkened face. 'Aye, well ... there'll be beds of a kind in yon fort I've no doubt, sir. It's a better prospect than a bivouac up here. When do you wish to move out, sir?'

'Now. It's dark enough, and no moon yet. We'll go down at the rush and in single file. I'll lead, you bring up the rear, Colour. When I lift my arm, get the men into cover. All right?'

MacTrease spat on his hands and rubbed them together. 'All right, sir,' he said.

The 114th Highlanders were ready to move out when a fleshy figure was seen hurrying from the lines of the Kohat Light Horse.

Passing in front of the companies assembled in column of route, he found Andrew Black.

'Your colonel,' he said, peremptorily. 'I must have words with him.'

Black recognised Keeley. 'Follow me, sir,' he said, and turned about. He led the cavalry Colonel to Lord Dornoch's tent: the Scots were not striking their camp, which would remain in being under the charge of a colour-sergeant and a small guard, the battalion going into night bivouacs on the march to the east when necessary. Dornoch was about to leave his tent when the Adjutant approached.

'Colonel Keeley, sir.' Black saluted.

Dornoch stared coldly. Keeley said, 'You're about to march out, I see.'

'Yes.'

Keeley hesitated. 'I've changed my mind. I've come myself to say so.'

'You mean you intend moving out your regiment?'

'Yes.'

Dornoch caught Black's eye, saw relief in it. The presence of cavalry would be a comfort to the Adjutant. Dornoch, his voice still cold, asked, 'What's made you change your mind, Colonel?'

Keeley said, 'Soames.' He, too, looked towards Black. 'May I take it—'

'You may speak freely. My Adjutant is in

my confidence.'

'Ah – of course. Well, Soames came to see me, Dornoch. Things spread in camp as you know. He's heard – and has urged that we ride out in support.'

'Why?'

Keeley shrugged. 'He appeared simply to be keen for action, and—'

'Then I suggest you consider this: he wishes to place himself closer to the Wolf so that he's handily situated to desert the Colours – and join his master as soon as he sees danger to himself!'

'Perhaps. Or perhaps he means to kill the Wolf, and destroy the evidence. In which case, he'll lead us where we want to go.' Keeley shrugged again. 'It seems my first decision may have been a poor one, Dornoch!'

Dornoch smiled, and there was warmth in his eyes now. 'Your view had much to commend it, my dear fellow, but I'm delighted you've changed your mind.' He added, 'Soames is going to need careful watching, but that's your affair, of course.'

'Don't worry, he'll be watched all right! Now – I suggest I take my regiment a little south, then strike east through a pass lower down, and drop upon Fort Gaza while you advance through the valley.'

'A pincer movement – yes, I agree. And in

the meantime, neither of us has men to spare to inform General Fettleworth! Do you agree to that, Colonel?'

Keeley grinned. 'You're half-way to thinking along a cavalryman's lines already, my dear fellow!' Saying that he would be ready to ride within the hour but that the infantry should not wait for him, Keeley turned and went back to his own lines. Black, pulling at his moustache, looked anxious. 'Colonel, would it not be wiser to keep Division informed? Frankly, I see no point in *not* doing so!'

'I see plenty, Andrew. Our good Fettleworth would become ... shall I say, excited? We could be wrong in all our assumptions, and if Division were to react by diverting more troops towards Fort Gaza, it could give the Wolf his chance elsewhere.'

'But our present orders—'

'We have no *precise* orders, Andrew! We've already achieved our purpose here – we've flushed Soames, or we seem to have done so. In a sense, we were sent here to expedite and assist Ogilvie's own mission, don't you see?'

Black nodded, but looked dour. He was back to his continually simmering thoughts of nepotism: it was handy to have a father as General Officer Commanding – without that, in Black's view, no officer of captain's rank would be given the backing of a whole battalion in carrying out his orders! Dornoch broke in on his sour reflections. 'Since the cavalry are moving out, I'll leave no men behind. I'll risk the tents! Inform Colour-Sergeant Gaunt he's to join the march with his guard, and send word to Colonel Keeley that I suggest he follows suit.'

In the lead of his small force, Ogilvie advanced through the night in total silence, his attention fixed upon the outpost ahead. With its whitened walls and tower it could just be seen as a lighter loom in the darkness. His chances, he knew, were in fact no more than fifty-fifty: surprise could be achieved, or it could not. All along he had had in mind what every man on the North-West Frontier was aware of – the constant tribal watch from behind the peaks of the mountain ranges. Someone during the long day's wait would have spotted them, however good their cover. Their disguise as natives might well have held, yet they would be seen as an intrusion, as natives who should not be where they were, and contact might have been made with the Wolf. Currently in the pitch darkness they were safe enough, but the outpost's garrison might have been warned of strangers in the vicinity. However, it was a risk that had to be taken and there was nothing unusual in it: the Raj could not be tied down by brooding fears of what might happen if it moved...

The advance continued, slowly and watchfully, all rifles held ready across the men's bodies, each with a bullet up the spout for instant action. It was a very silent night, disturbed only by a cold breeze funnelling along the valley from the hills behind. Scrubby bushes got in their way from time to time, and small living creatures slithered or scuttled across the path of the horses. In that almost total silence the men's breathing sounded heavy, even the water remaining in the bottles could be heard gurgling as it swayed to the movement of the riders, and the occasional clink and creak of a rifle sling sounded, in Ogilvie's ears, like the advance of a battery of artillery. He took a grip on his nerves, clenched his teeth against a call for yet more silence. As silent as their own advance was the cautious encircling movement of the enemy: no one among the Scots had heard a sound when the bayoneted *jezails* came out of the surrounding dark and the rusted steel blades pressed hard into each man's spine.

Fifteen

'You were a bluidy fool to show fight, sir. With respect, sir.' MacTrease eased cramped limbs on the filthy floor; the rattle of chains sounded in the cell's blank darkness, darkness even greater than that of the night's abortive advance. 'We had no chance, sir, from the moment the buggers closed.'

Ogilvie felt the caked blood round his mouth when he opened his lips to answer. 'In retrospect, Colour, I see you're right!'

There was a grunt from the Colour-Sergeant. 'What do we do now, sir?'

'What *can* we do?'

A short laugh: 'Nothing!'

'Then that's what we do, Colour. We await developments.' Ogilvie added, 'I'm sorry to have got you into this, all of you.'

There was a silence; the Scots were being dourly grudging. After a moment Mac-Trease said, 'Dinna worry, Captain Ogilvie, sir. You were not to know. None of us did. And we're all fit enough. Except maybe you, sir.'

'Oh, I'll survive.' Ogilvie shifted in his chains. He was, in fact, in a certain amount of pain and discomfort though not, he believed, seriously hurt. When the attack had come he had rounded on his man, bayonet notwithstanding, in an attempt to use his drawn revolver. The dirty bayonet had scored across his back, drawing blood that was caked now on his native clothing; his revolver had gone spinning from a savage blow on his wrist, and then the *jezail*'s butt had been swung up to take him a glancing blow across the mouth and he'd gone down from his horse, flat on his back. After that, hoisted roughly to his feet, he and the rest had been marched in front of the *jezails* and daggers all the way east along the valley, with their horses being led by their attackers. Lance-*Duffardar* Akhbar Mohammad Khan had been separated from Ogilvie and the others upon arrival, and was still being held elsewhere, no doubt under interrogation. And this, their second arrival at Fort Gaza, had scarcely been as regimental an entry as their first...

MacTrease chose that moment in Ogilvie's reflections to underline the point, bitterly and without tact. 'Full circle, sir. Though this fornicating cell isn't the Sergeants' Mess. Good Christ, what have we come to!'

Ogilvie snapped, 'For God's sake, hold your tongue!'

'*Sir?*'

'I think you heard me, Colour-Sar'nt. And it was an order.'

'I'll be buggered—'

'You will be,' Ogilvie said harshly, 'the moment we return to cantonments, if you don't obey the order.'

'Good grief, I'd chance me arm...' Mac-Trease's furious voice died away into impotent silence. Never in his career had an officer told him to hold his tongue, and in front of the men ... but he wouldn't chance his arm and he knew it; his arm carried too much – the crossed flags and chevrons of a colour-sergeant could be lost in the ignominy of a return to the barrack-room and the anonymity of a private soldier: he was not, like the Regimental Sergeant-Major, an unbreakable warrant officer. And, one day, he wanted Mr Cunningham's appointment for himself, and to achieve that his arm had to be intact and his nose the cleanest in all India. Besides, Captain Ogilvie was a fair officer normally, a decent officer who must just now be feeling touchy. MacTrease grinned to himself: bloody fool was right! In a moment his thoughts of fairness were vindicated: he heard Captain Ogilvie's voice.

'I'm sorry, Colour.'

'It's all right, sir. No bones broken.'

'I don't like this any more than you do. Have you noticed the livestock?'

'Good grief, have I not? Fleas and bugs. Lice too, I've a feeling. There'll be nothing left, if they leave us here too long, sir.'

It was the cell that Blaise-Willoughby had used – so recently though it seemed years ago now – for his torture of Abdul Qadir of the Salt Department's cavalry. The door was thick and strong, and there was no window, no other opening at all; and the binding chains were secured to heavy ringbolts set deeply into the walls. To Ogilvie, it all began to look hopeless. With escape out of the question, at least until they were brought out into the open when some chance might come if they were lucky, it was odds-on they faced torture themselves. From scraps of conversation from the tribesmen, much of it in a dialect beyond his understanding, he had gathered that the Wolf of the Salt Range was not currently in the fort; he had a feeling that either the Wolf would come, or that he and his men would be taken into the hills to be confronted by the Wolf. The only hope appeared to be that Lord Dornoch had got his message and that he would have moved the regiment out. Yet if he did that, there might be wholesale slaughter of the

Scots. Further scraps of talk had led Ogilvie to believe that the Wolf had strong forces in the vicinity; and he had seen with his own eyes, as they were marched across the courtyard from the gate, past the former Officers' Mess, that the fort was stuffed to overflowing with men and guns, the latter being a mixture of light machine-guns, Maxims, Gatlings and Gardners, and heavy field artillery albeit of highly antique pattern. Fort Gaza, in the name of the Wolf of the Salt Range, was now much better garrisoned than ever it had been in the name of Her Majesty the Queen-Empress ... Ogilvie, shifting against the close attentions of the livestock, hungry little beasts, and feeling the pain of the bayonet-opened flesh, did the only thing possible: he tried to find sleep that would bring him freshness and renewed strength.

With the 114th Highlanders as they left the camp went the cavalry's attached field guns, Keeley retaining his battery of horse artillery for his own support when action came. It was a fair division freely offered by the cavalry Colonel, and when the combined force converged upon Fort Gaza it would be a reasonably formidable one and well-balanced. Dornoch's hopes were high enough as he rode with Major Hay ahead of the infantry column and its silent pipes and drums. There was, of course, no hope of their not being spotted and reported ahead; but as he had remarked earlier to Colonel Keeley, the very fact of their advance before the rising started should have its effect upon the Wolf's plans. Dornoch had a strong inner certainty that his moves had been sound and that, of all the variously dispersed formations in Northern Command, his and Keeley's were about to strike the first blow against the Wolf in person. Of success he could not be so certain; but there was no virtue in thinking of defeat. His Scots were good, and would fight as well as they always did, and would never give in. To concede a battle was never the Scots' way; the Scottish regiments stood fast and their endurance was epitomised by the Thin Red Line at Balaclava, when the Sutherland Highlanders, 93rd of the line, had stood fast to bring enduring glory to British arms ... Dornoch smiled at his thoughts as he led the column into the pass between the peaks, with the pickets ahead scaling the sides. He must not be too parochial: the English, Irish and Welsh regiments of the line were every bit as tenacious in battle, but each man was naturally wedded to his own territory, and his was Scotland.

At his side Hay said, 'I think we might

increase the pace, Colonel. We'll be hard put to it to reach Fort Gaza in time.'

'It won't help if we arrive tired out ... but perhaps a little more forcing at this stage.' Dornoch turned in the saddle and called for his runner. 'My compliments to the Adjutant and Mr Cunningham. I'd like words with them in the van.'

'Sir!' The runner saluted and turned away, moving fast down the line of advance. The Regimental Sergeant-Major marched up ahead of Black, as smart in his dress and movements as if back on the parade-ground in cantonments.

'Sir! You wished me, sir?'

'Yes, thank you, Sar'nt-Major. As I shall also tell the Adjutant when he arrives ... ah, there you are, Captain Black. We shall increase the pace, gentlemen, but not to the point where the men begin to fall out. A close watch, if you please, Sar'nt-Major.'

'Aye, sir. Will you rest the column during the night, at all, sir?'

'As soon as Captain Black or yourself reports the necessity, Sar'nt-Major. A short halt, no more.'

'Aye, sir.'

'Carry on, if you please, Mr Cunningham. Captain Black, one further word.' For a moment Dornoch listened to the voice of Cunningham as the RSM marched away down the column, passing the word to the company officers and instructing the colour-sergeants. Then he turned again to Black. 'There's a need to move fast, as we all know, Andrew. I shall be forced to drive the men, but to exhaust them would be only to frustrate the march itself. I rely upon you to strike the happy medium, and to keep me fully informed as to their condition.'

'Very good, Colonel.'

'One more thing: we shall make no special issue of smartness. Do you understand me?'

There was a curtness in the Adjutant's voice as he answered, and as Black turned his horse and rode towards the rear Dornoch gave a sigh: Andrew Black had perhaps never been the best choice as Adjutant. The man was efficient, conscientious, jealous of the regiment's reputation; but he irritated officers and men alike by being overpunctilious in matters of detail under difficult circumstances. But for the word of warning Black, the moment the dawn came up, would have been riding down the line, frowning, criticising, drawing the attention of weary sergeant to the set of kilts, to the correct angle of the glengarries, to the dusty state of leather equipment, to talking in the ranks – all the things that could never be tolerated in cantonments but didn't matter a tinker's curse when force-marching into action. Black couldn't bear to see men march at ease; he seemed to take it as an affront, almost as an act of dumb insolence directed towards himself ... Dornoch shook himself free of thoughts of Black and projected his mind ahead. Ogilvie's message had indicated that, with MacTrease and the lance-*duffardar* and his four remaining men, he was halted at the end of the pass; the regiment should pick those men up during the coming day, when more information might become available.

Ogilvie heard the sounds from outside, the approaching footsteps and the rattle of *jezails* and bayonets. Then the heavy door was unlocked and the outside bolts were drawn back protestingly, squeaking in a lack of oil. Two armed guards stood in the doorway, big men, swarthy tribesmen in filthy garments, men with heavy beards and eyes that glittered with menace in the light of the lantern carried by a third man.

One of the armed tribesmen spoke in Pushtu: 'Which is the British officer sahib?'

No one answered; the fact that they were British had been established on their arrival in the fort – for one thing, the boot-polish had become very self-evident – but they were not going to give away Captain Ogilvie's identity if they could help it.

'Come – speak, or there will be torture.' The bayonet was jabbed forward, pricked into the thigh of the nearest soldier. The man's body jerked, but he said nothing, simply staring back into the dark eyes of the guard, his own eyes frightened. Every man had his breaking-point, and a soldier's perennial fear along the North-West Frontier was not of the torture itself so much as that he might be brought to that point of dishonour. Ogilvie spoke up: there was no value in silence; they would find out sooner or later.

'I am the officer,' he said, using the guard's own language.

The bayonet moved again, pointing down towards Ogilvie's chest. 'Come.'

'You'll have to unchain me first, won't you?' Ogilvie said coolly. The guard turned his head, said something to the lantern bearer. The third man entered the cell and bent to unlock Ogilvie's chains from their ringbolt in the wall. Ogilvie got to his feet, clumsily, feeling the stiffness in back and knees. His wrists, roped like the others behind his back, remained tied as he left the cell. Before the door was banged shut again and bolted, he heard MacTrease call out to wish him luck.

Between the two guards he was taken out into the light of day, a bright, cold day with

clear skies and a sun that could not overcome the sharpness of the wind, which
eddied around the courtyard between the
high walls of the fort. He was taken across
to what had been the Officers' Mess during
his short occupation earlier, pushed ahead
of his escort past the pantry and along the
passage. In the mess – it still contained a
portrait of the Queen-Empress, the broad
blue ribbon of the Order of the Garter
crossing her breast – beneath Her Majesty's
stony gaze sat the man who was, fairly
obviously, the much-vaunted Wolf of the
Salt Range. Olgilvie looked at this man with
a good deal of curiosity, almost with a sense
of awe: in his own territory the Wolf appeared, at any rate by repute, to have an
authority equivalent to that of the Queen-
Empress herself, and now in his person he
looked just as regal, just as compelling, as
the old lady above his head – and that in
spite of clothing as ragged as that of his
tribesmen and an appalling smell of dirt and
sweat and grease. He was a man of enor-
mous height, which was apparent even
though he was seated, and with shoulders
like a bison. But, as ever, it was the face and
above all the eyes that commanded attention: the head was big, the hair concealed
beneath a greasy turban, and the jaw was
long, the nostrils flared like those of a horse,

the forehead was deep. Heavy lines of will and authority drove down between the eyes ... the eyes, dark and large, held Ogilvie as if in a vice of steel. A loose shirt hung, would reach the knees when he stood up, draped over baggy trousers of blue cotton gathered at the ankles. The feet were thrust into rope sandals and the man wore a fancily decorated bandolier, plus extra belts of cartridges wound like snakes about waist and chest. A dagger was stuck into his belt and in his hand he held the inevitable rifle. Ogilvie found himself remembering the many stories told about this man: the murders by *jezail* and bayonet and by *thuggee*, the villages plundered and laid waste, the rapes, the tortures, the bloody killing of his own young son. A man to be reckoned with, a man to fear, a man who for the security of the Raj had to be overcome.

Currently, a tall order...

The Wolf, speaking at last, and speaking in excellent English, showed long yellow teeth, truly wolfish. 'You are the British officer, leader of the men who came to spy.'

'Not spy—'

'Silence, dog!' The voice was like a whiplash, cruel and decisive. 'There will not be denial. Is it not your own British concept of war that those not in uniform in their opponents' territory are regarded as spies?'

An immense hand was smacked into a palm. 'Is this not so, British officer?'

'There is no war,' Ogilvie answered, 'yet. And if it comes, it will be of *your* making, not—'

'No!' The Wolf got to his feet, made a dramatic gesture of flinging both muscular arms towards the portrait of the Queen-Empress. 'Not mine, but hers! The great memsahib, mother of the East, suckler of all the world with her teats, who has suckled *us* of our lands and our rights and our possessions. Is it war, to fight for our own, British officer? I give you the answer: it is not. Your Queen Victoria must retreat to her own lands and fortunes. As for us, we no longer wish her or her armies to remain in India. And they shall not! Now: some questions and the answers to them, British officer.'

The Wolf sat down again, staring at Ogilvie. From behind, Ogilvie felt the pricking steel of the bayonets, one of them exacerbating the wound of the night before, which was swollen and throbbing.

'First,' the Wolf said, 'your name and rank.'

'I am a captain in Her Majesty's Army. That is all I can tell you.' It was the old fear, the fear of being identified as the son of the General Officer Commanding the Northern Army; pressures could be applied, and

271

though Ogilvie knew his father was not the man to give way before them, he feared for their effect upon his parents. 'My name is not important. But there are others that are.'

The pupils of the Wolf's eyes appeared to contract. 'Name them.'

Ogilvie said, 'Captain Soames sahib.'

'Soames sahib?' There was no apparent change in the eyes. 'I know of no Soames sahib. Who is he?'

'Of the Kohat Light Horse. And I believe you know him very well.'

'Why do you say this?'

Ogilvie shrugged. 'The Raj is wide. The Raj has ears. Things are told to us. By the same token, things are told to you.'

'This last part I do not deny. I, too, have many ears! But this Soames – I do not know of him—'

'But you know Lance-*Duffardar* Akhbar Mohammad Khan, also of the Kohat Light Horse. Where is he?'

'I have nothing to say to you, British officer. These things are not important. I wish to know other things, and you will tell me. You will tell me where the armies of your Raj are placed, you will tell me whence you yourself have come, you will tell me all that is known to the British of what I plan to do. And now I shall tell one thing to you:

272

from this moment you are on your own, an officer without an army, a Briton in a hostile land, with soon no Raj to look after you and fight your battles for you, a Raj that will never come to your assistance.' As he finished speaking the Wolf's eyes widened, their strange luminosity seeming to hold some weird hypnotic power. Ogilvie found himself swaying a little, felt his skin flush, was conscious of a curious and intense inner heat and a drumming in his ears. And in the same moment, as if symbolically for the British Raj, the room darkened as cloud began to roll across the sun, bringing a coldness and setting a long black shadow across the portrait of the Queen-Empress. Into the sudden cold gloom dropped the voice of the Wolf of the Salt Range, uttering more threats of torture as the price of silence.

Sixteen

Far to the north at Divisional Headquarters in Nowshera, Lieutenant-General Fettleworth sat at his desk beneath another and more splendid royal portrait, one that gave him immense comfort and support in the cares and troubles of his rank and in his present efforts to hold the Raj together. God knew, his troubles were immense enough! Currently he was shouting them at his Chief of Staff.

'It's too bad, Lakenham! It's too damn bad! By God, I'll have his bloody regiment off him, damned if I won't! He'll face General Court Martial the moment he shows his damn face back in Peshawar – if ever he does! Damn it – I may not be a belted earl but I'm his superior officer – aren't I? Hey?'

'Yes, indeed—'

'But are you *sure of your facts*. Lakenham? Are you—'

'I am quite sure of my facts, sir!' Lakenham snapped, his face reddening. 'Had I not been, I would not have reported them to you. It's perfectly simple: the mounted runner from Kohat reports the encampment empty.'

Bloody Francis shook with fury. 'Dornoch's the senior as between him and Keeley. I suppose he took it upon himself to *order* the cavalry out! I'll have his guts!' He lifted his hands and shook them in the air, violently. 'If only we knew where he's gone!'

'But we don't, sir. What remains is to cope with the new situation, and if I may tender advice—'

'I know what your advice will be, thank you!' Fettleworth snapped. 'Do bugger all!'

'Exactly. In a tactical sense, there never was any real need for Dornoch and Keeley to go into camp. It was all designed to—'

'To flush out that bloody feller Soames – I know! But—'

'And that may have happened, may it not?' Lakenham was virtually barking at his General now: in his experience, most such conferences ended the same way. 'I suggest, sir, that we take no action that may frustrate whatever it is Dornoch and Keeley are trying to do—'

'Oh, balls,' the General interrupted. '*Frustrate – whatever*, a good choice of word since we don't damn well know and haven't been accorded the courtesy of being told – *trying*

275

to do! Try my arse! I'm not leaving all those tents to rot or be pinched by the bloody natives. Lakenham. Just think, the trouble there'd be with the QMG's department!' He sat back, arms outthrust against his desk, gnawing at a full red lip. 'Who's available, here or in Peshawar?'

'No one. All regiments are providing essential patrols, or remaining in defence of base.'

Fettleworth had turned deaf ears to this. 'Which regiment's the latest to join?'

'The 1st Wiltshires, sir—'

'Right! Take down orders for the Colonel of the 1st Wiltshires, Lakenham. Good exercise for a fresh regiment. He's to march out at once – or as soon as he's brought his patrols in – and take over that camp. He'll get further orders shortly.'

Lakenham shrugged; he'd had his say and to go further would be rank insubordination. Meanwhile, he knew that the word 'shortly' meant that Bloody Francis hadn't yet thought of anything for the Wiltshires to do when they got there ... With such officers leading its forces, the Raj might do better to look to the Chaplain General's department for an urgency of prayer!

Back in the cell, Ogilvie found he was shaking like a leaf in the wind: he had a fever, resulting from the infected bayonet-cut in his back. He had answered none of the Wolf's questions and had been brutally hit in the face by repeated backward jabs of the Wolf's elbow. In the end the Wolf had decided upon other means: as in the case of the Salt Department NCO, Abdul Qadir, who had put MacTrease rather than Ogilvie under threat of death, he announced that his knowledge of the British had led him to the view that officers disliked seeing their soldiers made to suffer in their place.

'You will be tortured by proxy, British officer.' The Wolf had then spat, full into Ogilvie's face, and Ogilvie had been removed.

He tried, through his chattering teeth, to talk to MacTrease, keeping his voice as low as possible. 'The regiment, Colour...'

'Aye, sir. I'd not be fretting myself, if I were you.'

'But if my message arrived by dark last night ... and if the Colonel moved out soon after...'

'Ifs, sir, all ifs. Rest your mind easy, now.'

'He may have moved, Colour. If he did ... he'll be well on the way by now. After dark, he'll reach the head of the valley.'

'It's possible, sir. It's possible. I wish you'd rest, sir.'

'So when the Wolf sends for one of the

men, he may not have too long to hang on. If it goes on too long, I'll talk.'

'And the man concerned, sir, will never forgive you and nor shall I.'

Ogilvie shifted his position on the hard stone floor. The fever was bad, distorting his thoughts; if only he could start to sweat, it would help. He was surprised, and so had MacTrease been, that the Wolf had needed to ask questions, unless he wanted a check on Soames. As for the lance-*duffardar*, the assumption he had to make was that Akhbar Mohammad Khan was being held and questioned separately as yet another check, this time on any answers Ogilvie himself might have given, and might yet give if things got too near the bone for the luckless man chosen for the torture. He tried to fight through an increasing delirium, was only just aware of MacTrease speaking anxiously to the others. Without medical attention, he knew, he could only get worse, whether or not he sweated. The infection was in the suppurating dirt of the wound, and must spread until it was cleaned out. He clenched his teeth against the shivers that racked him in spite of the increasing fire within his body.

He had no idea how much time went by before the cell door was opened again; he had slept, a nightmare sleep, and was woken when a foot was driven hard into his side. He cried out with the pain of it, heard Mac-Trease's voice, hard and savage, swearing viciously at the native who had kicked out. Then he was dragged to his feet in the lantern's light, the binding chain was unfastened from the ringbolt, and he was taken outside the cell between two armed men as before. When he and his escort had cleared the cell, two more men pushed past and went inside, unshackled one of the soldiers, and brought him out to join Ogilvie. The man they had chosen was one Private Fairbairn, the young soldier who earlier had cringed away from the prodding bayonet. Now as then, his eyes showed fear, and the mouth was slack and trembling. The Wolf's men had chosen well: under stress, Fairbairn would crack, and Ogilvie wouldn't like the result.

He met the man's pleading but silent gaze. He licked at his lips; there was nothing he could say that would not sound banal. It was Fairbairn who spoke, in a hoarse, high voice: 'Where's the Colonel, sir? Where's the bluidy regiment, for Christ's sake, sir?'

'No one, sir. The end of the pass is empty, sir.' The runner, sent back from the advanced scouting party, sweated from the effort of his fast dash to the rear.

'No sign of Captain Ogilvie and the others?'

'No, sir.'

'And the valley?' Dornoch, his face anxious, had opened his map case and was unrolling the map. 'Any movement at all?'

'No, sir. It appears empty too, sir. The forts are in view, sir, and Mr MacGillivray says he can see no sign of the garrison of the nearer outpost through his field glasses, and—'

'And Fort Gaza's too far off to be seen in detail?'

'Yes, sir.'

'All right.' Dornoch gave a nod of dismissal. 'Rejoin the scouts, and tell Mr MacGillivray to remain where he is and to keep in cover – for what it's worth! He'll have my decision shortly.'

'Yes, sir.' The runner saluted, turned about, and doubled away between the jagged sides of the pass. Dornoch studied his map, deep in thought. It was obvious enough that by now the defenders of both the forts would know a force was coming through, would know also that the Kohat Light Horse were riding east and south of them. It was merely one of the dangers of Indian fighting that had to be coped with, but Dornoch cursed the distance between himself and Fort Gaza: he was as yet most of a day's march away, and there was no knowing what might have happened to Ogilvie.

'What do you think, John?' he asked, glancing at his Second-in-Command.

'I'd outflank, I think, Colonel.'

'The side pass, back there?' Dornoch waved a hand to the rear. 'The maps show a route, that's true, but it'd take a damn sight longer and we'd still be observed and reported ahead. Andrew?'

Black frowned. 'I suggest we ride ahead and look at the valley for ourselves, Colonel. A personal viewing is always better, when possible, than a report.'

Dornoch nodded. 'Right you are! We'll leave the battalion where it is. Fall the men out to rest, if you please, Andrew, then we'll ride on.'

Black saluted and rode down the column, passing the order to the company commanders and indicating, officiously, the need for alertness on the part of the pickets and sentries. Rejoining the head of the column, he rode towards the valley with Dornoch and Hay, and soon they reached the scouting party, all of them in good cover from any sniping from the peaks. Black remarked on the absence of any kind of hostile action. 'It's as though they're leading us on,' he remarked gloomily.

'Well, we must always beware a trap.' The Colonel returned the salute of the officer in command of the scouts as the latter emerged from behind an immense boulder. 'Now, Mr MacGillivray, what's your assessment?'

'It's too quiet, Colonel. Much too quiet.'

Black gave a nod. 'Almost my own words, Colonel.'

Dornoch said nothing, but rode on some twenty yards to look down into the long valley stretching away into far distances beyond Fort Gaza, which was no more than a pinhead viewed from the upper slope of the pass. He looked for a long time through his field glasses, scanning every inch of the territory ahead of him, scanning the great hills that reared to either side of the valley, brown and barren, a scene of utter desolation. it would be a nasty prospect to march a battalion of infantry through that valley, under whatever guns might fire from the nearer fort, ultimately straight into the ready guns of Fort Gaza...

At his side Hay said, 'The hills, Colonel.'

'What about them?'

'They could pour down men and gunfire. We wouldn't have a chance.'

'Keeley should be just south of the valley by now, John.'

'I doubt if he'd be enough, Colonel. And

when – if – we reach Fort Gaza, the Wolf will have flown for a certainty!'

'There's still Ogilvie. I've a strong feeling he's in one of those forts – and likely Fort Gaza.'

'Perhaps, Colonel. It's no more than supposition, though.'

'But a likely assessment all the same.'

Hay took a deep breath. Reflected sunlight glinted from his major's crowns on either shoulder, from the buttons of his field service tunic. He was conscious in that moment of those crowns: as Second-in-Command, he had a right to express objections, and he expressed them now. 'It would be the valley of death, Colonel, all over again. *Guns to the left of them, guns to the right of them, guns to the front of them, volleyed and thundered* ... I think you cannot sacrifice a regiment for seven men.'

Dornoch's face was expressionless. Black, giving a small cough, put his point of view: 'We have two other alternatives, Colonel. Either we can do as the Major suggested and outflank to the north, or we can delay till nightfall. Night should give us a better chance, Colonel.'

Ogilvie had been taken out into the courtyard with Private Fairbairn; once again, he came face to face with the Wolf. The tall native was mounted on a big, rangy horse, and two more mounts stood ready and empty between a strong escort of riders each carrying a *jezail* across his body. It was difficult to read the Wolf's expression, but there was obvious tension in the courtyard; the firing-step running below the walls was manned along every foot of its way, with the long-barrelled, bayoneted rifles protruding over the top. Apparent facts penetrated Ogilvie's reeling mind: there seemed to be an indication that troop movements had been reported, and that could mean that the regiment was moving in. Under the Wolf's eye, Ogilvie waited to be told what to do.

His orders came: 'Mount the horses, quickly.'

'Our wrists...'

The Wolf gave a further order; the guards heaved Ogilvie and the private on to the horses. More rope was looped around their bodies and hauled taut, with the ends held by two of the riders. Ogilvie slumped sideways in the saddle, almost fell from the horse: he was shaking uncontrollably now from the burning fever's effect. He tried to pull himself together but it was no use; the Wolf, making some remark about weaklings who were unfit to ride, ordered him to be taken down. 'You,' the Wolf said, indicating one of the most powerful-looking of his men. 'The British officer shall sit your horse in front of you. Hold him fast, and be responsible for him.'

Nothing more was said; the Wolf, while the transfer was made, showed much impatience. The moment Ogilvie was up, held helpless by a strong arm and feeling desperately ill, the gates of the fort were opened and the cavalcade rode out, heading east. Through Ogilvie's brain drummed the one coherent thought: at midnight – however far ahead that might be – the rising was due to start and the whole of the North-West Frontier, from the plains of Swat to Baluchistan, would erupt in blood and flame. Nightmares came to him, fever-induced, hallucinations of plunder and ravage in a war-torn India that the Raj would have failed to protect when the moment came, of an India that would neither forgive nor forget afterwards but would drive the Viceroy's court from Calcutta in fulfilment of the Wolf's ultimate wish: that Queen Victoria should retreat to her own lands. The seizure of the salt deposits and revenues was only a start, an excuse perhaps to inflame the imaginations and the deep aspirations of the mob. As the horses rode on, going fast, Ogilvie slid into unconsciousness. He woke at last to darkness and a cold wind, and something icy being poured over his head and face: the contents of a water-jar. Forms bent over him, hairy faces, foul breath swept him though he scarcely noticed. Everything had lost its outline in a hazy blur. There was no moon, and the faces were dim in any case, and in a moment disappeared in a blood-red light that was the child of his own fever, an internal thing to interfere with his vision. He heard movement around him but it meant nothing; as the Wolf realised.

'The British officer is very sick, and will soon die. There is a reason, as for all things. I am told he was wounded ...strip away his clothing, and we shall look.'

Rough hands tore at the dirty native clothing and a torch was lit, flaring and smoking behind the cover of a large cleft in the rock face – they were high up in the hills now, south and east of Fort Gaza, and many tribesmen were gathering with their *jezails* and bayonets and daggers and light machine-guns captured from the Raj in earlier battles or in pillaging forays upon outposts. The light of the torch, held close to Ogilvie's body, showed the bayonet-slash across the back – far from a deep wound, but suppurating, red and swollen.

'There is poison,' the Wolf said. He thought for a while, frowning, fingering his dagger. 'The flesh should be cut away ... but first the poison shall be sucked from the wound.' He looked up, staring at the ring of watching tribesmen. 'One by one you shall suck mouthfuls, and spit away the poison. Start now.'

He stood up. 'You will not fail to save this life. You all know what was told to me by Akhbar Mohammad Khan: this is the son of the great General sahib who commands for the British Raj in Murree.'

The onward march of the Royal Strathspeys was conducted in all possible silence, and in the darkness as recommended by Andrew Black: reluctant of the delay involved, Dornoch had yet felt unable to commit his regiment to the hazards of a daylight advance. As the last of the light went, he had passed the order to move out, and the men and the guns made the steep descent from the pass down into the valley. Reaching level ground, the regiment was split: four companies with the artillery provided by Keeley moved to the north side of the valley, the others to the south. The orders were that they should march independently towards Fort Gaza, each attacking from its own side simultaneously when the Colonel gave the signal by firing star-shell to burst over the fort and illuminate it. Major Hay went in command of the advance to the south; Black remained with the Colonel to the north – a lugubrious and anxious Black who, half expecting to be attacked at any moment from the hills or the floor of the valley itself, was in fact the more worried when no attack materialised. He was still convinced of a trap; and said as much, once again, to the Colonel.

'We're here for action, Captain Black,' Dornoch said with a snap in his voice. 'We would be of precious little value in bivouacs in the pass! We must keep our eyes open – that's all.' He added, 'I'm doubtful of a trap. I'm inclined to think now that the Wolf will have gone back to the hills – as Colonel Keeley suggested. So that, too, was not unexpected.'

They rode on ahead of the marching men. There would be no halts, but even so they could scarcely reach Fort Gaza in less than five to six hours of forced marching, and even that, as Dornoch knew well, might be to push the men to the point of total exhaustion. It was a pity about Black; discontented murmurings and cautious advices were of little help to a commander in the field!

As they began to come within the ambit of the first of the forts, Dornoch despatched his runner to the artillery, warning the Major in command to stand by his guns, and to be ready to halt and lay on the mud walls, and open at once, if and when a single revolver-shot came from the infantry behind him. In the event there was no interference from the fort, which, in the moonless night, could be seen only as a faint and insubstantial smudge against the hills.

'Evacuated, I fancy,' Dornoch said with a sigh of relief.

The advance went on: here and there after a couple of hours men fell out and were lifted on to the commissariat camels and mules. Right in the rear strode the Regimental Sergeant-Major as a kind of self-imposed longstop to ensure that no straggler was left behind.

The sucking went on; the wound, afterwards, appeared even more red and swollen than before, but the suppuration had gone, giving place to blood, healthier blood. Still unconscious, Ogilvie had no knowledge of what was taking place, did not know that curious native remedies were being applied – weeds and grasses picked from between the rocks, and pounded until they liquefied into a mess that was rubbed into the raw wound. But after a while he came through his unconsciousness to find himself in a heavy sweat and with an appalling pain in his back and intent dirty faces peering at him in the light of the flare.

'You are better, Captain Ogilvie?'

To hear his name used was a shock, bad enough to sharpen his reeling wits. It was clearly no use to come out with a denial: someone had told the Wolf – and that someone could be Private Fairbairn, he supposed. In any case, it couldn't be helped now, and he answered the Wolf's question coolly. 'I am a little better.'

'To sweat is good.' A filthy garment, stinking to heaven of all manner of things nasty, was dropped on him. 'Keep warm against the night wind, Captain Ogilvie, son of the great British General sahib!'

'What do you want of me? Still the same questions, which I'll not answer?'

There was a loud laugh, a laugh with gloating triumph in it. 'The time for that has passed, Captain Ogilvie sahib, as will soon pass the days when the word sahib was used to you British devils! I am aware now of the dispositions of your forces in the vicinity – for you, there will be other uses, and for the forces, there will be slaughter.'

'And the rising?'

The Wolf said, 'Soon now midnight will come, and the rising will be signalled – by two happenings. When these happen, Captain Ogilvie sahib, the British Raj begins to meet its end.'

He went off then, saying no more. To Ogilvie it seemed likely enough that the Colonel had moved the regiment out: the Wolf would have had word of its coming, reports from his watchful tribesmen in the hills. He seemed entirely confident of his approaching success; Ogilvie, lying on the ground beneath the smelly garment, tried to concentrate his mind on his duty. It was up to him to escape if possible – and if possible to bring the Wolf out with him. It would, on both counts, be an uphill task! The place where he found himself was alive with the Wolf's men, with sentries placed all around the perimeter; and Ogilvie himself was not especially mobile though the fever was a good deal less and he felt some semblance of life returning as the heavy sweating continued. Time passed; there was still no moon coming through the cloud, but Ogilvie felt it must be close on midnight when once again the Wolf approached, accompanied by an escort of four armed tribesmen, and looked down at him.

The Wolf confirmed his thought: 'The time is upon us, British officer, son of the General.' Turning, he gestured to his escort. Two of the men came forward and roughly seized Ogilvie, setting him unsteadily on his feet and holding his arms fast. The Wolf turned away, smiling, and Ogilvie was led along behind him, feet dragging a little over the rock and scrub. It was difficult to see for far ahead, though there was a faint loom of light at the fringes of the heavy cloud above that slightly relieved the darkness of its totality; and after a while Ogilvie was able to make out some change in the ground ahead, some difference in the landscape, as though a pool of lesser dark – of lesser substance was perhaps more accurate – was coming up in front of him. A few steps farther on, he was halted by his guards. Looking round, he saw the Wolf, standing to his right. Then his eye was drawn ahead and down ... down into an immensity of empty space: he was almost on the brink of a long, long drop into the valley – on the edge of a precipice, he believed, a sheer rock side running down for possibly several hundred feet. A few moments later he heard footsteps coming up from behind, and the sound of heavy breathing.

He looked round: Private Fairbairn was being brought up between more guarding tribesmen. The soldier was taken to the brink of the drop, between Ogilvie and the Wolf, while more men came up on either hand. Four of them carried flares, ready to be lit. Ogilvie was conscious of rising sound, a sound as of many men on the move. Looking to right and left as far as he could peer through the darkness, he saw the tribesmen assembling on the edge of the drop into the valley, a weird, almost ghostly coming together of men who made no sound at all beyond the shuffle of their feet on the rock, men who awaited something, some happening, some signal; and Ogilvie had no need of the Wolf's words when the native said, with triumph and exultation in his voice, 'All along the North-West Frontier, Ogilvie sahib, men are waiting, men who stand ready to strike and kill. They will pour in through the passes out of Afghanistan, they will rise in Waziristan, they will pillage in Kohat and Peshawar, in Nowshera and Bannu and Mardan. The Raj is finished, British officer! All now awaits the signal, which—'

He broke off suddenly. From far below, from a westerly direction Ogilvie believed, had come the urgent sound of gunfire in the night, distant but heavy and foreboding, the deep voice of field artillery in action. And as Ogilvie looked towards the Wolf, he saw the leader's face in the light of a flare that had just been lit: the face showed anger, surprise, and a mounting fear.

Seventeen

'Captain Black!' Dornoch's voice rose hoarsely through the gunfire, through the scream of shells, as his horse reared beneath him. The attack had come as if from nowhere, as if from the very earth itself, the orange flame spouting from the gun-barrels ahead of their advance like some gigantic and devastating Guy Fawkes celebration. 'Captain Black! Where—'

'Here, Colonel.'

'Fan out the men – extend on both flanks. Tell the gunner Major to get into action immediately – he's too damn slow!'

Black saluted and rode away, yelling orders. As he went the British guns opened ahead of Lord Dornoch, splitting the night's darkness with flash and flame and exploding shells to add to the appalling racket from the enemy. Everywhere, it seemed, shells were digging their great pits: in the light of the explosions Dornoch could see men's bodies lying shattered, or being blown to fragments in the terrible blasts. A burst of star-shell from the British gunners lit the scene ahead with its descending balls of fire, and Dornoch was able to make some assessment of the enemy's strength: some dozen field guns, some light automatic stuff, and numerous dismounted tribesmen lying flat on their stomachs in the open or firing from behind rock cover. It was impossible to make any good guess at their infantry strength, but the rifle flashes were coming thick and fast. Dornoch turned away and rode along his extended flanks, encouraging the men, his sword in his hand as a symbol of what they were fighting for. He found the Regimental Sergeant-Major, minus his headgear, doing something similar.

'Have a care, Sar'nt-Major. Take cover with the rest.' Dornoch rode on, not waiting for the reply, knowing what it would be in any case: Cunningham had never been the man to hold back. Dornoch's thoughts were bleak; the casualties looked heavy. It would not be the first time in the long story of the Raj that a regiment had been decimated, left only with its name and the sad task of rebuilding itself under the same Colours and the same badge. To think of that happening to the 114th was cruel: Dornoch forced his mind away from such negative processes. As he rode along the embattled flanks, disregarding the whine of bullets, he listened: without orders the pipes had started playing, and their music gave him heart as it beat strongly out into the night to cut through the sound of the engaged guns. Then, into one of those lulls that seemed so often to occur without reason in any action, Dornoch heard other sounds: the thunder of horses' hooves as Keeley came in from the south, and the heavier sounds of limber wheels as the horse artillery turned to swing their guns and halt to the order of Action Front. Beyond that, more pipes and drums, the other half of the Royal Strathspeys coming in under John Hay...

Ogilvie made the guess that the regiment was in action in the valley: he knew of no other force likely to be marching towards Fort Gaza unless some fresh intelligence had reached Fettleworth in Nowshera and he had reacted speedily. Whatever it was, it had clearly not been expected by the Wolf, who had been thrown off his stroke and looked sheerly murderous. For a while he stalked up and down the edge of the drop, his face working in the light of the solitary flare, completely undecided as to what he should do next. Then he halted, looking down into the valley, remaining still for some while. Turning at last, he spoke.

'Here we shall remain until we know what

is happening. We are safe in the hills.'

'And the signal?'

'Yes, the signal.' The Wolf seemed again undecided: Ogilvie could imagine his processes of thought. This action was localised it was true, and might not amount to much; on the other hand, it was an indication that something had gone wrong. Similar actions, attacks by the British on the Wolf's prepared positions, might be taking place in other sectors of his planned front. Should he, therefore, abandon his plans or stick to them? Would a better time come again, or should he risk all now that, at least, he had full support from all the many tribes, a degree of unanimity and co-operation that could not always be counted upon? Ogilvie smiled to himself; the Wolf was facing what many a commander had faced in the past and would face again.

The Wolf made his decision: 'We are ready. We shall act. It is fortunate that we have with us the son of the British General. The signal will be given now.' He raised an arm, his garment falling back to show thick hair and sinewy muscle. 'The flares, and quickly!'

The four flare-bearers came forward again. Each carried two flares, as yet untouched by flame. In the grip of his guards Private Fairbairn was brought back a little way from the edge of the precipice: Ogilvie saw the terror in the man's eyes, but both he and Fairbairn were unprepared for the Wolf's next announcement.

'The signal, British officer, was to be the descent of a pattern of eight flares down the hillside. The flares were to be tied to a frame of wood ... and the sight of them reported onwards throughout all the frontier lands. Fortune has brought me another way to achieve the same end, and when *that* word spreads from my people here with us tonight, the effect will be the greater.'

'And this other way – what's it to be?'

The Wolf smiled, his long yellow teeth visible in the light of the single flare, now burning down to its end. 'The human torch, the human frame perhaps I should say – your soldier, the symbol of your British power, of your British queen's service, burning like the Raj itself shall burn.' He turned, and clapped his hands. 'Tie on the flares. Do not light them till the man is at the edge of the precipice, and ready to be dropped.'

The four men went up to Fairbairn; the soldier was in an obvious and natural state of funk, but no sound came from him. None came from Ogilvie either: both of them were helpless, though Ogilvie's wrists had been untied when his back was being attended to;

the guards were watchful for the smallest movement. And the Wolf would never be moved by words.

Down in the valley beyond Fort Gaza, the counter-attack from the flank was heavy and sustained; cavalry, infantry, artillery, field pieces and the heavy limbered guns – breech-loading twelve-pounders with rifled barrels firing three-inch shells up to 6,000 yards: these kept up a sustained fire that cut into the native ambush, scattering them wholesale, and it was followed up by a bayonet charge through the smoke of the guns, a dash by yelling Scots who hardly needed the pipes to urge them forward. Abandoning their guns, the tribesmen fled in disorder, pursued by the cavalry and infantry until Dornoch ordered the bugles to sound Stand Fast.

'They'll not try again,' he said to Black, then turned as Keeley rode up. 'My thanks, Colonel,' he said, holding out a hand. 'You were in excellent time!'

Keeley smiled. 'I always try to be, Dornoch. What now? Shall we advance and take the fort?'

'That's the idea,' Dornoch said. 'Advantage to us, I rather think! The word will go ahead of us, I'm sure.'

'Yes.' Keeley brought out his watch and

held it close to his eyes, then struck a match. 'It's just on midnight, Dornoch. D'you suppose that attack was the start of it?'

'I doubt it. I think it was a chance affair – a plain ambush, the sort of precaution the Wolf might well take. You know these people better than I, Keeley – you'll agree that they stick to their pronouncements.'

'Timing?'

Dornoch nodded. 'It's possible their synchronisation was poor, of course!'

'Yes, very possible.' Keeley hesitated, seemed to stiffen himself to go on, reluctantly. 'I have news, Dornoch, and it's not good. I'm sorry.'

'Well?'

Keeley answered in a hard voice, 'Soames. Soames has run. I'm damn sorry I repeat, but there it is. He cut and ran last night during our advance. I'll not make excuses – there was slackness. He slunk off in darkness and wasn't reported missing till daylight.'

At midnight all British units in Northern Command were standing to: there was no sleeping either in the field or in cantonments, or in the widespread outposts. Each man was ready with his rifle; every gun was manned and ready for action. Pickets and sentries were more alert than ever they had been before. In the cantonments of the big base garrisons the womenfolk were under a strong guard, and all city patrols had been withdrawn in the double interest of strengthening the cantonment guard and of keeping British soldiers out of the isolation of small units who might be caught in an unstemmable surge of city mobs; nevertheless, a careful if distant watch was being maintained on the outskirts of the native cities so that troops could if necessary be deployed around the perimeters to contain any outsurge from within.

At Division outside Nowshera, Lieutenant-General Fettleworth was closeted with his staff officers, grouped before a large wall-map of the Frontier lands. Fettleworth kept looking at his watch, his florid face filled with a deep anxiety as the hands approached midnight.

'Nothing more we could have done,' he muttered. 'Hey, Lakenham?'

'Nothing more, sir.'

'They can't blame me. I've kept on saying, I need more troops. They're a bloody stupid bunch in Calcutta.'

'The troop trains are on their way, sir, from Ootacamund and—'

'Too late!' Fettleworth broke in bitterly. He hitched at his Sam Browne belt: tonight he had foregone mess dress in favour of field service uniform, brandy in favour of total commitment to saving the Raj. He was in a desperate position in his own eyes: the Divisional Commander who lost the Raj would never be given another appointment and never mind whether or no it was his fault. Cheltenham, Tunbridge Wells, or Leamington Spa, and old age in a bath chair, dishonoured – no knighthood, spurned by Her Majesty, black-balled by his clubs, he'd be better dead! And dead he might be; but he was able to brush this aside. With all his faults, Bloody Francis was no coward.

Lakenham said, 'Midnight, sir.'

A moment later sound came: clocks, and more distantly bells. Fettleworth prowled the room, gnawing at the trailing yellow-white ends of his walrus moustache. He said, 'Well, the buggers are late at all events.' No one responded to this, but Brigadier-General Lakenham rolled his eyes to heaven: it had never exactly been expected that the Wolf of the Salt Range would attack Divisional Headquarters itself on the dot of midnight, and it might well be a matter of hours before the reports came in by runner or the field telegraphs.

Division's clock crawled on. The tension was immense, a coiled spring such as worked the clock itself. Fettleworth bit his finger-nails and longed for a *chota peg*. Just a shout for his bearer or corporal of servants ... but no. Then they couldn't say afterwards ... Fettleworth gave a jump as a loud knock came at the door and his ADC went over to open it.

'What is it?'

'A runner from the officer commanding the perimeter guard, sir. The city's restive, the mobs are out—'

'We expected that, didn't we, Lakenham?'

'We did, sir.'

'Well, go on,' Fettleworth said to the ADC.

'Riot is likely, sir. Major Weston suggests we evacuate the traders.'

Fettleworth blew out his cheeks, gnawed again at his moustache. Damn the traders! They were useful, yes; they were loyal to the Raj, too, though that loyalty was entirely profit-orientated. If they'd had any savvy, they would have gone already: it was unlikely the trading community wouldn't have got the word through their own grapevine. Well – they had stayed put and must take the consequences. Fettleworth pronounced: 'I shall not put our troops in hazard for a bloody bunch of bazaar-*wallahs*. Tell Major Weston he's to assist any who leave the city through his lines, and have 'em taken to safety in cantonments, but there's to be no penetration of the town itself.'

The runner went off. Fettleworth paced the room back and forth, anxiety preying more and more on his mind. No one spoke; all watched the clock and awaited more reports. None came in. From the direction of the city, however, came ominous sounds: the firing of rifles, howls and screams, the manifestations of the mob on its demented rampage through the streets, plundering, killing. Lakenham, looking through a spyhole in one of the big shuttered windows, reported burning. Someone was getting it; probably the traders, those who had over so many years succoured the Raj. Fettleworth closed his mind to it.

Fairbairn sweated, stared pleadingly at Ogilvie as the eight flares were secured with thin rope to his person. The valley could be seen clearly now, for at last the moon had sailed into view. Helpless between his armed guards, Ogilvie tried not to look at Fairbairn, looking instead around the high peaks as the moon bathed them in bright light, bringing them up sharp and stern and jagged, menacing in the very immensity of their majestic loneliness.

Yet now they were not alone.

All along those peaks men, clearly visible

in the moon, were waiting. There must have been thousands of them – many thousands, silently waiting with their *jezails* and their daggers, waiting for the signal from the Wolf of the Salt Range, the weird flare-signal that would send them to join his standard and advance in a huge mass against the might of the British Raj. The Raj was vast and powerful, yet at the same time weak; numerically it was outnumbered a hundredfold and more, and its reserves of men and arms came largely from outside the borders of the sub-continent – whereas the Wolf's replenishments were handily domestic and fruitfully plentiful. And the Wolf had fervour and fanaticism to fight for him as well, the bounding aspirations of a whole set of peoples who could be presumed to sink their differences at any rate until victory had been won.

Fairbairn was pushed closer to the edge. From the rear a tribesman approached, carrying a single lighted flare. Sounds came from Fairbairn now, a low cry that seemed to tear at Ogilvie. Straining against the grip of the guards, Ogilvie felt that grip tightened cruelly, felt the nick of steel in his back, prying again into his raw wound. There was nothing he could do, literally nothing, but watch the end come. In that moment, Private Fairbairn as a man almost ceased to register: he was to be just one casualty amongst the hundreds of thousands that would go down with a sinking Raj, just one more soldier, an obscure Briton to add his bones and his blood to all that had sown India in the past. But to think of the Raj ending here on this desolate mountain peak, to think of all the endeavour and courage and self-sacrifice on the part of loyal Indian and Briton alike, all going for nothing – that was unbearable. Ogilvie looked towards the Wolf: the man was standing some twenty paces clear of Fairbairn, his face lit by the moon so that the hawkish features stood strongly out – the nose, the bearded jaw, the greasy hair's ends visible below the turban – tall and straight and devilish, silhouetted against the night sky, surveying, like Attila the Hun of olden times, what he was about to conquer...

Without turning head or body the Wolf gave his order: 'Touch flare to flare now. The time has come.' He lifted his hands towards the heavens, spread wide, his head now lifted also, bathed in moonlight. He seemed taller than ever, seemed to assume gigantic proportions in his moment of action. As he stood there, a noise came from the rear, the sound of heavy running footsteps, but the Wolf appeared deaf to any interruptions. Ogilvie, as the first of the flares was lit on

Fairbairn's trembling body, looked towards the source of the noise. He saw a man coming, a man with a revolver in his hand, and a tribesman at his throat. The revolver came up, was fired; the tribesman dropped down, clutching at his chest, but in his falling knocked away the revolver and sent it spinning across the rock. The other man raced on; everyone seemed taken by surprise, and the Wolf remained in his strange attitude at the top of the precipice – until it was just too late. Like a bullet the running man came at him, took him like a target, wrapped his arms around him and then, still carried on by his own momentum, bore the screaming Wolf clean over the edge into the long drop.

Eighteen

Ogilvie's reaction had been instantaneous: the scene was pandemonium, uproar, panic. He swung the guards inwards in front of him with strength that seemed heavensent, and smashed them hard together. Their grip fell away and Ogilvie ran, his body bent low, for the revolver lying not far away. Picking it up, he ran back for Fairbairn and caught him just before he fell. The two of them went down, and Ogilvie rolled their bodies away from the brink, over and over until they were safe. Ogilvie, feeling again the onset of a shaking fever, sat up groggily.

He looked around. They were almost alone; the Wolf's men were streaming away, deeper no doubt into the hills, away from vengeance. The farther peaks were emptying as fast, most of them already bare of the assembled warriors, once again stark and lonely in the moonlight. Ogilvie shook his head in wonder at the last-minute deliverance: and deliverance it was! No signal, and the spreading word, as fast as lightning from those who had been near enough to see for themselves, of the undoubted death of the Wolf of the Salt Range.

And Ogilvie had recognised the man: the turban, the cavalry boots, the stars of rank of Captain Soames, late the Kohat Light Horse.

Ogilvie had lost consciousness, going out as totally as the one flare that had been lit on Fairbairn; it was Fairbairn who nursed him through the night and kept his body warm as the cold wind of the dawn eddied round the peak; Fairbairn who kept watch on the valley and saw with immense relief, not long after the next day's noon, the advance of a British force along the floor of the valley from the west. When the troops had closed the distance enough, Fairbairn fired a round from Soames' revolver and stood in full view, waving his glengarry and shouting as loud as he could. Soon after, he saw the head of the column turn inwards and begin to close the ground at the foot of the sheer drop. Then he saw the details of infantry moving independently out from the column towards the hills, searching for a way to the summit. Two hours later, with Ogilvie laid in a *dooli* carried by four Scots ahead of him, Private Fairbairn rejoined the regiment, reporting personally to the Colonel after the latter had had words with Surgeon Major Corton.

'We've found the bodies,' Lord Dornoch said. 'The Wolf himself ... and another.' He paused. 'Did you see who the other was, Fairbairn?'

'No, sir. I never set eyes on him, sir. I had my back to him, sir.'

Dornoch nodded, his face grave. 'That's all right, Fairbairn. You did very well – you and Captain Ogilvie. I can't express my gratitude enough. You'll find General Fettleworth grateful too, I promise!'

'It was Captain Ogilvie, sir—'

'And you to share his laurels!' Dornoch, smiling, reached down from his horse and shook Fairbairn's hand warmly. 'Rejoin your company, Fairbairn, after reporting to the Medical Officer.'

'Yes, sir. I'm all right, though, sir. Will you tell me, please, sir – will Captain Ogilvie be all right?'

'I understand so, but we must reach a hospital without delay. Off you go, Fairbairn.'

'Sir!' Fairbairn saluted smartly and turned about with a crash of boot-leather.

Dornoch gestured to the Adjutant sitting his horse alongside him. 'Pass the word, if you please, Andrew – that Ogilvie's life depends upon speedy marching. We can rely on the men to respond.'

'Very good, Colonel.'

'And a mounted runner to the telegraph at Kohat, to ride with all speed. A message for our Divisional Commander: the Wolf of the Salt Range is dead and the rising's over before it started.'

Black raised an eyebrow. 'Colonel, if I may suggest it, is this not a little premature?'

'Premature be hanged, Andrew! Don't you know the Frontier better than that?' Dornoch laughed. 'The runner, and quickly! And a happier face upon it, too. Good God, man, don't you ever celebrate anything?'

Black flushed, saluted, and was about to ride off when he paused and faced the Colonel again. 'Captain Soames, Colonel. Do you wish his death to be reported to Division?'

Dornoch rubbed at the side of his face, which was again troubled at the mention of Soames. 'Report the death, yes. No details – none at all. That business is far from ended yet! I'll say no more, and report no more, at least until I've had a talk with Keeley.' He added, 'There is one more thing: the runner's to ensure the hospital at Kohat's ready to take charge of Ogilvie, and you'd better report his condition to Nowshera. Have a word with the doctor first.'

★   ★   ★

The march was fast: everyone in the regiment wished Ogilvie well and there were few grumbles at the speed of advance on Kohat. Ogilvie in his *dooli* remained unconscious, deep in his high fever only slightly relieved by the poultices of the Surgeon Major and the attentions of the medical orderlies. The wound had been properly cleaned out but the poison was widespread around his body. It was three full days after reaching hospital before Ogilvie began to come round, hazily, slowly, and feeling desperately sick and with a pounding headache. It took him some while to focus on the nurse at his bedside and to realise where he was. The nurse smiled at him and continued cooling his forehead with a cloth dipped in iced water.

'Don't try to talk,' she said. 'Just sleep and you'll feel a lot better when you wake up.'

He closed his eyes again; the hospital bed heaved like a ship at sea, the room revolved, his eyes were filled with bright and startling colours that whirled and twisted strangely. It was another twenty-four hours before he was able to hold a conversation and that evening the nurse asked him if he felt up to visitors: there was one waiting.

He asked cautiously, 'Who is it?'

'Mr Cunningham.'

His face lit up. 'I'll see him, of course!

Delighted.'

The nurse smiled. 'I shall tell him he must tone himself down first, Captain Ogilvie. This is a hospital – and he's like an earthquake!' She left the room, and after an interval the Regimental Sergeant-Major, in uniform but stepping lightly, appeared in the doorway.

'Sir! Are you better, Captain Ogilvie?'

'I'm fine, thank you, Bosom. Come in and sit down.'

Cunningham advanced and lowered his bulk into a basket-work chair by the bed. He seemed both out of place and ill-at-ease in a hospital, but he gave Ogilvie the news he wanted. The regiment was back in cantonments and all trouble was over. During their night advance along the valley they had stormed Fort Gaza and re-taken it more or less intact. The garrison, Cunningham said, had seemed rattled by the absence of the promised midnight signal. Colour-Sergeant MacTrease and the rest were all right if dirty, and had been released intact.

'And the lance-*duffardar* – Akhbar Mohammad Khan?'

Cunningham said briefly, 'Skedaddled, Captain Ogilvie. Buggered off with the rest.'

'Buggered off?' Ogilvie stared. 'Or forcibly removed, for vengeance' sake?'

Cunningham hesitated, frowning. 'I'll not

say for dead certain, sir. I'll not say that in case he's suffering now. But I'm not usually wrong, sir, and it's my belief he ran for his own safety.'

'That's strange,' Ogilvie said. 'You know about Captain Soames, of course.'

'Of course, sir.'

'What do you make of it?'

'That's not for me to say, Captain Ogilvie.' Cunningham gave a cough. 'I understand you'll have more visitors tomorrow if the doctors agree: the Colonel, and Colonel Keeley. I think you may guess what they're coming about, sir.' Once again, Cunningham lifted a hand and coughed. 'And there's another in the offing too, sir.'

'Who?'

'A Mrs Archdale, sir. From England. It seems the bush telegraph met her off the train from Bombay, sir. She sought passage here in an ordnance wagon. I happened to encounter her, and it seems she had a recollection of me from when she was last in Peshawar.' Cunningham paused. 'She wishes to see you, Captain Ogilvie.'

'And I her, Bosom – but not yet. Not till after the others have been – the Colonel, and Colonel Keeley. And certainly not while they're with me.' Ogilvie met Cunningham's eye. 'May I leave it to you?'

'You may indeed, Captain Ogilvie.' Cun-

314

ningham indulged in talk of the regiment for a few more minutes before a nurse came to usher him out. He shook Ogilvie's hand and went off with a look of release about him, moving with a proper quietness still. Tired, thinking of Mary Archdale, Ogilvie drifted off into sleep. Next day he was feeling a good deal better, and during the afternoon his official visitors arrived, their arrival accompanied by the indignant tones of a sister outside in the corridor. The hospital, she was saying, was not a zoo; an altercation that could mean only that Blaise-Willoughby was present. Deprived of Wolseley, the Political Officer entered the room with Keeley and Lord Dornoch.

'You're looking fitter than when I last saw you, James,' Dornoch said. 'They tell me you'll be back with the regiment within a week or two.'

'Yes, Colonel.' Ogilvie was sitting up, propped with pillows. Talk was exchanged about his progress, and Dornoch spoke, embarrassingly but with sincerity, of the regiment's pride in what he had done, a sentiment in which Keeley joined. Ogilvie's response to that was to say that it had been Soames who had taken the initiative and performed the final action: none of the credit was his own. For the moment the question of Soames was not taken up;

315

Blaise-Willoughby, in his capacity as Political Officer at Division, had much to ask, and noted down Ogilvie's answers for his report to Fettleworth, a report that would eventually find its way to Sir Iain at Murree, then to the Commander-in-Chief, then to the Viceroy in Calcutta and finally, no doubt, to Whitehall. Ogilvie's movements and assessments duly entered into Blaise-Willoughby's notebook, Soames was cautiously mentioned by way of the lance-*duffardar.*

'As I understand it,' Blaise-Willoughby said, 'Akhbar Mohammad Khan deserted to the enemy.' He tapped a pencil against his teeth. 'Makes one wonder.'

'There's no evidence of desertion, Major,' Ogilvie pointed out. 'Mr Cunningham's view – and he was there – was that ... there was some doubt.'

'A view in which I think your Colonel would not necessarily concur, Ogilvie, but we're not likely ever to learn the truth of that.' Blaise-Willoughby paused, then asked directly, 'Tell me, what's your view of Soames now?'

Self-consciously, feeling the triteness of his answer, Ogilvie said, 'He died well.'

'Yes,' Blaise-Willoughby agreed with a sardonic smile lingering around his mouth. 'He died well, saved the Raj by his sacrifice, turned up trumps at the finish! Is that it – more or less?'

Ogilvie nodded. 'More or less.'

'Or he saw the end coming, and he decided his way was better than the firing squad or the self-inflicted bullet in the head,' Blaise-Willoughby said brutally. 'Or, again, he didn't mean to die himself. Just to polish off his master before his master could shop him. Didn't realise the precipice was quite so close. How's that?'

'It's all possible, Major. Isn't it a case of taking one's choice?'

'Yes.' Blaise-Willoughby was smiling his sardonic smile still. 'There's something to be said on both sides. But what we lack is what we lacked after Chakwal – proof either way. Isn't it? That Salt Department NCO, Abdul Qadir, never identified Soames positively – he spoke only of "a white officer", you'll remember. There's Akhbar Mohammad Khan, now in the hills, there's his story of what happened in London. There's Sar'nt Zachary in Dartmoor gaol, and his story. All hearsay in basis! There was the fact of Soames's listening outside your Colonel's tent – or did he?' Blaise-Willoughby shrugged. 'If Soames were alive, I've a feeling he could cover that. His meeting with the tribesman in the hills afterwards – that would be harder for him. But we have no proof he wasn't passing *false* information. We have no proof the villain wasn't Akhbar Mohammad Khan, who could have been making up yarns to put the blame on Soames – and making a fool of you into the bargain, Ogilvie.'

Ogilvie felt suddenly weary and sick. He asked, 'Does it matter? The man's dead, isn't he?'

'Justice never dies,' the Political Officer said. 'It's of great moment to the Raj, and to General Fettleworth, who has despatches to compose. And recommendations to make.' His dark eyes brooded on Ogilvie. 'I think I know what *I* shall recommend.'

'Well?'

Blaise-Willoughby closed his eyes for a moment and sat back in his chair, fingertips together. Opening his eyes again he said, 'The British Raj, Ogilvie, is a very great institution, a tremendous force for peace and progress in a backward India. It's important, I believe, that it should not be sullied unnecessarily. At the last, Soames may well have had this in mind himself, you know.'

'So—'

'So I shall report to General Fettleworth that his mind may rest easy.' Blaise-Willoughby swivelled his eyes to meet those of Lord Dornoch and Keeley. Both officers nodded, and Blaise-Willoughby continued, 'It's a pity about the climate. Soames is already buried, so we can't have a grand military funeral, a hero's parade in the Fettleworth sense ... pity, that! But his name will be published in orders as a splendid example ... the man who saved the Raj. He'll not have died in vain. And there'll be a recommendation from Division for a posthumous reward for bravery. His widow will appreciate that, at all events, poor woman.'

All three officers left soon after this announcement; alone, Ogilvie stared across the hospital room towards a green-painted wall and out through the opened slats of the shutters into a hard blue sky. From so many points of view it was the best way out, some might have said the only way out if there was any doubt at all. Yet to Ogilvie it seemed a little premature. The next week or so might bring change, and with it embarrassment for the Raj: if Akhbar Mohammad Khan was in fact a loyal soldier of the Queen-Empress, his broken body might well be placed where it would be found by a British patrol. And if that should happen it would be only the hovering vultures and the diligent prowling jackals that might prevent the dead Wolf of the Salt Range having the last laugh at Her Majesty's expense...